A JAR FULL OF LIGHT

AVELINE BOOK TWO

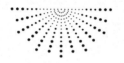

RAE WALSH

SMALL SEED PRESS

PROLOGUE

"Mom?"

Theresa held her phone with trembling fingers, closing her eyes at the sound of her daughter's voice. She took a deep breath and opened her eyes to look at the sky outside her kitchen window. It was showing off again with deep, luscious sunset colors—fuchsia, purple and tangerine. Theresa tapped her fingers on the side of the sink and prayed that her voice would hold.

"Hi, Little," she said. Her voice was quiet but steady, a relief after a few long days of not saying a word out loud to anyone. "How are things?"

There was a pause. "Pretty good," Maddie told her. Her voice sounded the way Theresa's heart felt, full of ragged edges and question marks. Lack of sleep. Theresa's heart wanted to burst out of her ribcage and fling itself across the country to her baby. Maddie's shoplifting and Theresa's subsequent meltdown had led to Theresa sending her daughter to live with her grandmother, across the country in Aveline, Theresa's hometown in California.

"I finished writing my apology letters," Maddie went on.

Theresa let her eyes drift shut as guilt washed over her in a hot wave. "That's good," she said. "That must have been hard to do."

"It was. It feels good to have it over with. But Mom? I miss you."

"I miss you too. Are you ready to come home?"

"I was wondering..." There was a long pause. Theresa readied herself for whatever Maddie was going to say. The last months had been good and hard. With Maddie gone, Theresa had dug deep into counseling, scheduling herself with two different therapists. She had made some break-throughs and spent hours journaling, painting, and throwing pots. The months had been good for Theresa. But she was worried that she had given up too much when she sent Maddie away. Theresa's mother hadn't even allowed Maddie to come and live with her, sending her to Theresa's little brother Sam, instead. Living with Sam had gone okay for Maddie, except for another shoplifting incident, something Maddie assured Theresa she would never do again. She was done with stealing for good.

But would Maddie ever want to come home, now that she knew what it was like to have a normal life? With normal people? Theresa steeled herself as Maddie went on talking.

"I don't want to come back to Minnesota," she said. "I don't think it's good for me."

Pain bloomed somewhere near Theresa's sternum, and she breathed, the way she had learned, trying to allow it to flow over her, rather than pulling her under its current. But Maddie wasn't finished.

"I don't think it's good for you either, Mom. I miss you so much. Will you please move here? Then we can all live here together."

Theresa's eyes snapped open. She stared at the sky—now half swept over by the indigo night. She pushed away from the sink and walked to stand at the fridge, staring at the wedding invitation she had taped to the door.

Move back to Aveline?

Aveline still beat hard in her heart. Some part of it traveled with Theresa everywhere she ever went. She had never really become accustomed to the winters in Minnesota, though she appreciated the numbing of the cold.

"Mom?"

Theresa shook herself. "I don't know, honey," she said.

"You're coming, next month, though, right?"

"To the wedding?" Theresa traced the edges of the gold invitation with her fingertips. Sammy was finally getting married, and she was happy for her little brother. "I was thinking about it. Maddie, there were a lot of hard things in Aveline..."

"I think you need to believe that you can move past those hard things," Theresa's fourteen-year-old told her definitively.

Theresa snorted out a little laugh. "Oh, I've missed you so much, feisty girl."

She left the kitchen and opened the screen door to walk outside in the late summer evening. The air smelled of fields, of cut grass and sunshine.

Maddie didn't yet know that some hard things never let you go. Theresa shivered.

"I'll come to the wedding," she said. "And we can talk there. We need to live together, you and I."

Maddie broke in. "And we can do that in Aveline. It's so good here, Mom."

Theresa didn't need her daughter to tell her how good Aveline was. If she closed her eyes, she could see it, smell it, taste it. Home. The jewel of a lake. The smell of redwood needles underfoot. Sleepy afternoons, star-filled nights. Dancing on the shores of the lake. And... danger. Her arms prickled as she remembered. But she would do anything in the world to keep Maddie happy and safe.

"I'll see you at the wedding, Little," she said. "Do you have a dress yet?"

Maddie took a breath and launched into a long ramble about how she was a bridesmaid, and the dress was amazing, and the food was amazing, and everything was amazing.

Theresa paced her backyard, listening to the change in her daughter, growing more and more sure that she was going to have to move back to a place she had thought she left forever.

CHAPTER ONE

Sheldon stood on the sidewalk in front of his shop and looked down the street. Any minute now, Lucy would arrive, and then they could walk to the church together. But Lucy was always late. He huffed a sigh, looking down at his suit and smoothing the embroidery on the cuffs, reliving the night before in excruciating detail.

Sam and Katie's wedding rehearsal had gone smoothly— or at least Sheldon thought it had. He had been a little preoccupied, hardly able to think straight. Theresa was coming to the rehearsal dinner. It was all Sheldon had thought about for days. Theresa was returning to Aveline after ten years.

Sheldon had fumbled through the ceremony rehearsal, staring blankly at Francisco when the reverend asked him for the vows. After Francisco asked for the copy of the vows for the third time, Sheldon pulled them out of his pocket with a start, only to find that he had carefully folded and carried the menu for the rehearsal dinner, not the vows.

Sam shook his head, but the rest of the wedding party

burst out laughing. Needless to say, Sam and Katie had practiced with made-up vows. Despite Sheldon's jumpiness, Theresa hadn't shown up when they were at the church.

The wedding party and family walked to the Aveline café, Katie's restaurant, where the rehearsal dinner was held. Sheldon thought it was strange to have a rehearsal dinner at the home and restaurant of the bride-to-be, but Katie wouldn't have it any other way.

"Control freak," he muttered at her, passing her in the doorway. She elbowed him playfully.

Inside the café, Sheldon couldn't settle down. He tried to enjoy the hors d'oeurves and wine Katie's employees had served, but finally, he jumped up and walked back and forth in the second dining room, which was blissfully empty. Why wasn't Theresa here yet? How long was a man supposed to have such crazy anticipation before his head exploded?

After a while, Sam came and stood in the doorway, leaning on the doorjamb with his arms crossed.

"You're pacing," he said.

Sheldon flashed his best friend an irritated look.

"You're not," he retorted. "What's wrong with you? Aren't you nervous?"

"To marry Katie? Are you kidding? Of course not."

"Fine then, never mind." Sheldon continued to pace, now just the tiniest bit irritated that his friend was so levelheaded.

"Do you have a plan?" Sam asked after a few minutes.

Sheldon looked up. "A plan?"

"For when you see her?"

Sheldon stared. How could you plan a thing like that?

While he tried to formulate an answer, he noticed that of all things, Sam had grown a short beard. He had even trimmed it, rather than shaving it off like he usually did when he was too lazy for grooming for a short while and then realized his mistake.

"Are you going to shave that off before the wedding?" Sheldon asked.

Sam shook his head, leaning forward and fixing Sheldon with a look. "Shel. Don't try to distract me. Do you know what you will do when you see Theresa for the first time in ten years? Don't forget how many times I had to hear you talk about how you were waiting for her and were never going to stop waiting. What were you planning to do when you saw her again?"

Sheldon was opening his mouth to reply, but just then, Maddie skidded breathlessly into the room.

"Mom's here!" she said. "She's pulling onto the street." She was gone before the words finished echoing off the vaulted ceilings.

Sam raised an eyebrow at Sheldon.

"Better come up with something quick," he said. And he straightened and motioned with one hand. "Let's go welcome my big sister."

"I still don't know what you mean," Sheldon muttered as they walked to the front door. "What good is a plan? Isn't human decency enough?"

"If you say so," Sam said, and then his face broke open in a smile and he hurried forward. Sheldon breathed to try to ease the knot in his stomach, and his eyes landed on someone coming in the front door, and all thoughts... well... he reached for thoughts, for one single thought, but his head had emptied itself.

Theresa. Vaguely, Sheldon saw Maddie throw her arms around her mom, and blurrily, he saw Sam bend to give her a hug. Fuzzily, Sheldon sensed Katie come to stand beside him. Then Katie was moving closer to Sam, greeting Theresa. Sheldon came out of his fog to see Katie staring with her mouth open. Staring and staring at Theresa, who shuffled her feet and turned a bit red.

"You're taller than I expected," Theresa said bluntly, and suddenly Sheldon could breathe again. This was the Theresa he had always known. Hearing her blunt words took the edge off the sharp pain Sheldon felt when he looked at her face— her absolutely...

"You're more beautiful than I expected," Katie said in reply. She was still staring at Theresa. Again Theresa shifted her weight from foot to foot, looking up at the ceiling.

"Beauty is only a construct," she said. "You might not think I was beautiful if I had a giant plate in my lip, but some people would think I was very, very beautiful."

Katie laughed a little under her breath. "Yes, but, Sam, Sheldon, you didn't warn me. You could have told me that Theresa looks like a painting."

Sheldon flinched. He knew how much Theresa hated this. She hated it when people stared at her. Hated being called beautiful. She looked as though she was holding her breath, and her hands were tightening into fists.

"You should have asked Katie if she had a plan," he murmured to Sam, lurching forward toward Theresa. Sheldon knew she was on the verge of running, and he had to keep her here. He had a feeling that if she ran, she would never come back.

"Picasso," he said. "Right, Reesey? Maybe you look like that woman in the Picasso painting with three chins and four noses?"

Theresa looked at him then, color coming back into her face, and Sheldon saw her eyes light up with relief. She wouldn't run. But oh, she was looking at him, and he was going to freeze again. Theresa was shorter than any of them, even shorter than Maddie. She was average height really, or maybe a little under average, but nothing else about her was ordinary. She had grown her hair out, he saw. It brushed her waist. That was new. But her hazel eyes, so startling, her cheekbones, her perfect face... they were all the same.

"I do have a lot of noses," she told him. "I left some at home."

And she held her arm out to him so they could walk into the dining room together.

"Purple," a voice said in a wry tone, and Sheldon jumped, bringing himself back to the present. He was not at the rehearsal dinner with Theresa. He was standing on the side-walk, waiting for Lucy, so the two of them could attend Sam and Katie's wedding. Lucy stood in front of him now, eyes wide as she stared at his suit.

"There you are," he said. "Shall we?" He held his arm out to the older woman. Lucy, his short, spirited friend, was Thai-American and wore her hair spiked with some kind of prod-uct. Her lipstick was the red of fire halls. She narrowed her eyes at him but took his arm without further comment. They began to walk in the direction of the church.

"To answer your question," he said, "if it was a question: Yes. Purple. This is a wedding, after all. Most people have forgotten how to dress for weddings." He looked down at her. Lucy wore a brilliant yellow dress, covered in large roses. "Present company excepted, of course," he added.

Lucy reached her free hand out to pat at the embroidery on the cuff. "This is exceptional, even for you, Sheldon. Any reason you're pulling out all the stops?"

He frowned at her. "My best friend is getting married. That's not enough for exceptional?"

It was true that his suit was divine. Rich, old purple velvet, embroidered at the cuffs and collar. Part of the reason Sheldon had been excited about a wedding, was that it gave him a chance to wear this suit.

Lucy changed tactics.

"How was the rehearsal dinner last night?" she asked. "I'm sorry I couldn't make it. I was getting Larry settled in his new dorm."

Sheldon blinked. He opened his mouth to say it was fine, just fine, but he couldn't say a thing. He started to cough, choking on God knew what, and bent down to tie his shoe and recover, remembering. Blast Lucy.

He straightened and took the water bottle Lucy held out to him, trying to regain composure.

"The dinner was fine," he told Lucy after he had his breath back. "Katie's menu was delicious. Even her parents were impressed. And I think they're warming up to Sam."

He thought of how he had pulled Katie aside after dessert.

"She hates being called beautiful," he told his friend. "She hates being beautiful."

Katie's mouth drew into a miserable line, and she crossed her arms over her chest. "I'm sorry," she said. "I wish Sam had told me. But how could anyone hate looking like that? It's impossible. She's perfect."

"I don't know," Sheldon had said, sighing. "But she has always hated it. She told me once that her outsides don't match her insides."

Lucy looked at him but didn't comment, and they reached the church without anymore coughing fits.

CHAPTER TWO

Before they reached the church, Sheldon saw Francisco, his reverend friend, standing at the church door greeting people as they arrived.

"Bride or groom?" he asked them as Sheldon and Lucy reached him. Lucy snorted.

"Nice try, Frankie," she said.

There was no way to choose between the bride and groom. Though both Sheldon and Lucy had known Sam longer, they had come to love Katie with a fierce, protective love. Sheldon knew he would kick Sam in the kneecaps if he ever broke his vows to Katie.

Frankie laughed at Lucy's response. She sniffed and walked past him, turning briefly to Sheldon. "I'm off to find Katie," she said. "Let me know if you need me."

Francisco grabbed Sheldon in a hug, then stepped back and looked at him, raising his eyebrows.

"Nice suit!" he said. "I didn't think you could still shock me, but this is magnificent."

"I'm so glad Sam didn't make us all wear the same thing," Sheldon said. "I hate it when wedding parties look like clones. Whose idea was that, and why do we let it continue in the enlightened age?"

Francisco stepped back and regarded Sheldon with crossed arms. He was taller than Sheldon, which was saying a lot. Sheldon was very tall. "It's interesting, the term 'enlightened age,'" Frankie said, "but we can save that conversation for another time." He paused, looking at Sheldon.

"What?" Sheldon asked, pulling back a little.

"Sam's sister,'" Frankie said, his voice low and significant. "She's the one you've been waiting for."

"I wouldn't say waiting for," Sheldon protested.

"You said—and I quote—'I'm waiting for a woman to come back. I will wait and wait, and I will wait until I am dead, and then I will wait some more.'"

"Did I say that? That doesn't sound like something I would say. Well, yes, I have waited for her to come back. But I don't think coming back for a wedding counts."

Frankie continued to look at him, arms crossed over his chest. Sheldon squirmed. "Oh look!" he said, spotting George and Mercy coming up the steps behind him. "More guests to greet! See you!"

Francisco smiled an infuriating smile, and turned to the lawyer couple, complimenting Mercy on her hat.

"Maybe it will be you, next," Sheldon heard Mercy say to Francisco, and he smirked, but his smile faded when he heard Francisco's reply.

"I was actually thinking Sheldon might be a good bet for the next groom."

Sheldon squared his shoulders and set off to find Sam.

The ceremony was everything a wedding ceremony should be. From his place beside the groom, Sheldon had an excellent view of the warm faces of the people sitting in the old pews. Lucy cried in the front row, her handkerchief soaked through within minutes, and others wiped away tears as well, including Juanita and Carlo, Aveline's real estate agents. George beamed and held Mercy's hand tight. Katie's mom cried into her dad's shoulder. Dorothy wept next to Theresa, but Sheldon couldn't see her because he was focusing on keeping his eyes away from Theresa.

Katie was gloriously beautiful, her hair a riot of red-gold curls. Maddie, the maid of honor, was elfin and lovely in her dress, and Sam had a happier look on his face than Sheldon had ever seen on his oldest friend. He could almost forgive Sam for not keeping their monk life vow.

Francisco gave a short sermon on love, calling it enduring tenderness. Sheldon allowed his heart to open the tiniest bit, to wonder if what he felt for Theresa was love.

Enduring tenderness. That sounded right. Sheldon's heart just about exploded with tenderness when he thought about her. Seeing her felt like catching sight of a rare bird. But Reesey hadn't felt the same way about him, so how was his love helpful? If someone wouldn't receive your tenderness, if someone didn't answer your phone calls, returned your letters unopened? It was like the love hit a wall. What was she thinking about these words, out there, partially obscured by Mercy's incredible hat? Sheldon craned his head, unable to stop himself from trying to see her. Sitting beside Mercy, Faith gave him a knowing look, her eyebrows raised. This whole town was the worst.

He kept his eyes on Sam and Katie for the rest of the service, forcing himself to be happy for them.

MUCH LATER, Sheldon finally talked to Theresa. The reception was held at the lakeside park, with tables and chairs set up under the trees. The guests ate, drank, and talked with the sun setting in the background. Sheldon's nerves didn't allow him to eat more than a bite or two, but the food was incredible. It could be no other way at Katie's wedding, he heard people murmuring to one another.

He wondered if people of the town had taken to Katie so well because she fed them. It was possible. People in Aveline loved good food. It seemed as though everyone from the whole town was dancing under the trees, lit by fairy lights.

Sheldon wandered with a glass of wine, stopping to listen to his friends in the Aveline Swing Band. George on trumpet, Carlo the lead guitarist and vocalist, Francisco on the drum set, and Daniel on bass. Sheldon wanted to join the group on the dance floor. It would be a waste not to dance in this suit, but he spotted Theresa sitting by herself on the lakeshore, and he knew he couldn't leave her there by herself.

Theresa wore a cranberry silk dress, and in the distance, she looked like a sculpture that an angel had dropped carefully onto the pebbles of the beach. A heavenly art installation. As Sheldon drew closer, though, the sounds of the band receding behind him, he saw that her eyes were filled with tears.

"Can I join you?" he asked.

She looked up, startled, but seemed glad to see it was him.

"Of course," she said. "The shore belongs to everyone." She blinked, and the tears that had been gathering spilled over. She swiped at them with the backs of her hands.

He didn't know what to say, so he simply sat down beside her, making sure to leave some room between them. They were silent for a long moment. Sheldon didn't know what to talk about, after so many years.

"So..." he began, reaching for something, anything. "How has life been treating you?"

She turned to look at him. A smile crept over her face. "You always were so kind," she said.

"Kind?"

"You haven't brought up the unanswered letters," she said.

He felt a twinge of pain. "Oh, well," he said. "We don't need to talk about the past."

She turned to look out at the lake, leaving him gazing at her perfect profile. "I remember swimming here every day of every summer," she said. "This town used to feel like it was mine."

"What changed?" he asked. He couldn't keep his voice steady.

She only shook her head. Then she answered his first question.

"Life is going well. Did Maddie tell you that I'm a potter now?"

"She did. I've read a bit about you... over the years. I can't think of anything more perfect."

She smiled at him, and his heart thudded. He swallowed.

She went on. "Maddie asked me to move here, you know."

If Sheldon's heart had been acting up before, now it felt as though he had fallen down a set of stairs.

"What?"

"She doesn't want to leave Aveline, but we need to be together. It makes sense for her. I want her to have this place to hold her, the way I did. I haven't seen her this happy in a very long time."

Sheldon just stared at her. Hope bloomed inside him, and there wasn't much space for it. It pushed against his rib cage painfully. Theresa's eyes skittered down and away, out toward the calm waters of the lake.

Sheldon tried to breathe.

"You're saying you might move to Aveline."

"What do you think? Do you think it would be good for Maddie?" she asked, and he could hear what she needed him to say.

Reesey needed him to tell her she was forgiven, that he would start over and they could be friends or neighbors or something. She wanted him to tell her that he wouldn't hold onto anger about all that had come before. It was ridiculous. How could that ever happen? He had been waiting for so long for her to come back, but now that it was happening,

Sheldon thought maybe he didn't want it. How could he be near her and not with her?

"Maddie asked you, didn't she?" It was mean of him to hold back, not to give her the assurance she needed, but he did it anyway. "Obviously it would be good for Maddie."

She frowned at the pebbles by her feet, picking up a handful of the small smooth stones. She poured them into the lap of her cranberry silk dress, then chose one stone and brought it up to her lips, smoothing it over them. It was a very Theresa thing to do, as familiar to him after ten years as it had been in the days they walked these beaches together. Its familiarity made Sheldon angry.

"I told you when I left that there was absolutely no hope for us. That is still true, Sheldon. We can never be together. But I know you mean a lot to Maddie, and you have always been a good friend to me." She turned her gaze on him, her hand closed around the stone now. "Can you work with that?" She managed to hold his gaze for the space of a few seconds, then dropped her eyes, turning her attention back to the stone in her hand.

Her bluntness, as always, came as a shock. Theresa had always been deficient in the art of gentle conversation.

I told you when I left...

He could remember it well. Her face, pale as a sheet of paper as she stood before him with her arms twisted behind her. Her hair had been short back then. She looked like Amélie or Audrey Hepburn, but with more anguish.

I can't tell you why. Just trust me.

There is nothing that could be bad enough that you need to do this. Just tell me what it is.

I can't tell you. I'm leaving, Sheldon. Maddie and I are moving far, far away.

Did you cheat on me? I would forgive you...

No, of course not, no never. I'm sorry. I'm going now, we're all packed up. Don't try to contact me.

And then she was gone. Sheldon hadn't really believed that Theresa would pull herself away so completely, but she had. She hadn't turned back, hadn't contacted him, had ignored all his calls and letters, and had never returned. Until now.

"Does Maddie know that you're likely to leave without saying why?" he asked.

Reesey looked at him, startled. She looked so different with her hair long, caught today in a braid that fell over one shoulder. The lines of her face were firmer, stronger with age. She was one of those people who was more beautiful in her thirties than she had been in her twenties, which was unfair and impossible. She had a tattoo of a fir tree that stretched from her elbow upward, disappearing into the folds of her dress.

"I suppose I deserve that," she said. She stood, and the stones dropped out of her dress and clattered on the shore. Sheldon flinched at the sound. "I hope you change your mind, Tazzy. You were the best friend I've ever had."

She was gone. Again, she was gone. Worse, she'd used Sheldon's nickname, the name only she called him. How could she not understand how painful this was? He shook his head, staring out at the lake. A bit of mist hovered over it. The stars were very bright. He didn't think he even had the power to change his mind. His mind wasn't really involved at all.

CHAPTER THREE

O n the morning that Theresa arrived back in Aveline
to live, she woke up in a soulless hotel, the very last
place that anyone should ever have to wake up.

Looking at the terrible striped wallpaper in her cheap
motel, Theresa felt like a shell of a person. Ugly things made
her despair. She had been driving for days, going from stale
room to stale room, but the end was nigh. Tonight she would
be in Aveline, the town that still had her heart, even after all
these years.

She stood and stretched, unzipping her overnight bag and
pulling out her last clean clothes. She pulled a soft T-shirt
over her head and buttoned up a pair of baggy corduroys,
heading to the bathroom to brush her teeth. She could hardly
believe she was moving back to Aveline. It felt like a decade's
worth of longing had been fulfilled. A day hadn't gone by that
she hadn't longed for the lake, for the lacy edges of the trees
against the dusk sky, and the stars coming out one by one. She
wasn't sure that she could trust it, and in a way, she couldn't.

The danger—everything she had fled—was still there. She stared at her pale face in the mirror before braiding her hair and splashing her face with cold water. The dangerous element in Aveline had lain dormant a long time. Surely it would allow her this much grace. Surely.

She ordered coffee for her thermos at a nearby coffee shop and slipped out once she got her order, ignoring the barista's attempt to chat. She climbed into the moving truck and started it up. She had wanted to make this journey on her own, though Maddie had asked to skip school and come help, and Sam had even volunteered to cut his honeymoon short, which was ridiculous. No, Theresa had told them both.

She needed this long solitary drive. She needed to find new ways to think about Aveline, her birthplace and her only real home.

Therapy over the last weeks had helped. Theresa had packed her house so quickly, leaving time only for eating and sleeping and going to see her therapist. In the last months, she had learned a lot about her own mind. Theresa's therapist had given her ideas for working with her mind, approaching simple things that had always evaded her, and not disparaging her brain for what it was. Theresa had always loathed her differences and had put herself down her whole life. She had hated herself for so long, but she was learning a different way—acceptance and love of herself, her brain and its unique characteristics. Loving herself felt like the relief of a cooling swim in the lake on a scorching day. She couldn't believe it had taken her so long to find this relief, the sweet symmetry of it as it lit her up from the inside.

She steered the heavy truck through forests that were as

familiar as recurring dreams. The last golden light of a day in late fall fell on her in flashes. A golden light. She was warm inside the cab of the truck, listening to Joni Mitchell, occasionally singing along. Bunches of sage and pinion that Theresa had picked up in the deserts of Nevada hung from the rearview mirror, along with a few feathers she had found on the side of the road.

She drove and drove.

A yellow diamond sign. *Curvy road ahead.* 15 miles to go.

Was she going to be able to use her new skills in a place that carried as many traumas as it did jewels? She felt a flash of self-loathing and pushed it away. Not here, she told it. You're not allowed in my heart. She felt real fear for a moment, terrified of going back to the past, but then she remembered that she didn't need to figure out the future or all the plans or relationships. She only needed to do the next thing— get to her new house.

THERESA DROVE SLOWLY through the streets of Aveline, heading for the house she had bought. The last months had been a blur of change. Buying a house based on pictures that Carlo had sent to her. She needed a place with a studio, and Carlo had found the perfect place. She bought it without even walking through it, while doing ten million other things, closing up life in Minnesota to come back to California. There! She read the address on the fence post. Her new home.

It was beautiful—a one-story Spanish villa that sprawled

over the property like a giant jungle flower. Theresa loved it. She had loved it from the moment she saw the photos, partly because it was so different from the wooden craftsman-style house she had grown up in, and it felt like a place to grow new memories. The house had rounded walls and doorways, with no sharp edges. A hug of a house.

She parked and turned to open her passenger door, just then seeing her welcome crew. Maddie stood under the oaks that spread over the sidewalk, with Severus—Sam and Katie's dog, Theresa's mother, Francisco, Carlo the burly real estate agent, and Lucy. No Tazzy.

She supposed she understood why Tazzy hadn't come. He had loved her once, but maybe he didn't want to be her friend anymore. Too much time had passed.

Theresa took a deep breath and remembered to smile as she fell out the door into Maddie's arms.

After she squeezed Maddie for at least five minutes, she stepped back to look at her daughter. "You must be exhausted," Maddie said.

"A little. Mostly hungry. I couldn't bring myself to eat the weird hotel breakfast," Theresa said, "I've mostly been eating apples and sunflower seeds today."

"Oh, Mom. You know I've told you that you can eat weird food once in a while if you have to."

"I can't," Theresa said.

"What will happen if you're trapped in a small town in the Midwest one day and you've never built the skills to eat weird food?"

Theresa shrugged and grabbed her daughter to hug her tight again. "I guess I'll starve. Stop trying to take care of me.

We've talked about this. I'm the mom, remember? Are you all moved in?"

"Not yet. I'm waiting until Sam and Katie get back because I have to take care of Severus."

Theresa tried to register that. Her vision of arriving hadn't included moving in alone.

She turned and hugged her mother. Dorothy smelled like perfume and laundry soap, the familiar smells of Theresa's childhood home. Dorothy pulled back to look at her.

"I can't believe you're here," she said. Theresa could see tears standing in her eyes. She squeezed her mother's upper arms and let go.

"I know," she said. "It's surreal."

Maddie spoke again. "Mom, do you know Reverend Francisco? His church and house are just a block away from here, so he's kind of your new neighbor."

Theresa looked up at the tall reverend. He had brown skin, rumpled hair, a young face, and a wide smile.

"I don't know him," she said. "But I have met him. At the wedding. Hi." She moved forward to shake hands, but he said, "Actually, I'm a hugger," and caught her in a hug. She stiffened, but relaxed after a moment. He was a safe person, and she had had a long day. To her surprise, she felt tears rise to the surface. She backed away quickly, trying to maintain control.

"I do know Lucy," she said, and she hid her weakness in a hug with Lucy.

"It's good to have you back," Lucy said. "It's not right for you to be away. But I did think Sheldon would be here to meet you."

Theresa let Lucy go and smiled at her. "No matchmaking," she said. "That ship has sailed. That's what people say, right?" she looked around at Maddie and Francisco for confirmation. Maddie was glaring at Lucy, and Francisco was grinning.

"If you say so," Carlo said, putting his hands in his pockets, his long beard tapping at his chest with his words. Beside him, Dorothy was grinning.

Theresa narrowed her eyes at them. Then she let her breath out in a huff.

"Okay," she said. "We'd better get this truck unloaded before I collapse. I'm assuming you're all here to help."

Maddie sighed and tucked her hair behind her ears. "What she means to say is "Will you please help?""

Francisco and Carlo chuckled as Theresa opened the back of the truck and climbed in.

"I understood," Francisco said. He paused. "Ah, just in time!" he exclaimed after a moment.

Lucy made an explosive sound with her teeth. "Sheldon, you are in so much trouble," she called.

Inside the truck, Theresa felt every muscle in her body stiffen.

CHAPTER FOUR

From inside the van, Theresa could hear Sheldon greeting the others. She gradually relaxed her muscles and dropped her head to her chest. She could do this. Seeing Sheldon was a part of her life again. Theresa needed to adjust to her new reality.

She rubbed her sweaty hands on her pants, looking around at all the boxes stacked in the van. There were boxes of pottery tools and supplies, boxes of books, kitchen stuff. All her worldly possessions. Theresa was tired from the drive and overwhelmed by the thought of socializing and unloading all of it at the same time. Especially socializing with Sheldon. What kind of mood was he in? How had he decided to be with her?

Replace the old memories with new ones, her therapist had told her.

Theresa took a deep breath and left the van, jumping lightly down from the back bumper.

Sheldon stood at a little distance from the others, hands

in his pockets. His curly black hair was as wild as usual, and he wore dark-rimmed glasses. He didn't meet her eyes. His attire was more subdued today— ripped jeans and a pink velour shirt she remembered from long ago. It wasn't Sheldon's fault that the shirt had been one of her favorites, that she could remember exactly how it felt when he slung his arm around her, wearing that shirt. Theresa frowned. Maybe it was. Maybe he remembered. She took a breath.

"Hey Sheldon," she said. "I hope you don't mind getting dirty. We have a lot to do."

He nodded, and she thought she saw a small smile creep over his face.

Carlo ceremoniously handed Theresa the keys, giving a short speech about ownership and wonderful first days. Theresa had absolutely no idea how to respond, so she took the keys and turned to look at her new home.

She sighed with happiness as she walked through the gate and under the adobe arbor with the fuchsia-colored bougainvillea cascading over it. Seeing the house was almost too much— Theresa had never lived in such a beautiful home. Carlo had warned her of things that needed to be fixed, telling her that the only heater was a wood stove in the living room. The winters could be damp, he said. Theresa shook off the warnings. After facing such intense fear about moving back to Aveline, she felt invincible, as though she could do anything, fix anything.

The gardens around the house were overgrown, but a riot of color, even now, in the fall. There was a Japanese maple in one corner, a row of spruce, a bay tree and an oak tree, more bougainvillea, and bushes full of tiny orange flowers.

Theresa gazed at it all, trying to take it in.

"This is wonderful," her mother said from beside her, and Theresa nodded, not trusting that her voice wouldn't break if she tried to speak.

After a moment, she unlocked the door and walked into the little villa. It sprawled around the property, one room leading to another, with long hallways—big enough to be rooms—connecting each space to the next.

Francisco, Carlo, and Sheldon hauled Theresa's sofas and chairs into the house. The dining room table and chairs. Her kitchen boxes, filled with mismatched pottery she had collected over the years, a collection of cast-iron pans, and a lot of jars in different sizes.

Dorothy opened boxes and put things in cupboards. Theresa wondered whether she should tell her mother to stop, but decided that she could just rearrange things later.

They carried in her mattress. "Is this it?" asked Lucy. "No frame?"

"I prefer sleeping close to the floor," Theresa told her. Lucy blinked at her. Dorothy wandered over to see what the fuss was. She shook her head at the mattress.

"She's always been like that," Theresa's mother told Lucy. "I used to find her on the floor all the time until I learned better and just took away the bed frame."

Theresa smiled at her mother, remembering.

"Yeah," she said. "I remember that. I would make a nest under my bed, and you could never find me."

The men carried in a lot of the heaviest stuff, but Theresa made sure she and Maddie worked as well, hauling boxes until their muscles shook.

"Where do these go?" Sheldon asked at the truck, pointing at the boxes that were labeled "Studio."

Theresa looked at the one outbuilding on the property—a little shed-like house with glass windows in the front and a large room in the back. This building was the real reason Theresa had bought the house. In it, she could see the perfect studio and shop for her pottery.

"In that building," she said, pointing. "Here, let me open it."

Sheldon followed her as she waded through waist-high grass to the door of the little building.

"I would have imagined Carlo would take care of the yard work before you moved in," he said.

"I told him not to touch a thing," Theresa told him.

"Of course you did," Sheldon said, as she finally got the door open and swung it out so he could carry the box inside.

She frowned at the back of his head. "What's that supposed to mean?"

"You know what it means. You never let anyone help you."

"I like things to be how I like them, Tazzy," she told him. She felt an ache in her stomach. "I'm not going to let people make me feel bad about it."

He straightened from placing the box carefully on the ground. The day was ending, and in the last streams of sunlight, dust motes danced in the air. Theresa looked around. There were a few places where boards had been used to replace broken panes of glass. Sheldon was lit from behind, his face furrowed as he looked at her. Theresa drew in a breath at the sight of him. She couldn't tell what his look meant.

"Telling you I've noticed something doesn't mean I want you to feel bad about it," he said after a moment.

"In my experience, when people tell you things they've noticed about you, it means they want you to change," Theresa said. She felt a twinge of pain as she said the words, just a ripple of memory at how many times it had happened to her.

Sheldon looked at her. Theresa still couldn't read his expression.

"What?" she asked, trying to keep her voice soft, and he opened his mouth to speak, but just then, Francisco, Lucy, and Maddie walked in carrying boxes of fragile pottery. Theresa was distracted by the need to show them where things went and caution them to be careful, so she didn't hear what Sheldon would have said next.

FINALLY, after all the boxes were in and the house was closed up, Theresa was alone. They had finished unpacking just as the pizza delivery guy had shown up, and Theresa, who had ordered pizza for her helpers, had eaten three pieces. Now she felt like her stomach was full of rocks, but tomorrow would be a better day, she promised herself. No more driving, no more bad food, no more hotel rooms.

She walked from room to room, turning off lights and looking at the immense amount of work in front of her, strange happiness welling up in her heart at the thought. She lingered in Maddie's doorway. How would it be for them, living together again?

Maddie seemed so changed, so content to be in Aveline. She still wore a lot of black, but her eyeliner wasn't as thick, and she had lost the giant overcoat. She had zipped on a fitted down jacket before she left, and Theresa had exclaimed over how cute it was on her. It showed off her slight stature, rather than hiding her in meters of cloth.

"Katie helped me find winter clothes," Maddie told her mom, and Theresa felt a swift stab of jealousy. She sighed it away. Of course, Theresa couldn't be everything to Maddie. She hadn't been here.

It was nothing but good for Maddie that she had a new aunt who could help her with things like clothing, but Theresa still found herself blinking back tears—a sure sign that she needed solitude and sleep. Theresa had hugged her daughter fiercely and said goodbye to the whole group.

Right before Sheldon left, he had turned to her and said, "Before, when we got interrupted..."

She crossed her arms over her stomach. Sheldon went on.

"I was going to say, 'I don't know whether to feel sorry for you or be angry with you.'"

She blinked, the tears startled away.

"Blunt of you," she said, smiling a little.

"You seem to appreciate bluntness," he said, and he smiled the tiniest bit in return, the first time he had aimed a smile in her direction since she had seen him at the wedding. Her own smile grew wider.

"That's true. Thank you."

She thought of him now, of that tiny smile.

"Don't go there, Reesey," she told herself. "You know you can't."

But she still felt warmth all through her. She fell into her bed with her clothes on, closed her eyes, and was asleep immediately.

CHAPTER FIVE

Theresa dreamed of fear.
I will hurt him.
Please don't.
Watch me.

When she woke, she could still taste and smell the terror that had been her close companion for so many years. Light streamed into her room, though, making delightful tree-shaped shadows on the walls, and she blinked away the haze. She was nothing if not used to nightmares. After a while, the fear began to fade, and her breath came more easily.

She stretched, willing the stiffness out of her muscles. Her stomach felt as though she had eaten socks for dinner, but look at this house! Everything about it was beautiful, even the way the light hit the walls.

Could it really be hers? Theresa thought about her house in Minnesota—austere and square, with long wallboards that joined in tight corners. It had sheltered her for many years, but it had not felt like home, even after a decade. This little villa, on the other hand, felt like home from the first day.

She got out of bed and walked from room to room, looking at the soft curves of the whitewashed adobe walls, and the large terracotta tiles on the kitchen floor, cook under her feet. Some of the windows were made of many tiny panes of glass. They were dirty now, but Theresa would clean them. She went to the front door and threw it open to the porch. She, Theresa Lily Grant, had a front porch!

The crisp fall air surrounded her. Theresa closed her eyes and breathed it in.

Then her stomach growled.

You can't go around eating socks for dinner and air for breakfast, she told herself. She needed real food, right now, but she had nothing in her kitchen.

She went back to her room and dug through her suitcase. She pulled on striped leggings and a salmon-colored tunic, braided her hair over her shoulder, tied a scarf around it, and laced up her boots. She found her satchel and keys, and then paused, looking at the keys in her hands. Did she want to drive a moving van to the store? Nope. She'd walk. She got as far as the front door, then at another gust of wind, came back for a sweater—a soft ruby-colored thing she'd had for years.

The lock stuck, and Theresa sighed and simply closed the door gently behind her, leaving the house unlocked. Not wise, maybe, but moving back to Aveline hadn't been wise either, and she had done that.

Surely no one would rob her.

The day was juicy with beauty. Theresa wanted to drink the sky right up as she walked. She hadn't realized how thirsty she was for this specific kind of loveliness. Autumn in California was glorious. Giant oaks stretched over the old street, bougainvillea cascaded over walls and roofs, and there were a hundred kinds of flowers along the way. Even some leaves changing colors. Theresa filled her eyes with it all and gave a little skip of delight. She couldn't help herself.

At the corner, she saw the church where Sammy had been married, where Francisco was the reverend. The building was a humble little structure—stone and board in the shade of a massive redwood. Oh, there was the reverend now, standing on the steps with someone else. Theresa squinted. The man looked familiar.

Theresa hated bumping into people when she was on a mission. It distracted her, and sometimes she didn't even get to her original errand. There was always so much derailing small talk. But this was part of life in the small town of Aveline, and Theresa knew she needed to get used to it. She gave a little wave, hoping they would let her pass, but Francisco's face was open with a smile, and they both loped down to the sidewalk to greet her.

"How was your first night?" Francisco asked after he had given her one of his big hugs.

"I slept like a rock," Theresa told him.

He smiled his kind smile, and then gestured to the man beside him.

"Do you know Daniel?" he asked.

Theresa felt shock turn her face hot. "Yes, of course, I know Daniel," she said, "Daniel, you look so different!"

The man standing before her was a little shorter than Francisco, with sandy hair and brown eyes. When Theresa had known him, he'd had long hair and a massive beard covering his face, neck, and upper chest. Now his face was clean-shaven. It was not a bad change. He looked ten years younger than the last time she'd seen him, which was no small thing since he was actually ten years older. He grinned at her. He had dimples.

She spoke without thinking. "Daniel, you have dimples! I mean, you have a face!" She felt a plummeting in her belly. Oh, that probably wasn't the right thing to say. It was odd to tell an old friend that he had a face.

He smiled, though. "Decided it was time to show it," he responded gently.

Theresa had always liked Daniel. He was a master bass player who worked at the post office because he was too shy to live a musician's life, even though several bands had approached him in the past. He had been a friend to her and Sheldon when...well, no use thinking about that.

People in town had been suspicious of Daniel back then. He was too quiet, had too many tattoos, and was socially awkward. But Theresa had always known she could trust him. She wondered how things were for him now.

"Do you still work at the post office?" she asked.

"Absolutely," Francisco said, "We're the luckiest people in the world, to have our postmaster Daniel. What other branch has posters of the universe plastered to every wall?"

"Shhhh," Daniel said. "We don't want management to demand that I rip them off. So far I've been squeaking by, unnoticed. But speaking of the job, I'd better get myself over there. People have letters to send."

"And I need to go buy some groceries," Theresa said. "I'll walk with you."

"Do you want to have breakfast with my family?" Francisco asked.

Theresa stared at him. "Wow," she said. "That's a very kind offer. But I need to get settled and have real food in my own house. Not that you don't eat real food. I'm just eager to get going with my new life."

She flushed, feeling like she had messed that up. Francisco smiled at her.

"I totally understand," he said. "Next time."

A cool wind blew down the street, rustling in the tops of the tall oaks, and Theresa shivered, remembering the fear from her dream. She shook it off. There was no reason to be afraid, she told herself. Not anymore.

CHAPTER SIX

Sheldon strode around the front of his grocery store, Green's, barking orders at his employees. He had not slept well, and no one seemed to be listening to him at all. Finally, Lucy came to stand directly in front of him, putting her hands on her hips and glaring up at him.

"These kids are not going to tell you to stop being a jerk, but I will, Sheldon Green. What under the purple sky has come over you? I haven't heard you grump around the store like this since you were worried that Sam was going to get married and leave you...oh! Is this because Sam is on his honeymoon?"

"No," Sheldon muttered. He massaged his temples and wished himself far, far away, deep in the forest, maybe, with a pair of binoculars, spotting a rare bird for the first time...or at an antique show...Lucy elbowed him. He pulled himself back to the present. The young cashiers were motionless, watching Lucy and Sheldon with open mouths.

The store actually did look clean and ready for the day.

Just a moment ago, Sheldon would have sworn it was a hovel with dirt everywhere and empty boxes cascading at the ends of the aisles. He blinked. The windows shone, the displays were overflowing with color, and the store smelled like the orange oil in the natural floor cleaner. He sighed.

"No," he said again. "I'm happy for Sam." Sheldon knew precisely why he was falling apart, and it wasn't because of Sam. To be honest, he was surprised Lucy hadn't figured it out. He looked at her now, standing there with short, black, spiky hair and a look part of outrage, part concern.

Theresa was the one making him crazy, of course. Theresa lived in Aveline. How could anyone do anything when Theresa lived in Aveline? An otherworldly being had come to live among them, and everyone was acting as though life was normal.

"I'm sorry, Lucy," he said, and then raised his voice so everyone could hear. "I'm sorry, everyone. I shouldn't take my mood out on you. I'm a bit worn out." He tried to smile. "Back to work! I'll do the outside displays, as penance."

Lucy patted his arm and smiled, but her eyes were still narrowed, and she muttered under her breath, "How is that a penance?"

She was right to question him, Sheldon thought as he hauled the crates of oranges outside. The autumn air was gorgeous. Working outside wasn't a penance. But it let Sheldon keep an eye out for Theresa. And just like that, as though he had called her by thinking her name—there she was. She was down the street, walking under the oaks. She was with someone. Who was it? Oh! She was walking with Daniel, looking up at him as she walked.

Sheldon smiled, faintly, memories coming to him.

"He's definitely odd," Theresa had said, "but I see so much in him. Let's adopt him."

"Are you sure he wants to be adopted?" Sheldon asked, kissing the top of her head. She snuggled against him, leaning back against his chest as though he was a chair just for her. The lake glimmered before them. Theresa smelled of lavender and cinnamon. "And who are you to call anyone odd?" Theresa laughed.

"Everyone needs to be adopted," she told him.

And so they did, asking Daniel over whenever they had space for a third person. He was quiet, but when he spoke, his thoughts were deep and kind.

Sheldon's smile wavered. He hadn't meant to drop the friendship the way he had. But when Theresa left, he didn't have much heart for anything. He was trying to repair the friendship now, bringing Daniel to backyard night with the other men.

Sheldon glanced back at Daniel and Theresa across the street. It looked like Daniel was turning to walk to the post office, while Theresa was coming... here? Sheldon's heart began to race.

But then Daniel reached out and squeezed her shoulder, and Theresa laughed up at him and gave him a hug. Sheldon's stomach dropped. He ducked into the store before they could see him. He felt feverish. He needed to hide, so he hurried into his office, flopping into his desk chair and grabbing the first stack of papers he found, flipping through them.

Soon he heard the bells on the front door, and a clear voice saying, "Hi, Lucy."

"Well, hello, darling. Oh my, I forgot you were really here now. Hmm. Things are becoming clearer."

"What?"

"Nothing. Is there anything in particular that you need?"

"Food."

"Well, we have that."

"Yes, I see. And I can smell it. Wow, this place is glorious."

"Thank you. You can tell Sheldon if you like. He's in his office, right over there."

Sheldon swore under his breath. Lucy was a meddling, annoying old woman...he held his breath, waiting, looking at the papers that were blurring before his eyes.

Sheldon felt Theresa before he saw her. He could feel her hovering there, like the remnants of an excellent dream.

"Tazzy," she said in a low voice. He dragged his eyes away from his sheaf of papers and up to her face. No, that was a mistake. He looked back down at his papers. Sheldon wouldn't have believed that Theresa could be more beautiful than she had been ten years ago—Lord knew Sheldon wasn't more beautiful—but it only showed the limits of his imagination. Theresa wasn't quite human. She had come back to Aveline luminous.

"Yes?" he said when he could trust his voice.

He could hear her hesitation when she spoke.

"I wanted to say thank you for yesterday."

"Oh, no problem at all. Just being neighborly."

"Neighborly. Right. Well, I'm going shopping."

"Great," Sheldon said, his voice flat. He could hear that

he had hurt her, and it made him feel angry. Angry with whom, he didn't know. "Have a good time."

She lingered. Sheldon looked up at her again. Mistake! He flicked his eyes back down again.

"Do you...is there anything good right now?" she asked.

He groaned inwardly. She had him. Sheldon couldn't ignore the cry for help of someone who needed to know which vegetables were fresh. He stood up and walked past her, swiftly, making sure not to touch her.

"We have amazing eggplant at the moment," he said as he walked toward the produce section. He shot Lucy a look from a distance, and she smirked at him. "And the kale is lovely."

"Mm, kale omelets," Theresa said, her voice happy again.

She really did want to be his friend, Sheldon thought. Did she have no idea how hard that would be for him? Before Theresa left Aveline, the two of them were the very best of friends, but Theresa had killed that friendship. They were more than friends. Sheldon knew what her lips tasted like, what the nape of her neck felt like under his hand. He had believed he was going to be Maddie's father. Then the lovely woman beside him had ripped it all away without an explanation.

"Our eggs are over here," he said, taking a shortcut through the kitchenware aisle.

Sheldon realized Reesey wasn't beside him anymore and turned back. Green's didn't have a large selection of kitchen-ware, but they carried some mugs and bowls, a few pots and pans, an assortment of utensils. Some towels.

Theresa had stopped by the mugs and stood there holding one of them in her hands, frowning at it. Sheldon sighed, letting his head drop forward. How was it possible to feel so jittery and so tired at the same time?

"This is poorly made," Theresa declared. "I can sell you better pottery, once I have my studio up and running."

He pinched the bridge of his nose. "Yes, I've heard that you've become quite the potter," he said. There were layers and layers of meaning in his tone. Theresa had left and found a fantastic new life somewhere else, and that made Sheldon bitter and angry. She blinked at him. He couldn't tell if she understood the subtext of his statement.

"I've heard that you've become quite the drinker," she said.

His jaw dropped. Then he pulled his mouth shut. "Yes," he said. "Well, I'm working on that."

"That's good. Too much alcohol isn't healthy."

"Why don't you put the poorly-made cup back on the shelf and I'll get someone else to show you the eggs?" he answered. "Lucy!" he called, striding away, angry again. "Can you show Theresa around the store? She seems to need a personal guide."

Sheldon ignored Theresa's little gasp as he went back to his office and slammed the door.

CHAPTER SEVEN

That evening, Sheldon sat beside the fire in Francisco's backyard, trying to ignore the fact that Theresa was in a house that was a mere block away. It was nearly impossible.

Sheldon could feel her presence in his bones and muscles, in the skin on his face.

The oak trees rustled, and Sheldon tipped his head back to watch the dancing leaves, breathing in the scent of the charcoal barbecue and the sizzling grass-fed beef steaks that Francisco had layered over it.

"You look haggard today," Francisco told him conversationally as he passed Sheldon a soda. His tone was much the same as if he'd said: "You look nice today."

Francisco had soda for Sheldon and beer for everyone else. Sheldon had been drinking more frequently, lately, and he wanted to break the habit, so he had started a ninety-day alcohol cleanse. Today was day five. Sheldon looked longingly at the beer in Francisco's hand. He may have neglected to think this through properly. With Theresa around, it was going to be a long three months.

"Thanks," he replied. "Observant of you."

"Come on, look alive, Sheldon!" George said, leaning forward in his chair. "This is it! Time to officially welcome Daniel to backyard night. We've waited a long time for this day."

Sheldon forced himself to sit up taller and look at Daniel. He smiled at the worried look on his old friend's face.

"Shall we toast?" Sheldon asked. "Raise your glasses for Daniel, our newest brother."

"To Daniel!" Francisco, George, and Carlo chorused.

They all drank, and Daniel smiled shyly. "Thanks, guys."

Francisco's mom, Lupe, came out with a pan of tamales, his daughter, Rosa, dancing behind her with a basket of napkins. Francisco stood to take the dish, dropping a kiss on his mother's head.

"Mama, I told you to take the night off," he said. "You can eat some of what we make."

"Shush, Mijo!" she said. "Let your mama cook. Hola, Sheldon, hola, George. Samuel is not back from his honeymoon yet? ¡Ay! They must be so tired..."

"Okay, Mamá," Francisco said, his cheeks turning red, "Here, take some steak for you three. Enjoy!"

"Thank you, Mijo. Thank you, Sheldon, for bringing fancy steak from your nice shop."

"No trouble at all, Mrs. Rodriguez," Sheldon said, grinning at the look on Francisco's face. He had been playing a game of 'high five, up high, down low, too slow' with Rosa.

The eleven-year-old was so fast that she nearly always got him.

"She loves to embarrass you," he said as Frankie's mom called Rosa and then slipped back into the door at the back of their house.

"She wants me to get remarried," Frankie muttered, "And thinks embarrassing me into it is a viable strategy. I have no idea why she thinks that will work. I'm not getting married again. Rosa is totally fine. She has all of us looking after her."

"That's right," Carlo said. "What preteen with a father, grandmother, and grandfather would ever need a mother?"

Sheldon inhaled. Carlo was overly direct at times.

Frankie passed his beer from hand to hand, quiet for a moment, then looked at Carlo. "Let's just say if I could be sure that Rosa would get a mother, not an ambivalent step-mother, like some of the women Mama tried to set me up with, I might be more open to marriage." He shrugged. "It's extremely unlikely, but Mama won't give up."

As THE STARS CAME OUT, they sat back in their chairs and grew more relaxed. Sheldon's stomach felt comfortably full. George had kindled a fire in Frankie's fire pit, and they all scooted their chairs closer than they had a week ago. Autumn was settling in. The talk ranged from work, to some new discoveries in physics that Daniel and George were excited about, to sports. Then a comfortable silence fell. The fire crackled. Sheldon thought again about how much he loved the smell of wood smoke.

"Let's talk deeper," Frankie said. "If you feel comfortable, you can tell us what God has been showing you about his love. What are you learning, lately?"

After a bit of a pause, George spoke. "Every day I'm more firmly convinced of God's passion for the people in the outer margins of society," he said. "I feel his love for them when I'm with them. This week Mercy and I worked in Billers, meeting with many clients who are caught in the cycle of poverty and crime. They're often treated worse if they are black, mentally ill, or a minority in some other way." He rubbed a hand over his forehead. "It's hard not to grow bitter, fighting for people and seeing how badly the structure of our society serves them. But Mercy and I are trying to direct our sadness into solidarity. God feels this ache, and we feel it with him."

Sheldon smiled at his hands. He felt privileged to be friends with George: someone who cared passionately and worked relentlessly for justice.

"It seems like hard work," he said.

George shrugged. "We're compelled to do it." George and Mercy were Aveline's lawyers, but they also worked in Billers or even as far as L.A. as civil rights or defense lawyers. Francisco and George had been working together on a program for at-risk youth, planning to launch it in the next few years.

Another silence fell. Sheldon heard an owl calling in the distance. Then Daniel spoke, surprising everyone.

"God is showing me love through you four, as well as Sam," Daniel said. "Many people don't trust me, but you welcomed me in."

"Welcomed you?" Carlo yelped. "We've been pursuing you for years now! We're so glad you're finally here!"

"It took a while for me to feel comfortable," Daniel said in his soft way.

Ten years ago, just before Theresa had left and Francisco had arrived, someone had gone on a crime spree around Aveline. Daniel had been dragged into the investigation when an anonymous person said they had seen him acting suspiciously. He had been cleared eventually, but some people in Aveline had never really trusted him again.

Sheldon had never known what to think about who had robbed seven homes in Aveline. He couldn't believe it was Daniel, though. Dan was shy and quiet. He had none of the characteristics of a thief.

George stretched a hand out and patted Daniel on the shoulder.

After a moment, Sheldon spoke. "I felt some of the wilder side of God's love today," he said, "when Lucy tore into me for being too hard on my employees." The other men chuckled.

"Lucy does a good job of demonstrating that particular kind of God's love," George said. They all laughed, then silence fell again. They waited.

Francisco spoke next. "I'm feeling God's love in having a new neighbor," he said. "It's good to have change in the neighborhood. We get too stagnant, otherwise. And we need practice because next year we get our refugees."

Frankie had campaigned for a long time and had finally succeeded in convincing the town council to sponsor a few refugee families. There had been a vote, and though not everyone was for it, they had the votes they needed. More than 70% of people in Aveline wanted to extend welcome to the new refugees. They would be responsible for helping the families settle in, find jobs, and become comfortable in their new home. Frankie was right. They needed practice.

Sheldon chewed his lip, frowning. Something about what Frankie had said didn't sit right with him. Sheldon didn't want Francisco to appreciate Theresa too much. He didn't want Daniel to like Theresa too much, either, for that matter.

He was speaking before he had time to think about the words coming out of his mouth.

"I saw you and Theresa looking pretty chummy this morning," he said to Daniel. "Catching up?"

George and Francisco burst out laughing. They roared with laughter, leaning back in their chairs and holding their stomachs.

"I'm glad you find this so funny," Sheldon said.

But Daniel was looking at him with gentle eyes. "I remember," he said to Sheldon quietly. Abruptly, Francisco and George stopped laughing, still wiping at their faces. "I remember what your love for her was like. You don't have to worry about me. I would never betray you."

Suddenly Sheldon was on his feet. "Thanks for the great evening," he said. "I'm pretty tired. Think I'll head out now."

He was halfway through the gate when he heard George's words. "Don't forget that the love of God takes a lot of different forms, Sheldon. You might open yourself up a little more."

Sheldon let the door slam behind him, the second he had slammed today. This was becoming a bad habit.

CHAPTER EIGHT

Sheldon was too worked up to go home, so he walked the streets of Aveline, stewing over the day, the sound of the men's laughter echoing in his brain, taunting him.

A long time ago, Sheldon and Sam had made a pact to be single, to live the monk life, and to leave the world of relationships in the past. They rashly vowed it back in the dark days when a woman had thrown Sam over, just after Theresa had driven away without explanation, taking Maddie with her and breaking Sheldon's heart.

The vow was nothing flashier than two broken-hearted men, hoping to shift priorities and focus on the spiritual life. Sheldon wasn't even a very good monk. He sometimes woke in the mornings for prayers, but he drank too much and yelled at his employees, and he was obsessed with antiques and Jeopardy.

Still, though, a promise was a promise. Sam had jumped ship, but Sheldon was still sailing. The world needed men who weren't chasing women, right? Who knew how to be people without having to be in a relationship? Sheldon had believed it, back when he, Sam, and Frankie were out on Sam's boat all those years ago.

The reverend hadn't promised anything about monk-hood, but he might as well have, for all the attention he showed to women. After losing his wife, it seemed that he simply had no interest in anything other than his work and his daughter.

Besides the promise, there was the matter of Sheldon's heart. He had masked his immense grief for years, joking around, leaning into the dramatic when the sorrow seemed too large. But nothing in life his had ever hurt him as much as Theresa leaving. Not even his mother dying in a mental hospital when he was still a youth, not losing his father years later.

He had wondered at himself for being so desolate. Why had Theresa's disappearance hurt him so deeply? Maybe it was because of all the questions it had left behind. Was it his fault? Why wasn't he enough to make her stay? He had written the questions all through those unopened letters, and he'd still never received an answer. Not knowing tormented him.

And now Theresa was back in this small town where he owned the grocery store, and was her brother's best friend, and couldn't help bumping into her every few days. Sheldon didn't know what to do. Was there a book that would tell him how this should go? He knew George thought their whole monk life thing was a huge joke that would pass like an identity crisis. Not that George didn't believe in a life dedicated to God. But he didn't think they needed to isolate themselves from love relationships to surrender themselves to God.

"A large part of God's heart is revealed through love for another human being," George had told them. "You might not be able to fully understand all of Jesus' love for people unless you are confronted with an angry woman and decide to walk into the room and sit down beside her, rather than running away." Then he had clutched at his arms and laughed himself helpless.

But Sam and Sheldon had been caught up by brotherhood and sorrow for the world at war and men who were cruel to women. They didn't want to be those men, so monkhood it was. Until Katie came along.

If Sam was still with him, Sheldon might know what to do. He felt alone, floating in a new sea that he hadn't been prepared for.

Theresa had killed part of Sheldon when she left. She had also taken away something he had come to cherish: a chance to be a father. It had been a terrible, monstrous thing for her to do.

Sheldon paced through the neighborhood toward the lake, muttering to himself. Reesey had wounded him, but still, he was helpless around her. He thought of her in his shop today, asking about vegetables. Theresa knew it was the only subject that would pull him out of his grumpy cloud when he was angry with her. It bothered him and touched him that she remembered.

Her face swam before him, and he sighed. Her face was lovelier than any he had ever seen; so beautiful that modeling agents approached her on the street.

Sheldon had seen her run from one agent, literally sprinting away as fast as she could go.

He smiled, remembering. They had gone to L.A. for an art show of one of Theresa's heroes. Standing outside the gallery, Reesey passionately told Sheldon everything she knew about the artist until a tall, impossibly thin woman had approached them and put a hand on Theresa's arm, interrupting her midsentence. Theresa had blinked up at the woman, clearly taken by surprise and unsure of what to do.

"I must know who represents you," the woman said. "Because if you don't have an agent, or you aren't modeling yet, I would love the chance to be your agent. Here—"the woman had blinked her fake eyelashes, reaching into her purse—"take my card."

Theresa had opened her mouth once, twice, before pulling away and sprinting down the street, leaving Sheldon standing with the woman.

"Sorry," Sheldon had muttered, and then he took off after Reesey. When he finally caught up to her, she was so panicked that she wanted to keep running, but after a few blocks of walking quickly, she finally slowed and laughed.

"I hope that taught her a lesson about accosting people at art shows," she said.

They went back to the gallery when Reesey calmed down enough to think it might be safe.

Sheldon remembered her face, open like a flower as she gazed at the paintings and sculptures of her hero. Now that he thought about it, she had lingered a long time over one display, a simple case from floor to ceiling, filled with pots and jars the artist had crafted. It was the most humble of the exhibits, and most people glanced it over briefly and then passed it by, but Theresa's eyes stayed wide with delight as she looked her fill.

"They all have some kind of mistake," she said. "Not even one is perfect. I love that."

Sheldon had slipped his hand into hers. Dorothy had been watching little Maddie and encouraged the two of them to take as long as they wanted. They went to a taqueria that night and sat devouring tacos, drinking Coronas, and dreaming.

Theresa had so many dreams. She was high on beautiful art, excited about the endless possibility of the artist's life. They walked around the city streets, holding hands, disappearing into shadows for quick kisses. Sheldon quoted poetry to Reesey, and she kissed him after every poem. The memory burned in Sheldon's heart as he walked through the park, aiming himself like an arrow for the lakeshore, the comforting sound of the water lapping gently on the stones. His heart couldn't take much more of this.

He didn't know why Theresa had left, or why she had hurt him so badly. But she was back.

And Sheldon loved her. He loved every single thing about her. Sheldon loved Theresa so much his heart ached with it. He loved her more than some vow he had made. He loved her more than the ache he felt at the memory of her betrayal.

He needed one last chance to win her over again.

He looked at the silvery reflection of the moon on the black water, testing the thought in his mind. A quest. A resolution. Yes, Sheldon would try one last time to see whether

Theresa could love him. If she couldn't, well, that would be that.

Sheldon had been waiting for her to come back. He had told all his friends that he was suspended in time until Reesey came again, and it wasn't only drama or self-protection that made him say it. Now that she was here, as whimsical and blunt and strange as ever, Sheldon realized that he hadn't really believed she would ever return. He couldn't miss this new chance to be with her.

If she were loved, all would be well, wouldn't it? Sheldon had convinced Theresa of that once. She had believed him, and she had loved him back. That was what she needed: to know she was loved.

CHAPTER NINE

Early one morning, about a week after her arrival in Aveline, Theresa pulled her favorite mug out of the cupboard. She traced its lines with her fingers, allowing memories to flow over her.

The day she made it, in the cold little studio in Minneapolis, where the heater never worked very well in winter, and when she worked with clay, her hands stiffened up until she had to breathe on them or jam them under her arms to warm them.

This cup had been her first successful wheel throw after she remade her entire life. She'd finished it while Maddie was at her new kindergarten. Back then, in her cold and lonely new life, her face had often streamed with tears while she worked on her pots. She wedged clay or centered and molded it on the wheel, she learned about glazing and firing, and all the while, she longed for what she had left behind.

Theresa had made hundreds of mugs since then, but she still loved this first one the best. This was the one, a sculpted depiction of a milestone: the first time Theresa had dared to let herself think she could do something more with her life after she fled...well. The first time she believed that she could become a potter and take care of Maddie, far off in the snowy wilderness.

The cup was round and gently tapered at the top, with a deep blue glaze, cracked in spots where it had fired incorrectly. It had a dent on one side. Theresa had deliberately pressed her thumb into the clay after she cut the mug off the wheel. Since that long-ago day, reviewers of her work had written about these little signature marks. She'd been praised for them, and she'd been criticized for what one reviewer called a conceit.

Theresa didn't care what they called it. She only knew that perfect symmetry made her teeth hurt, so she made an indent in each pot. Without the last mark, her work was not complete. Choosing where and how she made the mark was essential, a sacred step that Theresa took seriously.

She pulled her ceramic pour-over coffee filter out of the cupboard and set it over the mug, placing a cloth filter inside and turning the kettle on. She pulled a bag of coffee beans from Sheldon's store out of the freezer and poured some into her hand grinder, turning the crank, and breathing in the aroma of the beans releasing their oils. She felt her shoulders loosen as she moved through the slow ritual.

Theresa had unpacked carefully over the week, opening boxes, hanging art, and putting her belongings into her new cupboards. She had skimped over the last decade, living in a tiny house, spending next to nothing. Buying this house was her reward. Theresa was making the most of it, designing the home she had always dreamed of, as though with her care, she could guarantee this was the final time they would move houses. She did all of this while her heart thumped a warning, trying to tell her the new home wasn't safe. She ignored the message. Theresa knew her body. Her heart pounded warning signals even if none were needed.

The water bubbled in the gooseneck kettle. Theresa picked it up and poured, swishing the steaming water around the inside of the mug to warm it. She poured the used water out, then wet the filter. She added two scoops of coffee and put the cup on the scale. 60 g of water, clockwise.

Maddie sometimes made fun of her for this ritual. "It's just coffee," she said. "Honestly, Mom."

"How would you feel if someone forced you to drink tea from a tea bag?" Theresa countered.

"What? No one would, ever," Maddie said, pulling a horrified face.

Theresa smiled. She loved it when Maddie spoke fiercely. Her daughter had grown up around the scent of her mother's fear, which made her try to console and protect, rather than being her true fierce self.

A sudden wave of terror weakened Theresa's knees, as though even the thought of fear had made her afraid. She was foolish to think she could live here, in Aveline, that someone like her was allowed to have a life and a new house. She jerked compulsively, and hot water splashed over her arm. Gasping with pain, she rushed to the sink and held her arm under the running water.

The ends of her hair trailed in the sink, dampened as she leaned over, running the cold water, breathing in peace and breathing out fear, the way her therapist had taught her. It took nearly ten minutes for Theresa's heart to stop racing and the sting of the burn to ease.

She turned the water off and found the jar of aloe vera, daubing it along her arm in a long swathe.

Her coffee was ruined. Theresa started the kettle, washed the cup, washed out her cloth filter, and started again. Warm the cup. Wet the filter. Scoop the coffee. 60 g of water, clockwise. Wait 30 sec. 90 g of water, counterclockwise. Wait 50 sec. And then the next step. The coffee bloomed, the grounds expanding and rising in the cone. The fragrance reached her, and it was not a dangerous smell. She finished making the coffee and put the filter in the sink.

With her cup in one hand and leather journal in the other, she walked over to the open back door and stepped onto the tiled veranda. She had bought an outdoor table with two chairs: one for her and one for Maddie, who was still at Sam and Katie's house taking care of Sirius. Theresa had spent hours in the garden already, mowing, weeding, revealing hidden plants. She bought a birdfeeder and new plants that she dug into the earth with her bare hands.

These were not the actions of someone who hated herself.

Theresa opened her journal.

An incident in the morning. But not a full meltdown. I recovered and made my coffee because that is what I can do. Because I am strong.

There was a time when that wash of fear would incapacitate Theresa for the day. Maddie had known her that way for a long time. Even as a young girl, she had dealt with the aftermath of meltdowns. The familiar heat of shame prickled in Theresa's palms. But she pushed it away.

I have today. What will I do with today?

Oh! Sam and Katie were coming home. They would all have dinner together tonight, and after dinner, Maddie would move into this house. She hadn't seen her room yet—Theresa was keeping it as a surprise. Her fierce little girl. A memory came to Theresa: tiny Maddie, hands in fists at her waist, standing at Theresa's bedroom door. Lobbing a question like a grenade.

Who is my father?

You don't have a father. You have an uncle and a grandfather. That's pretty good, right?

Theresa took a shaky breath and stood. She needed to get dressed for her walk by the lake—the dog might be waiting.

It had become a rhythm, and Theresa needed rhythm.

"You need to find the middle point between rhythm and inflexibility," her therapist had said. "You have to take care of yourself, and taking care of yourself in this world, which is full of unpredictability, means finding that line."

Theresa was working on it. She threw on a loose indigo tunic and gold leggings, stepped into tall boots, and pulled a red beanie over her messy black hair. Washed her face. Brushed her teeth. Wrote herself a note on the mirror: After walk- breakfast! No more forgetting to eat. No more self-loathing.

CHAPTER TEN

T he air was fresh and bright outside, and the dog was waiting for her. The dog had been there every morning, tagging along as Theresa walked to the lakeshore.

"Who are you," she asked him, "and who is letting you wander?" He replied by wagging his tail and falling into step beside her, sniffing at every tree in their path. Theresa walked at her own pace, and the dog always caught up.

Once she reached the shore, she walked with wide steps, relishing the crunch of the stones under her boots. She prayed not to meet anyone while also trying to open herself to the possibility of meeting someone. It was tricky. *Don't be inflexible.*

When the therapist had first introduced the concept of flexibility, Theresa had responded by making a series of sculptures. She spent half a year on the project. When she was done, she held an art show called *flexible*. Each sculpture followed the other: Flexible 1, Flexible 2, Flexible 3... and so on. They looked a bit like elongated human creatures, but all were missing a limb. She didn't know why—they had just come out that way. Maybe the missing parts were wounds from not being flexible enough. Theresa knew the feeling.

"Just the fact that you're taking our talks into your studio shows that you're getting it," her counselor said, her round face flushing with excitement.

Theresa stared at her. Theresa had taken their talks about actually being flexible in life, and made a series of sculptures that all had the same name. It didn't mean she was progressing in actually *being flexible*.

"That makes you happy?" she had asked.

"Of course it does."

Theresa would never understand people.

The dog brought her a stick. Theresa threw it for him. He was a raggedy kind of dog, the type that had one ear pointing up and one ear flopping over. If she stopped to gaze out over the lake, the dog sat waiting for her, head cocked to one side. If she patted him, wrinkling her nose because he was dirty, he wagged his tail and yelped when she stopped. He was sweet.

"Where do you belong?" she asked him. She felt all loose and happy after walking. Talkative. Even if she was only talking to a dog.

The dog didn't answer.

Her *flexible* sculptures had all sold for incredible amounts of money. Theresa had an agent now, something that made her sigh and smile. She remembered how she used to feel about agents, back when they tried to contact her about modeling or acting. Once, Theresa had literally run away from one. She sighed, remembering that evening with

Sheldon. That art show was where Theresa had made up her mind to be a potter, right before she left Aveline.

Oh, Sheldon. Theresa hadn't wanted to hurt him.

She knew that she could never get involved with anyone in Aveline again. Not if she wanted to stay here, wanted to keep her house and not have to move on. She needed to make sure Sheldon was not holding onto any hope that there could be anything between them. But she did wish they could be friends. Besides Maddie, he was her favorite person in the world. It would be good to have a friend.

Just as Theresa turned to walk away from the lakeshore, she saw people in the distance and tensed up. As they came closer, though, she recognized George and Mercy, her long-time friends. Theresa waited, and hugged each of them when they reached her spot on the beach.

"We missed you," Mercy said. "Are you going to set up shop so we can bathe in your glory? We'll have a famous artist in Aveline."

Theresa blushed. "How did you know?" she asked.

"Oh, Sam has shown us headlines from Minneapolis," George said.

Sam. Theresa smiled, thinking of her younger brother, wondering if he knew how much farther her art had traveled recently. There was a twinge of uncertainty in her chest. Theresa had been gone forever—she had no right to complain —but what was it going to be like now that he was married? Married to an apparently perfect person, at that.

"I remember when you moved here," she told George and Mercy. "You came over to our house for Thanksgiving dinner."

"I remember that," Mercy said, smiling.

"I was young, though. We didn't talk deeply then. I remember babysitting Faith. It was hard for you at first?"

Mercy turned and looked out over the lake. "You remember we moved here for Mercy's health," George said.

"We moved because, as you know, we lost our son, and I wanted to kill myself." Mercy said.

Theresa blinked. George made a choking sound.

"I don't think I've ever heard you tell someone that straight out," he said to his wife, moving closer to her. She leaned into him.

Theresa felt a sharp pang somewhere in her chest. The dog came back. She threw the stick for him again.

"Theresa understands," Mercy said. "She has secrets of her own."

Theresa looked at Mercy quickly. "How do you know that?" she asked.

"No one disappears the way you did if they don't have secrets," Mercy told her. "And I can tell a lot of things without having them spelled out for me. I am a lawyer, after all. Let us know if you need help, okay?"

Theresa looked at Mercy. The older woman had started to wear her hair short and natural, different from years ago, when she had worn it long and straight. Short hair suited Mercy, showing off her dark skin and eyes and her beautiful bone structure.

Theresa wondered if the statement about secrets was a lucky guess or if Mercy knew more than she was saying.

"I did have secrets," Theresa said. "When I left. But everything is okay now, or I wouldn't be here. Don't worry about us. We'll be fine."

"Whose dog is that?" George asked, changing the subject. He held Mercy's hand in his and had one vertical line between his eyebrows.

"No idea," Theresa said as she threw the stick for him again.

"Looks like yours," Mercy murmured. "Have you seen Sofía, since you've been back?"

Theresa looked up, startled. "No," she said. "But I haven't talked to Sofía in a long time. Sometimes she sends me a Christmas card."

"That's a shame," Mercy said. "I remember the two of you playing with Faith together, all of you laughing yourself into a fit."

"How is Faith?"

They both smiled, suddenly, beautifully, as they thought of their daughter.

"She's doing well," Mercy said. "I don't think she eats enough, though. She's been seeing Maddie more often, now that Maddie's doing therapy with her."

"Yes, I heard that," Theresa murmured, feeling a wash of sudden shame. Mercy stepped forward and caught Theresa's hand in her own.

"We all do the best we can," Mercy said. Her eyes were shiny, and Theresa felt her own eyes fill with tears.

"What if our best isn't good enough?" she asked.

"It has to be," Mercy said. "Did you know we have a women's circle now? You should come."

"Oh, I don't know about that," Theresa said, dashing at

her eyes with the backs of her hands. "I don't like groups of people."

"These are good women," Mercy said. "You're welcome to join us if you ever feel that you can come."

Theresa remained at the lake longer than she usually would have, gazing at its blue, smooth surface and throwing the stick for the dog. She stood there until Mercy and George were tiny specks in the distance, and then she wiped at her face and took a deep breath. It was late. She needed to go straight to the post office. Breakfast would have to wait.

CHAPTER ELEVEN

The bells on the post office door rang as Theresa walked in, giving her an old shivery feeling that she imagined might come from years of picking up Christmas and birthday presents here. A feeling like some kind of lovely surprise was on its way. Then a beautiful surprise did come, as Theresa took in the effect of the post office walls.

Posters depicting space covered every surface with galaxies, planets, and nebulas. Theresa turned in a slow circle. The effect was magical.

"This is marvelous," Theresa said out loud.

Daniel appeared at the front counter.

"Hi, Reesey," he said.

"Hi, Daniel. I love your posters."

"You do?" He turned slightly pink. "Thanks. I'm hoping the head office doesn't make me take them down."

Theresa looked around. She could still see all the essential things—the signs, the posters that advertised stamps, the post office boxes.

"I don't see why they would," she said.

"Did you come just to look at my walls?" he asked her.

She approached him and leaned her elbows on the counter. Her stomach was rumbling with hunger now. "No, I wanted to know if there's anything I need to do to register my address or anything."

"Do you mean forwarding your mail from your old address?"

"No, I've already done that and changed everything."

"Then, no, I don't think so. Why?"

"I order a lot of my pottery supplies online. Glazes, tools, clay. Some days I'm not home."

"Oh. Well, that's easy. If you're not home, we'll deliver a notice, and you can come in and pick your packages up here."

That made Theresa feel better. She didn't like the thought of the boxes sitting on her porch. Maybe the dog was a chewer of boxes. You never knew.

"What time is the mail delivered?" she asked.

"To your house? Probably around two o'clock in the afternoon."

Theresa nodded. That was good. Maddie was still at school at two o'clock. If any strange letters came for her, only Daniel and the delivery person would see them. Theresa didn't want Maddie to see them if they came. Theresa had told Maddie the letters had stopped, and she hoped that they had, but she knew she couldn't count on it.

Daniel smiled at her. "It's good to have you back, Reesey," he told her.

"Yes, we oddballs need to stick together." Back when

Sheldon, Daniel, and Theresa were close friends, Sheldon had nicknamed them the oddballs. Theresa loved the name. It made her feel less alone. It had been so hard to leave their little circle.

"The other oddball doesn't want me to stick very close to you," Daniel said.

Theresa gasped. "Sheldon? Did he say something to you?"

Daniel grinned, and his dimples, so surprising, flashed in his cheeks. "Yes," he said. "But don't worry, I think I convinced him that we're just friends."

"I'm so glad we are," Theresa said, reaching out and catching his hand in hers. "I need friends, and Sheldon doesn't want to be my friend right now."

"Give him time," Daniel said. He rocked back and forth on the balls of his feet. "Have you hung out much with Katie yet?"

"No, not yet. I'm a little nervous. Maddie loves her, and she's so tall and beautiful and confident." She would never have dreamed of telling Sam that, or even Sheldon. She didn't like to admit how insecure she really was. But Daniel was easy to talk to.

"She's a good one. Don't judge her for her happiness. She has depth to her."

She smiled at him. "I'll remember that. You always know who to trust."

Daniel ducked his head, and Theresa turned to leave.

"Whose dog is that?" he asked.

"I don't know," she said. "Have you ever seen it before?"

Daniel shook his head. "Looks like he's yours."

Theresa frowned as she marched across the street to Green's. Why did everyone keep saying that? A dog couldn't just *be* hers, could it? It must belong to someone.

She was starving, she needed groceries, and Sheldon was going to get a piece of her mind.

The bells announced her arrival. "Why does everyone in this town have bells on their doors?" she demanded as she walked into the store. The young, baby-faced cashiers blinked at her.

"Is Lucy here?" she asked.

One of the cashiers shook her head. "She's got the day off."

"And next week she starts working at the Aveline Café again," added the other one helpfully.

Theresa blew out an annoyed breath. "Typical," she muttered. "Is Sheldon here?"

"In his office," the younger cashier said, rolling her eyes at the other one. Theresa narrowed her eyes at the young baby giraffe person.

When she reached Sheldon's office door, she stood outside for a few moments, staring at him, words momentarily failing her.

He sat at his desk, looking over papers attached to a clipboard. He wore brown cords and leather suspenders over a well-fitted white shirt with the sleeves rolled up. His black hair was messy and curly, and he was wearing Theresa's favorite glasses—a round tortoiseshell pair Theresa had found for him at an estate sale. He took her breath away.

He saw Theresa and jumped up, a little too casually, as though he had been letting her look her fill.

"Reesey! To what do I owe the pleasure?"

Her frown turned into a glare. He looked as beautiful as a beautiful man can look. And he was calling her Reesey again after sticking to Theresa since she had come to Aveline.

"Sheldon," she said, "why are you interfering in my friendships?"

"Hmm, what? I don't understand," he said, and he breezed past her, out of the little room, and into the store. Theresa followed.

"You need to leave Daniel alone," she said.

"Daniel? Why would I leave him alone? He's my friend."

They were nearing the front of the store. Sheldon turned back to face Theresa. Oh, her heart, that shirt. Theresa crossed her arms over her chest and refused to let her face relax out of a glare.

"You know what I mean."

"Whose dog is that?" Sheldon asked, frowning at the floppy-eared, asymmetrical dog that waited outside for Theresa.

"He's mine," Theresa said. "And you have all the friends. Can't you leave one for me?"

"What about Katie?" Sheldon asked.

"I don't even know her!" Theresa wailed, and she pressed her palms to her eyes. "You know what, never mind. I need to pick up some supplies, and then I need to be far away from you because you make me furious."

Sheldon shook his head, chuckling. "I wondered when your temper was going to come back out."

Theresa grabbed a cart and marched away. "I'll temper you, beast of the swamp," she muttered.

71

"I'll give your dog some water. It looks thirsty," Sheldon called to her.

Theresa went to the dog food aisle first, grabbing the biggest bag she could find. The ribs on that dog were showing. Then she stopped dead in her tracks. Sheldon had black chalkboards scattered all over the store. Some had prices on them, some had vegetable puns. (*Lettuce leave. Celery later.*) And some had quotes or poems.

The one in front of her was a poem.

Somewhere I have never traveled
Gladly, beyond any remembrance
Your eyes, they soften me
Your slightest glance easily will unfold me...
* e.e. cummings*

That was it. The poem didn't end there, Theresa knew, but it was all that was written on the board. Theresa did the rest of her shopping in a storm of rage. What right did Sheldon have to write *their* poetry on his chalkboards? What was his game?

She could barely admit to herself that part of her anger was at her own treacherous heart.

She had felt the old lift, the surge of happiness, at the sight of those words in that familiar handwriting. But Theresa could not go down that road. She simply could not.

CHAPTER TWELVE

Theresa took her groceries home and ate a handful of almonds and an apple, two slices of cheese, and a bag of baby carrots. She was shaky from hunger and seething from her talk with Sheldon. When the food started to have an effect, and she felt better and calmer, Theresa unpacked her groceries and put them away. She poured food for the dog in one of her own clay bowls. He fell on the food ravenously, prompting a twinge of guilt because Theresa hadn't thought of feeding him sooner. The sound of the dog's crunching gave her a good feeling, though.

Her anger had fizzled into a kind of blue haze that made her want to curl up on her bed and sleep forever. But Theresa had a lunch date with Sam, her mother, Katie, and Maddie, and today was the day that Maddie would come home to live with Theresa again. At first, Theresa had felt sad about Maddie staying with Lucy to housesit for Sam and Katie. She understood that it was important for her daughter to finish the time at her uncle and aunt's house well, so Theresa wouldn't have dreamed of protesting, but she had also come to appreciate having time and space for herself while she moved into the house.

She walked into Maddie's new room, straightening the pillows on the bed and looking the room over. Everything was in place.

Theresa pulled the door tight behind her, reflecting that she needed to oil the lock, so she didn't have to keep leaving her house open. Of course, the dog came with her when she left, his tail whipping back and forth as he gazed up at her. Theresa stood blinking at him for a few minutes before shrugging and heading down the street toward Katie's house. Katie and Sam's house, she reminded herself. It was Sam's house, now, too.

When she got close, Theresa saw Dorothy, Sam, Katie, and Maddie sitting around a table on the porch of the Aveline Café. Her steps slowed. They looked so lovely sitting there together that Theresa felt equally a pang of longing to join them, and the urge to run away.

The restaurant was closed for Sam and Katie's wedding and honeymoon break until next week, so only one table was set up, and no one else was there. Lucy would be back to manage the restaurant when it reopened, leaving Green's for the time being. Theresa knew that Maddie worked at the Aveline Café too, sometimes. She knew that Maddie had stopped her compulsive stealing. She knew that the big dog bounding toward her was named Sirius. Besides that, Theresa felt as though she knew nothing. She didn't know how to have this relationship with a daughter who was transformed after time living with Sam and Katie. She didn't know how to be a sister, a sister-in-law, a daughter, or a friend.

She nearly turned around to walk quickly back home, but Sirius had discovered Theresa's dog. While the dogs circled each other, sniffing, tails wagging like mad, Maddie spotted her mom and skipped down the steps, running toward her. Maddie hugged Theresa hard, and Reesey inhaled her daughter's specific orange-vanilla scent, holding her close. Maddie's steadiness in being Maddie, the way she had always been, her own particular self, nearly undid Theresa. She finally remembered to let go.

"You okay, Mom?" Maddie said. The worry in her voice made Theresa's chin come up.

"Great," she said lightly. "Our new house is wonderful. You'll like it, I think."

Maddie nodded, but Theresa saw her eyes drift back to the big Victorian.

Her life has changed there, came her therapist's voice. *She'll be bonded to it, to them. You have to make that a safe thing for her to feel. It's not about you.*

Theresa swallowed a lump in her throat and said, "You can come back to Katie and Sam's house to sleep over, you know. Anytime you want, as long as it's okay with your uncle."

Maddie smiled at her gratefully and then turned to look at the dogs, who were still greeting one another. Theresa's dog stuck his butt in the air and wiggled his whole back end, then leaped forward and gave a sharp bark, tearing off like a wild thing. After a moment, Sirius followed.

"Whose dog is that?" Maddie asked.

"He's mine, I think," Theresa told her. "Ours."

Maddie's face opened with joy and disbelief.

"Really? How? I thought you didn't want a dog."

The dog came running back, and she knelt to greet him. He began washing her face enthusiastically with his tongue, his tail like a mini whirlwind.

"I didn't want a dog. But I want this dog, and he doesn't seem to have anyone. He needs a name."

"Can we name him Remus?" Maddie asked, and Theresa grinned.

"Remus is perfect."

Dorothy was coming down the walk, with Sam and Katie following together, so Theresa took a deep breath and braced herself for the hugs. She hugged her mother first.

"Hey, Mama," she whispered.

"Hey you," her mom said. "You ready for the interrogation?" Theresa's eyes widened, and she stood back to look at Dorothy, wondering what she meant, but then Sam swooped in for a hug. His jacket smelled of warm sawdust, even after two weeks away from carpentry work. Theresa smiled at him, happy to see him glowing with love, then turned to Katie, who stood watching, biting her thumbnail.

"I want to apologize," Katie said.

"Apologize?" Theresa asked, puzzled. "Whatever for?" *You've practically been raising my daughter,* she didn't say.

"For making a big deal about..." she waved a hand around in the general vicinity of Theresa's face..."you know."

Theresa couldn't think of what she meant. She looked at Sam for help.

"Sheldon told Katie that you don't like it when people talk about how drop-dead gorgeous you are, like a model and a fashion star and an actress of olden days..." Dorothy elbowed him and he stopped.

"So anyway," Katie said, shooting a glare at Sam. "I'm sorry. I was just so stunned, because you're so beautiful, and I had never seen anyone who looked like you..."

"Katie," Sam said. Katie lapsed into silence.

Theresa stared at the tall redhead in front of her. Theresa had thought she had picked out Katie's type right when she first met her. She assumed her brother's new wife was one of those happy, confident, effortless people who never worry, who glide through life, knowing exactly what to say. The kind of person who understands how and why things work. Theresa had been relatively positive that they wouldn't get along. She was terrified of Katie's type of person. But Katie had spent her whole honeymoon worrying that she had said the wrong thing to Theresa. Theresa suddenly understood why Sheldon and Daniel thought Katie and Theresa could be friends.

She hadn't had a close woman friend since Sofía. It would be interesting to have a woman as a friend again. The mothers she had met at Maddie's schools, over the years, were usually first intimidated by her looks, which was ridiculous, and then put off by her bluntness, which she couldn't help. Men were easier, though it had been years since she had *anyone* she considered a true friend, she realized. The thought made her feel lonely.

"It's okay," she said to Katie now, surprised by the desire to make sure her new sister-in-law didn't worry for even one second longer. "It happens a lot. Mom says people see me and just have to say something. I do the same thing, but with other, even more awkward topics, like the surprising amount of dust in a person's living room."

"It's true," Dorothy said agreeably. "She does. Don't worry, you'll get used to her face and it won't look so perfect anymore. The rest of us have."

Katie stared at them for a moment, then threw her head back and laughed. Sam joined in, and Theresa watched them and felt the loneliness inside her grow a few inches, but then Katie linked her arm into Theresa's and walked toward the house with her.

"The food is getting cold, and I really want to feed you," she said.

"That doesn't sound terrible," Theresa said, unexpectedly relaxing into the woman's warmth. "I'm hungry."

"Did you eat breakfast?" came a soft voice behind her, and Theresa turned to look at Maddie.

"You don't have to worry about me," Theresa told her daughter. "I'm doing so much better, Maddie, and I want you to take a turn being the daughter. Then it will be easy for us to live together again."

"But did you eat?"

"A little," Theresa said. "I'm serious, though. It's not your job to make sure I eat."

Maddie gazed back at her. The two of them had a long road ahead. Theresa remembered the times she hadn't been able to get out of bed for days after a meltdown, and Maddie had brought her soup and tea and nagged at her to eat them. It was Theresa's fault that Maddie thought she needed to be the responsible one. Theresa felt a hot wave of shame, but she blinked it away, leaning toward the feeling of being loved, another thing her therapist had taught her.

Katie pulled out a chair, and Theresa kissed her daughter gently on the cheek, then went and sat down, closing her eyes and imagining standing in a circle of light, seen by God. *Everything he sees he loves.* She touched the love and felt its warmth. When she opened her eyes, the others were seated, and all of them were staring at her. The dogs bounded up the steps, toenails clicking on the wooden floor, and flopped on the porch, tired out from play.

"I can tell you more about the last months while we eat if you have questions," Theresa said.

Katie went to get the first course—a butternut squash soup that made Theresa sigh when she tasted it.

"You are an excellent cook," she said. "No, not just excellent. Unbelievable."

"Isn't she?" Sam asked. His voice was rough. Theresa looked at him. "I guess I do have questions," he said. "Or maybe just one. Why did you send Maddie to us without telling us what had been going on with her? Why did you put her on a bus? I know we talked about it when it happened, but I still don't understand."

Theresa let the feelings come. She picked up a warm piece of bread and smoothed butter onto it, then took a bite and chewed. She hardly ever ate bread, but this piece was perfect. She thought about what to say. How much to say. How much to leave out. She swallowed and took a breath.

"About two years ago, I found a therapist who was willing to help with my particular kind of disorder," she said, glancing at her mother. "I told Mom at the time, but no one else, really. It was a steep and intense learning curve. I had to find ways to understand how I work and why I feel the way I feel. I was undoing years of self-hatred and unhelpful coping skills. At the same time, Maddie was there just trying to make sense of who we were and who we had been. Her questions started boiling over, her unease was apparent in school, in her stealing. It was a cry for attention, but I knew I wasn't ready to give her what she needed. I wasn't even ready to communicate what I needed. So I put her on that bus, trusting that you would step in and take care of her. And you did. But I am very sorry. If it helps at all, I would never do that now. I'm so much better now."

She had closed her eyes as she spoke. The pressure of their eyes directed at her was too much, but she knew they needed to hear it all. So she spoke and inwardly begged them to understand. This was hard. She knew she would be exhausted later, that she would need all her tricks to not melt down after so much vulnerability. And so she poured her heart out and then waited in the silence.

CHAPTER THIRTEEN

Theresa opened her eyes and saw that Maddie had her face buried in her hands. Feeling a deep twist of pain and grief, Theresa got up and went to her, leaning over to pull her daughter close. Maddie softened into her, resting her head on Theresa's shoulder and crying into her neck.

"What is it, Little?" Theresa whispered.

Maddie pulled back, wiping at her face and sniffing. Katie handed her a tissue, and she took it, smiling at Katie, then looking back at Theresa with large eyes.

"You just sound so...good." Her face crumpled, and she started crying again. Theresa stayed with her, rubbing her back until she was finished. When Maddie's eyes were dry, Theresa went back to her seat and tried for composure. She breathed. She ate a mouthful of bread. She put another spicy, creamy spoonful of soup in her mouth. The soup was divine. Katie went into the house and came back with an enormous salad. She set it in the middle of the table. Theresa's eyes widened.

"Wow," she said. "Real food."

"My mom loves vegetables," Maddie said to Katie.

The words '*my mom*' were a tiny bit of salve on Theresa's exposed heart.

Theresa glanced over at her brother, but he wouldn't meet her eyes. She couldn't tell what his expression meant. Theresa looked at her mother, but Dorothy just shrugged.

"It helps if you say what you're thinking," she said suddenly, and Sam glanced up. "If you want to," she added. *Allow people an out,* came her therapist's words.

"I forgive you," Sam said. "I think I'm still a bit angry, mostly on Maddie's behalf. But some on mine too. We went through a lot here, and it would have helped to know Maddie had already been arrested for shoplifting. But I forgive you. Thank you for saying all of that."

Theresa nodded. Relief bloomed inside of her. She willed herself not to cry.

"Do you have a diagnosis?" Katie asked.

Theresa took a breath. "Yes," she said. "Aspergers. Or high functioning Autism, they call it now."

"What?" Sam asked, leaning forward, his palms on the table. "No way."

"What do you mean, 'no way?'" Theresa asked.

He stared at her. "I mean, isn't autism the Rain Man disorder?" He shook his head. "You're not like that."

"Sam!" Katie said, putting her hand over his. "If you don't know anything about it, maybe don't speak." She turned to Theresa. "I've actually wondered if you were autistic for a while. Maddie described a little of what life was like for you.

The things that were hard for you. The way it takes you a long time to recover."

Theresa shifted in her seat. She didn't like the idea of Maddie telling Katie all about Theresa's odd problems. But Katie went on.

"Back when I worked in HR, I helped two or three people who were on the spectrum, both at our branch and the New York branch. What Maddie described sounded similar to some of their issues."

Theresa's emotions shifted quickly from discomfort to relief at Katie's words. She couldn't hold back a genuine smile for Katie, who blinked at her and sighed.

"You really are so pretty. Okay, I'm going to get dessert and then you can tell Sam how many women have gone undiagnosed because doctors didn't know women could have Aspergers or how it presented in women, and then we can eat sweet stuff and talk about your dreams for the future, now that you live here." She shot Theresa a rueful smile, and gave Sam a look that Theresa couldn't interpret, then walked into the house, letting the screen door swing shut behind her.

"I always wondered if your dad had Asperger's disorder," Dorothy said suddenly.

"What?" Sam asked. Dorothy nodded, her mouth full of salad. Sam stared at his mother for a few beats, but she didn't say anything else. "Is it true?" he asked Theresa. "Do women go undiagnosed?"

Theresa nodded. "Mom, do you remember how I would cry if I had to wear my school uniform?"

"Of course I do," Theresa's mother said. She dabbed at her

eyes, and Maddie put a hand on her shoulder. "How teachers said I was mean to other kids, and I was baffled? How I would get so tired after a day of school that I slept all afternoon and then didn't get my homework done and failed classes that I was smart enough for? How it was so simple to deceive me..." she stopped talking with a glance at Maddie, who was gazing at her.

"You mean by my father, right?" Maddie said. "Do I get to know who he is now, too?"

"Maddie," said Katie, coming back with a pie in one hand and a bowl of whipped cream in the other. She laid the two dishes on the table and stood back, crossing her arms. "Am I the only one who can see how hard this conversation is for your mom? You and Sam might show a little compassion."

"My whole life," Maddie said, slumping in her chair, "has been about how hard things are for my mom. I'm tired of it."

Oh, there was Maddie's anger. Theresa had been expecting it, wondering when it would turn up. Theresa breathed, counting until she had breathed three long breaths through the pain in her heart. "Fair enough," she said. "But things will be different now, Madeleine Sky. I promise."

Maddie just looked at her. Theresa willed her daughter to remember the rest of their life together, not only the bad parts. Sweet days of playing on the floor, snow castles, popcorn and movies, candles and music in the living room while they danced. Finally, Maddie nodded.

"Okay," she said.

As Theresa let out a breath, she realized there was a piece of pumpkin pie with whipped cream on the table in front of her. She smiled at Katie and took a bite. It was delicious, but all Theresa wanted was to go home. How long until lunch was over? Surely the worst was past. She could recover from this conversation and then slowly, over a long time, show them she had changed. She was more aware of herself, her limitations. It made life more comfortable, and Theresa a lot easier to live with. At least, she thought so.

"So, Theresa, what are your plans now?" Katie asked. "I know I'm hoping that Aveline will have its own potter-in-residence."

Theresa smiled and nodded. "Yes, I want a studio and a shop at home," she said. "But I'll need your help, little brother."

Sam sat forward, his face changing as he heard her words.

"Yes!" Katie cried. "This is so exciting. I can't believe I have a potter for a sister-in-law!"

"Yes, that is wonderful, Reesey," Dorothy said. "I can't wait to tell my friends. They'll all shop at your store if I have anything to say about it."

An autistic potter who has estranged most of her family with bad behavior, and attracts the wrong kind of people, Theresa thought, but she was warmed by Katie's words. She could really use an ally in this town. One she hadn't damaged with her challenges.

"I would never have believed that I would have a professional chef as a sister-in-law," she said shyly.

Just then, the sound of singing wafted toward them. Theresa froze. She knew the voice and the song well. *Three Little Birds* sung slightly off-key. Slowly, she turned to look at the street. A tall figure wearing brown cords, a snug white button-up, and suspenders was walking up the sidewalk toward them.

Sam gave a low whistle and said, "Wow, what did you do to make Sheldon wear the Reesey outfit?"

"Sam!" Theresa hissed, horrified. "Be quiet!"

"That's the Reesey outfit?" Katie asked. "Wow, he does look stunning, doesn't he? Did you realize Sheldon was that handsome?" she asked Maddie, then frowned and shook her head. "Never mind."

"Gross," Maddie said.

"Sorry," Katie said. "My head has been turned by that shirt. He looks... ripped."

Sam frowned. "Stop looking at Sheldon," he said.

"He does look rather delicious," Theresa's mother mused.

"All of you shut up," Theresa said under her breath. Sheldon was humming his way up the stairs. At the top, he paused for effect and looked at the five of them.

"Hi—Oh, Theresa! I didn't realize you were here too!" His surprise was so fake, it was hilarious. Theresa narrowed her eyes at him.

"What is your game today, Taz?" she asked him.

"Mom!" Maddie groaned, her face turning red.

Katie stood. "Let me pull up a chair," she said. "You're just in time for dessert and Theresa's description of her plans for a pottery studio."

Sheldon gave Theresa a tiny wink, nearly imperceptible, as he sat down. He sighed with happiness over the pie Katie handed him.

"Pie is just what I needed," he declared.

"Even pie you weren't invited for?" Theresa asked, her voice sweet.

Sheldon choked. Maddie exclaimed, "Mom!" again, and

Sam narrowed his eyes at Theresa. Only Katie smiled, looking from Sheldon to Theresa and back. She sat back, chuckling.

"Sheldon has a permanent invitation," Sam said. "You should know that, Reesey."

"Do I?" Sheldon asked. "I should take advantage of it more often." He leaned back in his chair and crossed his arms. "I'd love to order whatever pottery you can produce for my kitchenware aisle," he said.

Theresa looked at him. "I'm not in the business of mass production."

Sheldon snorted. "Do I look like I am? If you have any spare mugs, though, I'd love to sell them."

"Thank you," Theresa said, feeling the way she had to force the words out of her throat. Why was she so annoyed with him? It was the outfit, she decided. The clothing and the poem. She realized that everyone was waiting for her to respond to something, and Theresa hadn't heard a word.

"Sorry, what?" she asked.

"I can start measuring and taking notes tomorrow," Sam said. "This is going to be fun. How much construction are you imagining?"

Theresa forgot Sheldon for a moment, leaning forward with excitement welling up inside of her. Having clay in her hands would make life so much better.

"I need large windows, and a lot of shelves," she said, "as well as a little room built for the kiln out back."

They sat and talked through plans over cups of excellent coffee, and then Maddie went to get her bag so she could walk home with Theresa. Sam said he would arrive first thing in the morning with the rest of Maddie's things, ready to start work on the studio.

"And we'll keep your room here for you," Katie said. "You can come and stay over whenever your mom says it's okay."

"Can I help carry anything?" Sheldon asked.

Theresa started to say no, but Maddie jumped in. "Yes! I'll get you a box."

Theresa rolled her eyes and hid a sigh. Sheldon gave her another wink, visible only to her. As they waited for Maddie to come back with the box, Katie hugged Theresa goodbye.

"When can we get together, just the two of us?" Katie asked.

"My schedule is open. You tell me," Theresa said, feeling shy.

"How about taking our dogs for a walk on Saturday evening?" Katie suggested.

Theresa thought about it. Thought about the lake, rocks clicking under their feet, stars, dogs running around.

"Yes," she said. "That sounds wonderful." She was surprised to find that it actually did.

CHAPTER FOURTEEN

Sheldon set out from Sam and Katie's house with Theresa and Maddie, just as the afternoon light shifted to golden. Despite the disapproval emanating from Theresa, Sheldon felt as though he was living a perfect day. He was walking beside a spunky kid, a friendly dog, and the most beautiful person in the world. *Be cool,* he told himself.

Theresa walked ahead with Remus at her heels, and that unique, forceful stride of hers, so familiar to Sheldon. He turned to Maddie for conversation.

"How's school going since you went back, favorite four-teen-year-old?" he asked.

"Not bad, not great," she said, smiling at him.

Maddie's smile was still surprising. Not too long ago, she hadn't smiled at all, and always wore a large black trench coat that resembled a trash bag. After the events of the summer, Sheldon knew she had worn it for the pockets. Maddie could slip any number of bottles of nail polish or tiny spoons into those pockets. But Maddie said she didn't steal anymore, and in the clear light of her eyes, Sheldon saw it was true.

A memory came to him. Maddie, four years old, just a couple of weeks before Theresa left with her. The little girl sat on the grocery belt at Green's, swinging her legs and shrieking with joy as Sheldon pushed the button to slide her along the conveyor belt.

Or, Maddie pushing a tiny cart around the store, piling it full of whatever ingredients she could reach. Table salt. Cream of tartar. Baked beans. A muffin pan. Insisting that all of these were her "fravrit" foods, her black hair swinging as she looked up at him over her shoulder.

Another memory—Maddie asleep in his arms on the shore of the lake.

"Shouldn't I know who her father is if I'm going to be her dad?" Sheldon had asked Theresa, gazing down at Maddie's eyes, which were squinched shut as though she was never at rest, even in sleep. Even then, she had been an intense, fierce little girl.

Theresa had choked on the tea she had just sipped from the thermos they took down to the lake on days like these. When she got her breath back, she looked at Sheldon with wide, terrified eyes.

"I'll never tell you," she said. "Sorry, Taz, but you can't ask me that. I can't. I can't."

Sheldon put his free arm around her stiff shoulders and tried to reassure her, though he was deeply disappointed. He did want to know who Maddie's father was. *Anyone would,* he told himself.

Two weeks later, Reesey was gone. And though Sheldon

was angry with her for years for leaving him so abruptly, deep down, he knew it was his fault. He shouldn't have pushed her. Sheldon had been well aware that there was a painful story behind Maddie's birth. Someone had taken advantage of Theresa's vulnerability. It wasn't hard to see. Stupidly, Sheldon had prodded the wound where Reesey hid Maddie's father's identity.

Sheldon had written Theresa letters of apology, but they all came back unopened. Sheldon spent years despising himself for what he'd done, then despising her for making him hate himself. Their story wasn't beautiful or tragic—it was merely ugly and unfinished.

"Hey, where'd you go?" Maddie asked, her voice soft.

"What?" Sheldon was startled to find himself walking beside the nearly grown girl who had fallen asleep in his arms all those years ago. She had returned to him, though she remembered none of the fun they'd had together. Tears pricked at his eyes. "Sorry."

"You missed Mom's big announcement," Maddie said, raising her voice so it would carry to Theresa, who still strode along in front of them. Remus loped beside her, reaching up to lick her hand every once in a while. She smiled down at the dog. *Lucky dog,* Sheldon thought.

Theresa's shoulders tensed and lifted at the sound of Maddie's voice, but she didn't stop or turn around.

"Aspergers," Maddie declared dramatically. "The answer to everything. Why Theresa can't be bothered to be polite, or take care of her child, or tell her child anything at all about her own life."

Theresa missed a step, nearly tripping. She regained her

balance and kept walking, still not looking back. Her back was rigid.

"Maddie," Sheldon said, his voice low and reproachful. He looked at her and saw that she had the decency to look ashamed. She was clearly fighting tears. Oh, these two beauties would have an uphill climb finding each other through the pain of the past.

"Hmm," he mused. "Autism. Like Daniel. I think I already knew." He pitched his voice so it would carry to her, like Maddie had done, except that he hoped his words would build a bridge to her.

Theresa stopped short, turning around slowly, her face intense.

"What do you mean, Tazzy?" she asked.

"I was listening to something a few years ago. A podcast or something," Sheldon said. He stopped just in front of her. "And it was talking about Aspergers, and I thought, 'Oh, that sounds like Reesey. Everything makes so much sense now.'"

The look on her face, blazing up at him. She was thankful, he could tell, though she didn't smile or touch him or say anything. She just stared at him, and he smiled gently into her face. Maddie sighed beside him.

"I guess I should have been listening to podcasts if I wanted to understand why my mom is such a weirdo."

Theresa snapped her gaze away from Sheldon and onto her daughter's face, her expression sad rather than angry.

"It will be better," she said. "I promise. Though I will never not be a weirdo. I may be a better weirdo. We can hope." She turned around and started walking again.

"Thank God you won't stop being a weirdo," Sheldon said. Theresa shot him a smile over her shoulder, and he felt as though she'd thrown him the sun.

"Speak for yourself," Maddie muttered beside him.

Sheldon couldn't understand what was going on with her. Why was she so angry? Theresa had moved here for her daughter—she was obviously trying her best. Sheldon was the one who had a right to a grudge if anyone did. He was about to ask Maddie about it, but a familiar voice called out to them.

"Theresa, Maddie," Francisco called, crossing the street with three long strides. He smiled at the dog, who shoved his nose into the tall reverend's hand. "Sheldon," Francisco said, winking at Sheldon.

"Frankie, what's up?" Sheldon asked.

Francisco replied. "I just picked up the flyers for the play. Aren't they beautiful?"

He held the flyers out for the others to see. The colorful papers read, "Maria and José, a refugee story."

"They're done," Sheldon said, taking one. "That's great!"

"They're lovely," Theresa said. "Who did them?"

"Justine," Sheldon answered. "It's a little early, but she was excited about them, and we decided to hold onto them until it's time to pass them out."

"I didn't know she could paint like this," Reesey said. "She usually paints whales, doesn't she?"

Reesey was right to be impressed. Justine had done a great job. Maria wore a torn pair of jeans and sat on an old mule, and the look on her face—weariness mixed with hope—

was perfect. Theresa leaned in to look over Sheldon's shoulder, and he held his breath so he wouldn't ruin the moment and scare her away.

"Do you know who's auditioning this year?" Francisco asked.

Sheldon looked up. "We have a few people on the list."

"You'd be the perfect Herod," Francisco said.

"Herod!? How dare you? Besides, I'm not *acting*. I'm the writer and director. You know that."

"I'm serious, Sheldon, your play needs a Herod who can be scary. You know you can be scary."

Sheldon turned his head slowly to look at Reesey. She was grinning, and even Maddie was smiling.

"I'm not acting in the play," he said with a mock scowl.

"I asked Lenny if he would be Herod, but he said no because of political reasons."

The smile had faded from Theresa's face. She looked off down the street.

"Lenny would say that," Sheldon said, scowling. "Don't worry, we'll find the perfect Herod. What about you, Maddie, will you audition?"

"You would make a great Maria," Francisco said.

"Me?" Maddie asked, putting a hand to her throat. "I'm a teenager," she said.

"So was Mary," Theresa said softly. She pulled her eyes out of the distance and looked at Sheldon. "We should go. I'm exhausted."

Sheldon nodded, and this time he stepped forward to walk with her, taking her arm like it was no big deal. She allowed it, which surprised him. He felt longing and love wash over him in waves.

"Look for a good Herod," Francisco called after them. "And consider the Maria thing, Maddie. You'd be great."

CHAPTER FIFTEEN

They reached the house soon after seeing Francisco. As soon as they reached the gate, Sheldon felt Theresa relax. He let go of her arm as she opened the wooden door, and she turned to him.

"Thank you," she said. "I needed support. It's been a long day." She looked at him for a moment, leaning on one foot and then another, as if considering. "Do you want to be there when Maddie sees her new room?"

In response, he reached out and broke a bright clump of bougainvillea off the bush that climbed over the arch around the gate. He leaned close and stuck it behind Theresa's ear. He could see her trying not to smile, but she lost the battle, and a grin spread across her face.

"Don't make me revoke the invitation," she said. "Come on, Little, I've been impatient to show you."

Sheldon gave Maddie a warning look as she slouched by. This was obviously important to Reesey, and he wanted

Maddie to stand up straight and be pleasant. What had gotten into the girl today? Teenagers were baffling.

But then Sheldon was distracted because the house was stunning. And not just the bones of the villa, but the warm lights Theresa had placed in all the rooms, the paintings on the walls, the way she had made it home. The kitchen was inviting, with jars of beans and grains on the tall wooden shelf beside the countertop, pots and pans hanging above the stove, and pottery everywhere.

Then Maddie's room. When they got to the doorway, Maddie dropped her surly act completely, gasping and exclaiming like a little kid. Freshly painted cream-colored walls. A hand-woven rug. A four-poster bed with a quilt the color of red wine, and hanging above it, colorful bunting and twinkle lights—twinkle lights everywhere. Baskets on shelves, a desk in the corner, a mirror over the dresser.

Sheldon walked in to get a better look and saw photos of Maddie as a little girl tacked all around the mirror, with a piece of paper that said, "You are beautiful, never forget it," taped to the top right corner. A large ceramic bowl, filled with flowers, sat on top of the dresser.

The window beside the dresser looked out into the garden, and Theresa's progress since moving day was obvious. The bushes had shapes and were separate from their neighbors, instead of tangling together in a mass of weeds. Despite all the work, there was still a mountain of work to be done.

Sheldon took a moment to get his face under control. All of this was new. The old Reesey barely remembered to feed herself. She lived in bare-walled apartments with cinderblock shelves. Sheldon didn't know what to do with all this new information: Theresa, an accomplished potter who effortlessly made a house feel like a home. A lot had changed in ten years.

It wasn't fair. Sheldon wanted to be close to her. His hand tightened on the windowsill.

Since he was a youth, Sheldon had often felt, in his low times, that the whole world was gray and dreary. People were wearisome; work was tedious. People walked around making inane comments about things that didn't matter.

Theresa was not boring. To Sheldon, it seemed as though she walked through a room trailing color behind her. She woke people up by saying things no one would think to say. He felt rather desperate. By becoming more domesticated, had she lost her wild self? By discovering she was autistic, had she dampened down the things that made her Reesey?

It was none of his business, though. By removing herself from his life, Theresa had removed the color from his world. He wasn't going to be able to keep it together. All of this was too much. Why had he even come in here? But then he heard the sound of crying, and he turned quickly.

Maddie was in her mother's arms. Theresa smoothed her hand down her daughter's back, murmuring to her. They stood like that for a long time, before Maddie pulled back to look into her mother's face. Sheldon wondered if he should leave, but they were blocking the door, and he didn't want to interrupt the moment. He stepped softly over to the bed and sat down.

"I'm sorry for being mean," Maddie said in a low voice.

"It's okay, radiant girl," Theresa said. "You can be mean if you need to. I know this hasn't been easy for you." She looked as though she wanted to say more, but stopped herself. After a moment, she said, "It will be better. I know it."

"You made a perfect place," Maddie said with awe in her voice. Her eyes were wide as she gazed around.

"Have a look," Theresa said. "I brought your things. I got rid of clothes that didn't fit you, and things I thought you might not want anymore are in that trunk over there, but most of your stuff is organized on your shelves." She paused, looking shy. "And some new stuff. I hope you like it. I went through your Pinterest boards to see what you like."

Maddie's back was turned to Theresa as she looked through her closet, but Sheldon could see the girl's face, and he couldn't help smiling at her radiance. He gave Reesey a thumbs up. Reesey's face was such a mixture of hope, sorrow, and vulnerability that Sheldon knew he had to leave, or he would kiss her.

Kissing Theresa was hopefully part of his plan, but Sheldon wanted to do it when she was ready, and it would ruin everything right now. He made his excuses and got out of there quickly.

CHAPTER SIXTEEN

Out on the boat the next day with Sam and Frankie, Sheldon killed the motor and sat back with a sigh.

"Beer?" he asked. They each took one.

"This new?" Sam asked, looking at the label on the bottle.

Sheldon nodded. "Just in. Tell me how it is, will you? I'm still only on day twelve."

He picked up a bottle of green tea and opened it with a sigh. It was good to be on the boat. The trees were casting perfect reflections over the lake, and the sun was warm on his face.

"How's married life treating you, Sam?" Francisco asked.

Sam shot them a wicked grin. "It's... wonderful."

"Great," Sheldon said sourly. "Keep it to yourself."

"I thought you were still a monk," Sam said. "You shouldn't be struggling with any jealousy over my wedded bliss."

"I'm not, that's for sure," Francisco said, shuddering dramatically.

"What are you talking about, Frankie?" Sam asked. "You've always been against the monk thing."

"Starting to think it might be a good idea," Francisco said, after swallowing a mouthful of beer, then grinned when he saw their faces. "Kidding. Sort of."

Sheldon didn't say anything. He reached over the edge and pretended to be absorbed in a bit of tar on the side of his boat, but Sam knew him too well.

"Not having second thoughts, are you, *Tazzy?*" he teased, and as Sheldon whirled on him, he burst out laughing.

"You're not wrong," Francisco said. "I think we're losing Sheldon, and now that I'm coming around to the monk life, I'm trying to recruit Daniel, but I think it's a losing battle. He says he never makes promises of any kind, ever."

Sheldon felt his face burning. He frowned at Francisco. "That's true," Sheldon said. "He doesn't. But I don't know why you want to recruit Daniel anyway. It wasn't a club. It was a promise made in a difficult time. Easily adjusted. I see no reason to invite more members."

"You two clearly have no idea of what a vow is," Frankie responded. "You don't 'adjust' vows."

"We made vows, Frankie, you didn't," Sheldon said, but Sam sat forward, his hands on his thighs, and looked very seriously at Francisco.

"Now," he said. "Now I can say I know what a vow is. Before, I couldn't say that."

"What good is a vow that keeps love inside, anyway?" Sheldon said. "Isn't it better to pour it outward? If my love can help Theresa, why keep it to myself?"

"How do you know your love can help her?" Sam said.

"She needs to know how loved she is."

Francisco chuckled. "If you can show her that I'll give you a job at the church. It's the number one thing everyone needs to know."

Sheldon shifted, taking another sip of green tea. "I don't exactly know how to go about convincing her. But I'm going to start by helping her with her garden."

"She agreed to that?"

"She will."

Francisco set his beer down in the holder on the side of the boat and leaned forward, also intense. "You have it all wrong, Sam. It's not about holding love in. It's about spreading it around. Having time for people. You have chosen to channel most of your love into one person. I also did that, and my love was taken to the grave with my wife. Now I feel that I want to offer love to my neighbors, my friends, and the refugee families when they come in the spring."

"I don't think it works that way, buddy," Sam said. "I don't think you have less love if you offer some to a person." He raised a hand when Francisco would have replied. "But, I want to get back to Sheldon."

"Me?" Sheldon said, frowning. He stared at his bottle. The glass caught the light and threw it into starbursts. He wished the tea were something stronger.

"You did this before," Sam said. "You thought you could fix her. Thought you could be Maddie's father when Theresa was terrified of Maddie's father, whoever he is."

Sheldon felt his stomach lurch. How could Sam bring up the most painful point in his life?

"You're not Maddie's father either," he said.

"No, I'm her uncle."

"I'm not doing it again. No one needs to fix Theresa. She's fine the way she is. I just want her to know that."

They fell into silence. Sheldon watched the light play across the ripples on the lake as a breeze grew, marring the perfect reflections of before. The wind chopped the water into shapes that glittered with sunlight. Sheldon closed his eyes and let the breeze blow over him, fighting the anger that rose up inside him toward his friend. Sam thought he *knew*, thought he understood love, now that he had Katie. But love for Katie didn't make him an expert in Sheldon's life, or in the long sad story of Sheldon and Theresa.

"So, Sam, are you going to audition for the play?" Francisco asked finally.

"I'm not. Katie might, though. She likes acting."

"Can I get your help with the set?" Sheldon asked. It felt as though he had to force himself to speak.

"Of course. Don't I always help you?"

"You do."

"Frankie's obsessed with the play, even though he doesn't have to do a thing to get it ready. That's all me."

Francisco held his hands up. "Hey, I printed the flyers out. I am obsessed, though. This play is important for our refugees. Few people remember that Mary and Joseph were poor, unwanted, and ended up fleeing to a nearby country for their lives. It will be good to tell that story."

"I heard that Cam threw the script and backed out of the play when he saw it," Sam said.

Sheldon looked up at that. "Cam, too?" At Sam's quizzical look, he said, "Lenny did the same."

"Yeah," Francisco said. "I was shocked. I thought Cam and I were friends, and surely he knows my parents were refugees from El Salvador. But he started spouting all this vitriol about the dangers of immigrants."

"Cam's mainly a good guy, I think," Sam said. "He hears this stuff from Lenny."

Sheldon frowned. Cam had grown up in Aveline, become successful as a banker, and was generous and friendly, giving to fundraisers and supporting the town, even though he had moved to Billers long ago. Sheldon had always felt funny about Cam. Maybe he had sensed the hypocrisy that seemed to be showing now.

He tapped the side of his boat, his anger turning into irritation. "Why do those who have nothing to worry about yell the most about danger and jobs? And why does he care? He doesn't even live in Aveline anymore."

Francisco sat forward. "Well, he moved back to Aveline not too long ago, Shel. And let's not dig into him when he's not here. I'll continue to pray that he changes his heart and mind about the families who are coming. God knows we need everyone to support this if they're going to feel welcome."

"Do we know where they're from yet?" Sheldon asked.

"We don't. We know we're hosting four families, most likely from the Middle East, and we know a general timeline, but nothing is certain yet. And the organization I signed up with is sending someone to help with the transition. She'll be here before Christmas."

"Four refugee families in this little town," Sam said with a low whistle. "You're right, Frankie. The play is important."

THAT NIGHT, Sheldon searched his loft apartment for the perfect thing to wear to help Theresa garden. Something to blow her away. He made his way through his shelves of antiques, every one of them with a story Sheldon wished he could know. Sam had made him shelves that divided the big loft, and he walked through the aisles of collections of model cars, stacks of books, and strange sculptures from different places in America. An old gas pump sat in one corner of the big room.

Tomorrow would not be an ordinary gardening day. Sheldon needed to show Theresa that he was serious. He opened his wardrobe, eyes scanning the clothes hanging inside. His eyes landed on the perfect outfit, the one that would change Theresa's mind about him.

"Yes," he said, and reached out to grab it, grinning.

CHAPTER SEVENTEEN

Theresa walked to meet Katie at the end of her street, moving quickly, so she didn't have a chance to chicken out of their date. Remus trotted along as well, making his rounds of the trees as usual. Aveline didn't have strict leash laws, and Remus was very well behaved when he was out with her, so Theresa felt comfortable leaving him off-leash.

She noticed, though, as she approached the corner, that Katie had Sirius on a leash. Theresa had a momentary flicker of dismay, as though dog etiquette was going to be another one of those things, like having a kid in primary school and trying to socialize with the other moms. All the rules that Theresa neither knew nor understood. She had a brief flashback of standing with a group of moms outside the playground and being asked if she was okay.

"Yes, why?" she had responded.

"Oh, you just have such a weird look on your face."

She had stared at the woman, who was blond and tanned, even in the winter. "This is just my face."

Actually, Theresa had been trying to figure out what the women were talking about. It was something about playdate rules of engagement, like which parent should feed the children, who should ask who, what should be reciprocated... and on they went. Theresa was hopelessly lost. And apparently, the feeling was right there on her face. Which didn't seem fair, because she couldn't read their faces. They all looked like blank sheets with eyes.

"Hey," Katie said, and Theresa snapped back to the present.

"Hey," she echoed.

Katie was frowning at Sirius, who was walking around her legs in circles, tangling her in his leash. "Sit, Sirius."

Theresa laughed. "People are going to think we're crazy when we're calling our dogs."

Katie grinned at her. "I guess that's what happens when you let a fourteen-year-old name your pets."

And just like that, Theresa relaxed. This was just Katie, not another situation where Theresa couldn't find her footing.

"To the lake?" she asked.

"Absolutely," Katie said.

Theresa thought they must have looked funny, walking along the lakeshore. Katie was so much taller than her, though Theresa didn't find it hard to keep up. She'd always been a speedy walker. Also, Katie threw a stick again and again for Sirius, who brought it back diligently, with Remus tearing back and forth and around in a frenzy of joy. If Remus ever found the stick first, he grabbed it and then took it somewhere else, prompting Sirius to turn and stare at Katie in confusion. Katie and Theresa fell into fits of giggles over the strange, lopsided game of fetch.

After a long walk, the two women sat. The dogs played in the distance, and Theresa began to make a pile of stones, balancing each precariously on the one under it. She was so intent on what she was doing that she nearly missed Katie's words.

"What, sorry?" she said, looking up.

"Did Sam tell you that I had a long episode of panic attacks last year?"

"You? No, he didn't." She looked back down at the stone in her hand. "You don't seem like someone who would have panic attacks," she said.

"Well, I don't know that you can tell that from the outside," Katie said, "but I didn't always have them. There was a whole series of events that led up to me falling apart... anyway. I only wanted to tell you that because Lucy asked me to try to convince you to come to the women's group."

Theresa looked up, startled. Katie made a funny face. "Sorry," she said.

"Ambushed!" Theresa said. "But no, that's okay. I'm just wondering what one thing has to do with the other?"

"She wanted me to ask you because I found it to be a safe place, even when I was suffering from the most intense anxiety."

"Yeah?" Theresa bit her lip as she placed one more rock on top of her pile. The pile collapsed, so she started over. "I can come if you both want me to. But it's not about whether it's a safe place. It's just so hard to sit in a group of people and feel like you don't understand all the currents of emotion running through the room. It's exhausting for me. I can often sense threads of feeling, but don't know where they come from or why they are happening."

Katie put a stone on Theresa's stone pile. It was a good one, hooking onto a small lump on the top of the rock under it, balancing perfectly, though it wasn't centered.

"That does sound exhausting," Katie said. "Maybe just try coming once, and you can decide whether it's worth it. It's at the Café this week, so it will be familiar, too. And there will be food!" She sang the last part.

"Well," Theresa said. "If there will be food, I'm in."

Lucy accompanied Theresa up the walk to the Café house several days later. Theresa was rigid with anxiety, and missing Sofía so much she thought she would burst of it. Sofía had always helped her with things like this. Lucy looped her arm through Theresa's.

"Chin up, Reesey," she said in a low voice. "We all know you're strong and can do this."

Theresa widened her eyes. "Strong like glass," she muttered. Lucy laughed and turned to go into Sam and Katie's house. Theresa stopped when she saw Katie at the end of the hallway, barefoot, wearing an apron, and holding a spoon.

"What's for dinner?" Lucy called.

"Wouldn't you like to know," Katie answered. "Go sit down, Lucy dearest, you're off duty tonight. Zoe and Ingrid are helping me in the kitchen. We'll be through in a minute.

There's wine on the table, but I'm sure Dorothy and Mercy will show you the way."

"As if I need to be shown," Lucy muttered, bustling in front of Theresa toward the open dining room on their left. "This is practically my restaurant."

Theresa stopped before a painting in a wood and glass frame, looking intently at it. It was a simple square, a mix of a subtle range of colors, moving from cream to ivory, to ecru, to beige. There was a painting next to it that was similar, but in shades of dark red ranging to black. Theresa stared at that one for a while, then her eyes refocused, and she realized she could see her reflection in the glass. Pale and heart-shaped, with large eyes, strong eyebrows, and a bit of an overbite. She thought, looking at the reflection, that maybe she should be a better friend to the woman in the glass in every way, including being nice about her looks. Perhaps she could even paint a self-portrait...one day.

"What happened to Reesey?" she heard Mercy ask, and then Lucy said, "She was right behind me. I hope she didn't run off."

Seconds later, Theresa's mother came bustling out of the large dining room to find her. "She's right here," she said, "looking at a painting." Dorothy looked at Theresa strangely, and then gave her arm a squeeze. "Some things never change," she said. "How are you, Reesey?" Theresa's mother was wearing a long silvery tunic over black leggings, and bright red lipstick. Her spiky gray hair seemed to be freshly shellacked.

Theresa gave her mother a shaky smile. "I'm all right," she said.

"Well, come in and sit down. You'll feel better."

Theresa allowed herself to be shepherded into the room. Lucy, Juanita, and Mercy were already seated in a cozy corner, fashioned from what looked like all the sofas and armchairs of the house. Theresa knew from visiting the café on other occasions that the soft seating was usually scattered more evenly around the rooms. This looked inviting, though. Couches were pulled up in front of a fireplace where a fire was crackling. A low table sat inside the half-circle of chairs and sofas.

Something like a long exhale moved through Theresa's body. She followed her mom over to the sofa and sat in the corner, tucking her legs under her, and taking the glass of wine Juanita handed to her. She looked around at the women, who were all looking back at her.

"Well," Theresa said. "This room is very yellow." Dorothy shook her head, and Juanita chuckled. Mercy beamed at Theresa. "That's it," she said. "I'm so glad you're here."

"Where's Faith?" Theresa asked.

"Couldn't make it tonight," Juanita answered because Mercy's mouth was full of the bite of food she had just taken. Theresa looked down to see plates of bread, apples, and brie, drizzled with honey, on the table in front of them.

"Oh, wow, what?" Theresa exclaimed, leaning forward to get some food. She placed a slice of brie on top of a piece of apple, and put the whole thing in her mouth.

Not long after that, Ingrid, Zoe, and Katie entered the room carrying saffron rice and paneer butter masala, with a beetroot and feta salad. Theresa's eyes nearly bugged out of her head, and she sat contentedly listening to the women chat, while the wine warmed her face, and the food filled her belly.

"This is absolutely delicious," Ingrid said.

"You helped make it," Katie said.

Zoe scoffed. "We chopped and did exactly what you told us to, that's not making food!"

Theresa smiled, and Katie noticed. "Come on, Reesey," Katie said. "Help me out here."

It was the first time her sister-in-law had called her Reesey, and it warmed Theresa even more.

"Sorry," she said. "I agree with Zoe."

"Thank you!" Zoe said. She turned to Theresa. "I'm trying to help Katie learn to take a compliment without deflecting it."

Dorothy and Mercy both raised their eyebrows.

"Theresa's not going to be able to help you with that," Mercy said.

"No, ma'am," Dorothy said.

Theresa narrowed her eyes at them.

"So, how do you know everyone here?" Ingrid asked.

"Oh—" Theresa's throat started to close. She felt like she couldn't get words out. She hated being put on the spot.

Katie jumped to her rescue. "Theresa is Sam's sister," she said. "Did you not know that?"

Ingrid shook her head. "Nope! I may have tuned it out when we talked about it previously."

"So she's my daughter," Dorothy added.

"Which means she's like family to us," Mercy said. "Ever since we moved to Aveline, Dorothy and I have been close, haven't we, Dorothy?"

"Yes, we have."

"And I know Theresa for the same reason," Juanita said with a shrug. "Lucy too. She grew up here. She's family."

"Speaking of family," Dorothy said. "Have you called Sofía since you've been here?"

Theresa stiffened. It was just like her mother to spring something like that in public.

"Who is Sofía?" Zoe asked.

"Reesey's old best friend from high school," Dorothy said. "She asked about you often, Reesey."

"I don't have her contact information anymore," Theresa said. "I've been thinking that maybe I'll go to her mom's restaurant in Billers. Do they still own that place?"

"They sure do," Lucy said. "Yum. Don't wait forever, hey, Reesey? A good friend is hard to come by."

As the evening went on, there was a lot more that happened. Talk about life and work. Prayer. Requests for help. But that was the moment that meant the most to Theresa. Those were the words that made Theresa realize she would come back. "She's family."

CHAPTER EIGHTEEN

Theresa and Maddie seemed to be adjusting well to living together again, Theresa thought, as she stood in the kitchen, in her pajamas, with a cup of coffee in her hands. Maddie was making a pot of tea, buzzing excitedly over her teapot, which, as she informed her mom, she had missed excruciatingly.

"Even Katie doesn't have a proper teapot," she said.

Maddie was also in her pajamas, an old pair of flannels that reminded Theresa of both good and bad times. Everything was entwined it that way, it seemed. All the good and bad woven together.

Maddie's pajamas were a deep maroon color, highlighting the new color in her cheeks. Theresa had bought the pajamas for Christmas one year, but after Maddie had put her new pajamas on, she'd exploded because of how lonely their Christmases always were, accusing her mother of ruining her life. Theresa had run out into the snow when she felt like she couldn't breathe, clutching handfuls of it to calm herself down. They had both spent time crying in their rooms, then come back to listen to jazz Christmas carols and finish their 1500 piece puzzle. They had worked late into the night. Neither of them had changed out of their new pajamas, and that Christmas had ended very late that night with a completed puzzle, candlelight, love, and laughter. So...a success? Theresa was learning that life was usually more nuanced than success or failure labels could describe.

Make new memories, came her therapist's voice.

Maddie's hair stuck up in every direction, and Theresa reached out and smoothed it, leaning over the island with her coffee in her hands, content to watch Maddie gracefully pour water into a teapot.

Light flooded the kitchen, Sam was going to start on her workshop today, an order of clay was due to arrive, and Theresa couldn't help feeling hopeful. Even as she experienced the goodness of the day, though, Theresa worried about when it would end.

"By the way, can you cut my hair, Mom?" Maddie asked.

"Sure. How do you want it?"

"Short and messy."

Theresa put her coffee down and lifted Maddie's hair off her neck, looking at the lines of her face, her graceful jaw. Maddie would look lovely with short hair.

"I can do it this afternoon. That'll look cute, Little."

The doorbell rang. Theresa went to get the door, expecting Sam. The last few days had been strenuous. Though Theresa had loved the women's circle, just going had taken a lot out of her. Today she had slept until seven o'clock, which was unlike her. At seven in the morning, Theresa was usually awake and had been sitting at her wheel for hours. She could hardly wait until her electric pottery wheel was set up, and her clay order arrived. She hadn't gone this long without making ceramics since she started working with clay.

When she threw the door open, Theresa found Sheldon instead of Sam. He stood on her front porch in a three-piece, vintage baby blue suit, and matching fedora. Theresa blinked at him. He looked gorgeous—breathtaking —with his cheekbones and startling blue eyes. His eyes had lines fanning out from around them now, she noticed, and it only made him look better. But why was he here? And dressed like that?

"What are you doing?" she asked.

Behind her, Theresa heard Maddie sigh. They were going to need to have a talk. Theresa didn't want her daughter to feel responsible for Theresa's lack of social skills.

During the last few months, something had shifted in Theresa, and she had realized that it was simply too hard to try to twist herself into something more palatable for the world. It was exhausting, and Theresa was done with trying. People could deal with her on her own terms. She needed to reserve her energy for creativity, not fitting in.

"I said I was coming to help you in the garden," Sheldon said. His voice was warm and deep, and without meaning to, Theresa put a hand to her throat.

"In that suit?" she asked.

He smiled at her, making her knees feel wobbly. "All for a good cause."

She narrowed her eyes at him. She knew what he was doing. The wretch. He knew her weakness for a well-styled man.

"No, Sheldon," she said. "Not in that suit, you're not. Go home and change."

She tried to close the door, but he stuck his foot inside and blocked her.

"What will you give me if I go change?" he asked.

"Nothing," she told him.

"What if I get to wear the suit at some time of my choosing, and you wear one of your vintage dresses? Wouldn't that be fun?"

"What are you talking about?" Theresa asked, standing back and crossing her arms over her chest. She tried not to look at his black hair curling under the fedora. "I don't owe you anything, so you have no room to bargain."

"Okay, you don't owe me anything. Will you go out with me while I wear the blue suit?" he asked.

She stared at him for a long minute. "Fine. Will you go home and put on something appropriate for gardening? You're going to get really dirty."

He twinkled back at her.

"Go home, Sheldon." She shut the door, and this time he let her.

She turned around to find Maddie staring at her. She shook her head in warning. "Not a word, Little."

Maddie held her hands up. "I didn't say a thing."

"You were thinking it. Okay, it's time, kid. Let's get ready for the day."

"It's Saturday," Maddie muttered.

"How right you are. And since you and I are still getting settled, we have work to do. Come on—I'll reward you with popcorn tonight."

Maddie muttered something inaudible, but she dragged herself to her bedroom and shut the door behind her.

Theresa went to her own bedroom and closed her door. She sighed, shaking her head, but then she looked around at her room and felt measurably more cheerful. She loved her simple bedroom.

A comfy mattress on the floor with lots of pillows and a dark teal quilt. A cranberry-colored rug. Three mirrors, more for reflecting light than for seeing herself. Theresa generally avoided mirrors unless she had to check her teeth. She put on a pair of old jeans and a threadbare T-shirt, braiding her hair and covering it with a red headscarf.

Theresa was an intense gardener and always ended up with dirt in her scalp if she didn't cover her hair. She groaned, thinking of Sheldon showing up in that suit, but as she left the room, she couldn't seem to stop smiling.

CHAPTER NINETEEN

When she went back to the kitchen, she found Sam wandering around, opening and closing cupboards.

"Ever heard of knocking?" she asked.

He smiled at her. "Your place is so nice, Reesey," he said. "You're all grown up."

"Thanks, I think?" she said. After a moment, she leaned in and gave her brother a hug. Sam looked surprised but hugged her back. He looked at her with an expression she couldn't read.

"What is it?" she asked.

"I'm just confused by you," he said. "You seem very... different. Plus, why did I see Sheldon jogging down the street away from the house in his special suit?"

She rolled her eyes. "He wore that to help with gardening," she said. "Can you believe him?"

Sam shook his head, smiling. "That's very Sheldon," he said. "Well, you can't blame him for trying." A shadow crossed his face as he opened her canned goods cupboard. "I can fix the hinge on this cupboard," he said, opening it and closing it several times before he turned to her again. "Are you going to break Sheldon's heart again?"

Theresa stiffened. Sam had never been a mean person, but over the last couple of days, she couldn't help thinking that he wasn't exactly tactful.

"I told him I only want to be friends," she said, crossing her own arms. "And then he told me he didn't want to be friends, but now he's the one turning up the charm. It's not my fault."

Sam leaned onto the countertop, letting his head drop forward. "You're right, Reesey. I'm sorry. It's not your fault, and it's between the two of you. But you didn't see how he was after you left. Or during year three. Or year seven. He's never gotten over it."

Theresa stared at her brother. She had been heartbroken when she left Aveline, but she had figured that Sheldon would be sad for a while, then realized he was better off with her gone. What gorgeous young man needed a single mother who couldn't pull her life together? Sam's words told a different story, and Theresa felt an unwelcome twinge of guilt at the thought of Sheldon hurting all these years. He didn't deserve it. He didn't deserve her mess.

Sam straightened, rearranging his face so that the frown lines were gone. "Right. We got a lot done yesterday, measuring and blocking things out. Let's go back out there and make plans. I brought some paper for sketching —you can tell me what you need, and I'll draw it out. I have a few wood samples. If we get to it, I have tools in the truck as well, and I can make a start."

Theresa rubbed her arms, feeling cold, but went gladly into the less fraught business of creating her studio. The planning was more natural than she had thought it would be. Sam was an intuitive carpenter with a gift for design, and he was also her brother, so he caught Theresa's ideas right away. She envisioned an open workshop in the back that opened up to a display in front, a journey from raw to finished, with customers able to see the different stages of work. Yesterday they had measured the dimensions of the shelves she needed and decided where the kiln could go. Sam would build a drying and firing room at the back of the shop, as well as concrete shelves and benches for manufacturing and drying her work.

"It'll cost you," Sam said, as they sat at the kitchen table. He rifled through the drawings and papers on the table, his face serious.

Theresa shrugged. "It's fine," she said. "An investment." She almost laughed when her brother's eyes widened.

She was pretty sure that none of her family understood exactly how successful she was as a potter. Her mugs and bowls formed the bulk of her work, and they did okay, but it was her fine art, her sculptures, which were genuinely profitable. Theresa didn't want to brag about that to Sam, though. She wanted him to build a workshop.

He didn't budge, though, just gazed at her. "I mean it, Reesey. It's going to cost a lot."

"Sam," she said, frustrated now. "I can afford it."

"She's right, Sam. Do you have any idea what her career is like now?"

Theresa turned to see Sheldon, back again, wearing torn-up jeans and a fitted white T-shirt. She frowned. Not exactly less beautiful, but she supposed it would do. When was the last time Sheldon had worn jeans and a T-shirt? He looked almost...normal.

"No," Sam said, drawing the word out. "Why don't you tell me, Sheldon?"

"Sculptures at her last show sold out within ten minutes. The largest sold for $20,000. The buyer turned around and sold it the next day for $30,000."

Theresa scowled. She understood that the customer making a resale was a good thing because it would cause the value of her work to increase, but she still found it tacky.

"She has buyers from three of the big collecting families in the U.S., as well as Europe and the Middle East." Sheldon put on a posh voice. "'Whatever Theresa Grant creates next will go quickly, and for a small fortune. Collectors greatly look forward to her next show.'"

The last sentence was a quote from the *New York Times*. Now Theresa knew where Sheldon got his information.

She smiled. "Thanks, Taz," she said gently. "That's probably enough for Sam to digest."

Sheldon winked at her, and she shook her head at him. Sam was staring at Sheldon with his hands folded on the stack of papers in front of him. He turned his gaze onto Theresa. She couldn't read the look on his face.

"Sam?" she asked. "What are you thinking?"

"I just...got such a different picture from Maddie. You puttering around in a shed, making stuff. Not this...fame. I mean, I knew about your shows in Minneapolis, but I didn't know about your success."

"I've never had a hard time with art," Theresa said softly. "It's the life part that's hard for me. Maddie sees me in terms of how I mother her. So from her side, she probably gave you an accurate picture. Plus, that big show happened during the last six months, while she was already living here."

Theresa looked back and forth between the two of them. Their eyes on her were too much, and she had to look away. She walked over to the counter and poured herself a glass of water.

"The thing about clippings and sound bites," she said after she had taken a long drink, "is that they only tell one story. I make things alone, glaze them alone, and fire them alone. Then my agent comes and picks them up, sets up a show that I attend, barely holding back a panic attack because of the hours of talking to a crowd of people, and customers buy the things I made with so much love, sell them again," she scowled, "and I go back to work. People all have assumptions about what a successful art career looks like. But to me, it looks like this." She gestured at the drawings of the little studio and workshop. "I just want to make stuff. It's like the face," she said, pointing to herself. "People have assumptions about what it means to be 'pretty' and what it must feel like. I'm sure I receive some of the advantages of being attractive, but I can't read people's reactions, other than unwanted attention. I don't know how to enjoy it, or how to make the inside match the outside. I only know how to make things. So that is what I do, and I try not to worry about any of the rest of it."

She smiled, suddenly, at their faces. She still couldn't figure them out, but they were dear to her.

Sam turned to Sheldon. "So when you offered to stock her dishes..."

"I was joking," he said. "I could never afford a Theresa Grant piece of pottery."

"Not true," Theresa said, swallowing the last of her glass of water. "I have a line of cups and bowls that are always affordable. But I have a mile-long waiting list for them."

"Your agent isn't going to let you do that for long," said Sheldon.

"My agent works for me. It's in my contract. I have to be able to make bowls and cups, or art will never come again. One feeds the other."

Sheldon pulled his phone out of his back pocket and started scrolling through it. "Yup," he said after a minute. "Here's a set auctioning for $3000 on eBay."

Theresa shook her head, hard. "I don't care," she said, her voice growing louder. "Can we not talk about this anymore? Sam, are you satisfied? I have enough money to renovate my workshop! And to pay you back if you want to be paid back for anything you spent on Maddie, and to pay you back for being a crappy sister, if that's what you need!" She sighed, tugging hard on her braid, trying to stay focused and in her skin. "Tazzy, I'll be in the garden if you need me."

CHAPTER TWENTY

Theresa paced back and forth in the back yard. Why did it matter that she was making more money now? Why couldn't her brother trust Theresa's own sense of her finances? Theresa knew that what she had done—sending Maddie to live with him without any warning—wasn't a responsible thing to do, but she didn't see how it had anything to do with right now, with building the studio and starting a new life here.

She blew out a short breath. And Sheldon, making a big deal about the shows and her sculptures selling. She grinned. It *had* been satisfying to see Sam's surprise. And annoying when he couldn't stop talking about it. She scowled.

Ugh. Theresa had nearly worn a path from one fence to another. It would be better to take her frustration out on the weeds. She took a breath, chose a section, grabbed large handfuls of unwanted plants, and pulled. And again. She pulled and pulled, and slowly, as her palms began to burn, her heart rate slowed. She started to feel better.

After a while of this, Theresa sat back and looked at her progress. A long swathe of the back garden was bare of weeds. She leaned forward to clip a few brown leaves from a hibiscus bush that already seemed to appreciate the extra space.

The garden was shaped like a shallow bowl, with a raised area along the rim that held perennial bushes, trees, and flowers. The center of the yard was filled with raised beds and grass. Even in November, some of the bushes were blooming.

Theresa turned and saw that Sheldon was next to the fence at the far end of the garden, a large pile of weeds beside him. Theresa hadn't even heard him come outside. She felt suddenly, fiercely grateful that Sheldon had allowed her to work without disturbing her. She watched him pull weeds. His black curly hair was messy, which was no surprise—it always was—but he also had dirt and clinging seeds smeared over his white shirt. He had earbuds in his ears and was singing along to a song Theresa couldn't identify, wildly off-key.

Theresa smiled, and just then, Sheldon looked up and caught her watching him. He winked at her. She shook her head without dropping her eyes, picking up her pile of weeds to haul to the compost.

Sheldon met her at the compost pile, dropping his own collection of weeds into the box. He pulled his earbuds out.

"Hug?" he asked. And because he asked, and because he was Tazzy, one of her dearest friends, and because he had cleared the weeds out of a significant section of her garden and left her alone when she wanted to be alone, Theresa walked into Sheldon's arms and hugged him hard. The top of her head reached his mouth, and Theresa could have sworn she felt a light kiss on her hair, but she ignored it, closing her eyes tightly, breathing him in. Sun-warmed skin, dirt, grass, a bit of sweat, the same soap he had been using for years. For a long moment, Theresa let herself relax into the hug, and then she heard a call.

"Mom! Daniel's here!"

Theresa was at the front gate in a flash. Daniel had pulled up in the little mail truck that he hardly ever used.

"You didn't need to bring it," she told him, grinning from ear to ear as he pulled a gigantic box out of the back of the truck.

"It's not far," he said, huffing as he hauled the box up to the porch. He laid it down and straightened. "Hey Sheldon," he said.

"Hi Dan," Sheldon said. "Oh! A delivery! That's great!"

Theresa looked at Sheldon sideways. Why was he smiling so big?

"Do you have any more boxes to carry?" Sheldon asked.

"Four," Daniel replied. Sheldon went to help, while Theresa did a brief foxtrot on the sidewalk, overwhelmed with delight. The boxes were packed full of the supplies and glazes she had ordered. She could hardly wait to begin throwing pots again, elbow deep in clay.

After Daniel left and the boxes were stacked in the back corner of the workshop, Theresa went back to the garden. She grabbed another handful of weeds, but Sheldon spoke from behind her.

"You're not going to keep going without lunch, are you?"

"Lunch?" Theresa asked, turning to look at him. She

smiled at the sight of him, face smeared with dirt, sticks in his hair. "What time is it?"

"It's nearly two o'clock, you workaholic. Sam went home to eat a long time ago. He said he would gather supplies from his store and meet us back here later in the afternoon. Come on, let's go to my shop and get some sandwiches."

Theresa considered it. Not a bad idea. She did have a gnawing feeling in her stomach, and the fridge didn't have much that would be fast. She nodded.

"Sure, let's go. Do you want to wash your face first?" she asked. Then she laughed as Sheldon put a hand to his face, as though he could *feel* where the dirt was.

"Come on," she said. "A mirror will help."

After they both washed up, they started walking. Theresa felt happy. This kind of friendship hadn't been part of her life in Minnesota. She loved the way she and Sheldon could just *be*.

"Who's looking after the store?" Theresa asked. "Isn't Lucy back at Katie's?"

"Not yet," Sheldon said, pulling his phone out of his back pocket. "I have one more week with Lucy, and I'm training a kid who has great potential. But Lucy's holding down the fort today...wait. I have a million messages. My phone was on silent."

"Is something wrong?" Theresa looked at him. He was frowning, scrolling through, and nearly tripped over a bump where a tree root had pushed the sidewalk up. Theresa reached out to pull him to a stop, and he let her.

"Something about the windows... Lucy asked if I looked

at the windows this morning? She's calling the police..."
What on earth? I leave for one measly morning..."

Sheldon put his phone back in his pocket and kept walking. Theresa jogged to keep up.

They turned the corner then...and saw the store. Theresa stopped dead in her tracks, and Sheldon swore softly under his breath.

All across the grocery store, ugly words had been scrawled in red spray paint. *Not welcome. Get out of town. Abomination. Terrorists go home.*

Theresa felt her stomach clench up. The blood drained out of her face, and she felt as though she might faint.

A couple of police officers stood on the sidewalk, talking to Lucy, whose fists were clenched at her sides. She was talking a mile a minute. Sheldon stared at his store.

"The brick," he murmured, and Theresa winced.

The ugly red words were spread all across the exposed brick of the store, even crossing the wrought iron decorations that held the vintage-style sign that said Green's in curling letters. The red paint covered the hand-painted sign itself.

Theresa was shaking. She wanted to run far, far away, but she followed Sheldon numbly as he walked to stand beside Lucy.

"I was just about to walk over to Theresa's house to find you," Lucy said.

"I'm surprised you waited this long," Sheldon replied.

"I didn't know how long you would be gone. Kept thinking you'd be right back. And it was a bit crazy around here."

"We have to get that off as soon as possible," Sheldon said. "I'll call Sam."

Theresa felt like she was going to throw up. The violence of the red words spread across Sheldon's beautiful building. The hatred behind them, she could almost feel it in the air.

"I have to go, Tazzy," she said, "I'm sorry." He turned and held out a hand, but she evaded him and started to run. She didn't stop running until she was in her bed, under the covers.

CHAPTER TWENTY-ONE

Over the next few days, Sheldon went back and forth with the police, looking at camera footage and answering questions. He listened to his customers, who all wanted to express their support and condolences about the hate-filled words. He tried to reassure them that this was a one-time event.

Eventually, life started to return to normal. Or rather, the new normal, which was becoming rather blissful. There were frequent Theresa sightings and little jokes forming between them. Their friendship sapling was growing leaves. Sheldon almost couldn't believe that Theresa was back in his life.

He found himself dreaming about her all the time. Sheldon knew he needed to put a lid on his expectations, but he didn't want to, so he ignored all the little twinges of grief that tried to make themselves known—the sorrow from the last ten years.

Enough of sadness. Theresa was back, she was becoming his friend again, and that was all he would think about.

The Aveline Café re-opened, and Lucy went back to work there. Sheldon was still in the middle of training a new employee, Raj, as his new manager, so he couldn't get back to Theresa's house to help with weeding. He bided his time and tried not to take his impatience out on poor Raj, who, despite being talented and savvy, couldn't retain a month's worth of information in one week. Pity.

Sheldon knew Theresa had been deeply shaken by the vandalism to his storefront. She always had been sensitive about things like hatred and cruelty, which made her curl up inside herself like a little snail in its shell. The rash of hateful graffiti and robberies that had rushed over Aveline right before Theresa left had affected her the same way. Theresa had been desperate and furious about Daniel being implicated but almost paralyzed by the fear the violence shook up in her.

Actually, at the moment, Daniel was the only bitter mouthful in Sheldon's tea. It wasn't the guy himself. It was the sharp spikes of jealousy Sheldon felt whenever he saw Daniel and Reesey together that tormented Sheldon. Daniel swore up and down that he wasn't interested in Theresa. He seemed miserable when Sheldon brought it up, but there was something so comfortable about the way the two of them related, and Theresa was so beautiful that Sheldon couldn't quite believe everyone wasn't in love with her.

What with all the emotions of the week, it felt great to be in Francisco's back yard with the guys on Friday night. The nights were growing chilly, and they all pulled their chairs close to the fire. George and Frankie watched the meat on the grill, while Daniel sipped a beer and Sam told Carlo about his and Katie's honeymoon—a few weeks of kayaking in Canada. Sheldon took a sip of lemonade. A comfortable silence fell. Sheldon had just about made up his mind to tell the guys about his trouble with jealousy. Maybe they would be able to help.

"I have another guy in mind for these evenings," Sam said.

"Who's that?" Francisco asked.

"Do you know Lewis?" Sam asked. "We've gotten to know each other because he supplies Katie with produce for her restaurant. He's a good guy."

Sheldon snorted. "Of course I know Lewis," he said. "He's one of my organic suppliers too. But do you think he'd want to come? Lewis strikes me as a bit of a recluse."

"Are you kidding?" Sam said. "Aren't we all recluses? That's the point."

George and Francisco laughed.

"Are you talking about the young farming brother who came out from Los Angeles a while back?" George asked.

"Yes," Sam said. "He's kind of a genius, really. His farm is incredibly productive, and he has great water conservation methods."

George nodded. "He's a good kid," he said. "He was a scientist, I think, and left the city after some mess happened."

"What was it?" Sam asked.

"Oh, you know," George said. "The usual."

Sheldon wasn't sure what that meant, and George didn't elaborate.

After a moment, Sheldon ruffled up his courage and spoke. "I have a question. How can you not fall in love with Theresa?" he asked the others. "How is it possible?"

"She's my little sister," Sam said, "that's how."

"You're excluded," Sheldon said. "And you too, George, Carlo, because you're married."

"To the smartest, most beautiful woman in the world," George said. Carlo raised his beer, and the two of them clinked bottles.

"What about you, Daniel? Frankie?" Sheldon added.

"You know I'm not looking for a relationship," Frankie said. He poked at the logs with a stick, causing the flames to jump up around the steaks. Francisco really was far too good looking for a reverend, Sheldon thought, narrowing his eyes at Frankie. Immediately, he regretted the thought. What was wrong with him? Frankie was a widower. Why did everyone seem like potential competition?

"I know you're really talking to me," Daniel said suddenly, glancing at Sheldon. "I don't know how to convince you that you're wrong. I am not in love with Theresa. She...well, she told you about being on the autism spectrum, right? I am too. So we connect because of that. We've always connected because of being odd and having a hard time in regular society. But there's nothing, Sheldon. She is like a nice old lady to me. Or a good book."

"No spark," George offered, while Sheldon tried to get over the shock of hearing his exquisite Reesey compared to an old woman. He didn't know whether he was insulted or relieved.

"Sheldon, stop harassing our brother about Theresa," Francisco said. He was laughing slightly, but Sheldon knew Frankie well enough to hear the rebuke under his light tone.

Sheldon shifted in his chair, realization dawning on him.

The purpose of this circle was hearing each other, challenging each other, and also to be a safe space. And yet Sheldon had spent the last two backyard nights quizzing Daniel, who was new, on his relationship with Theresa.

He looked at Daniel, and this time, he saw his old friend, not only the man who laughed so easily with Theresa. Daniel's lips were pressed into a thin line, his arms crossed over his chest. His shoulders looked tense.

"I'm sorry, Danny," Sheldon said. "The reverend is right. I'm hassling you. I don't know why I'm so insecure."

"That's easy enough to answer," Daniel said, shifting forward in his seat, his shoulders dropping a little. "You love her."

He did. Sheldon loved Reesey madly. And he didn't know how she felt, so he felt as though he was standing on shifting gravel.

"This is a change of subject," George said, after a moment, "but has any of that old nonsense come up since the graffiti, Daniel?"

Daniel rubbed his hands on his jeans. A few breaths passed before he nodded.

Sam shot Sheldon a look that Sheldon read easily as reproachful, then Sam leaned forward to put a hand on Daniel's shoulder. "Do you want to talk about it?" he asked.

Daniel darted his eyes toward Sam, then Sheldon, then back down at the fire.

"I got a few letters, that's all."

"By letters, do you mean hate mail?" Francisco asked.

Daniel nodded, eyes still on the fire.

Something changed in Sheldon at that moment. He saw

Theresa's approach toward Daniel in a different light, as though illuminated by the years of misunderstanding toward him in this town. She worried about him, the way the two of them used to when they had seen that no one really understood him. Theresa had never doubted Daniel, even when people thought he was clearly guilty of robbery and vandalism.

Sheldon had wondered how she could be so sure, but she always said Daniel would never do a thing to hurt another being. Theresa was still looking out for Daniel, even though Sheldon had stopped. The way Theresa loved others was one of the best things about her, and Sheldon wouldn't change it for anything. He made up his mind to rid himself of jealousy. It was like a sick, tired weed. He needed to pull it out as enthusiastically as Theresa weeded her garden, in great spiky handfuls.

As the men turned to pray for Daniel, Sheldon prayed as well, inwardly confessing that the weed of jealousy was overtaking him, and asking for help. He left Francisco's back yard late that night, his heart lighter and already turning back toward his old friend with affection.

The next morning, he was stacking apples at Green's when Sam and Theresa turned up together.

He looked up from his pile of apples and couldn't hold in a huge smile at the sight of Reesey. She squinted up at him.

"Why are you so happy?" she asked.

"I'm wearing my red glasses," he told her. "I'm always happy when I'm wearing my red glasses."

She crossed her arms and stared at him for a few more seconds. "Do you wear them because you're happy?" she asked, "or do you feel happy after they're already on? Because if it's the second, you should just wear them every day. I mean, why wouldn't you?"

Sam groaned and shook his head. "You two deserve each other," he said. "Can we please ask our question and get on with the day? I have stuff to do."

Sam's request seemed to surprise Theresa, but she nodded. Sheldon could barely tear his eyes away from her. She wore a bright red collared dress over a long-sleeved shirt and a pair of black and white striped tights. Her hair fell in a long braid down her back, and she had placed a red hibiscus flower behind her ear. Her cheeks were flushed. She looked like a queen.

"Sheldon!" Sam said. "Are you paying attention?"

Sheldon pulled himself back. "What?"

Sam threw his hands in the air. "You try," he said to Theresa. "This man is smitten and has apparently learned to tune out the sound of my voice."

Sheldon smiled at that. "Of course I have. Haven't you, Reesey? It's a survival technique."

Theresa laughed. "Everyone needs it. Let's teach Katie. Tazzy, we came to ask if you could help with my studio design. We need your expertise."

Sheldon put a hand to his chest. "*Moi*?" he asked.

"You," Theresa said. "You're so good with light and space. Sam's okay, too"—Sam elbowed her— "but we want your opinion."

"I would love to help. When do we start?"

"Right now?"

"How about tomorrow? I need to make sure Raj is up to

the task of handling the store by himself. One more day should be sufficient."

Reesey smiled in response, but before Sheldon could lose himself staring at her again, she turned and walked away. Sam cocked one eyebrow and shook his head slowly at Sheldon before he followed his sister out of the store.

CHAPTER TWENTY-TWO

Sheldon walked to Theresa's house under the oak trees the next morning, wearing his bowler hat and his red-framed glasses. He was happy. The sun was shining in a sudden burst of warm weather, birds were singing, and Sheldon was falling back into an old friendship. Over the last days, he had been feeling more free when he thought about Daniel, too. He had even spotted Theresa and Daniel talking on the street and hadn't felt the familiar stab of anguish. Sheldon liked his brain better when it wasn't tortured by jealousy.

At Theresa's house, he found Maddie sitting on the front step with a cup of tea in her hands. She wore purple pajamas and an irritated expression on her face.

"What's up with you?" he asked.

"Morning is offensive," she replied. But then she brushed her hair out of her eyes and smiled at him. "I like the feathers in your hat," she said. "And your suspenders."

"Thank you," he said. "They're bluebird feathers. My friend found them in the forest a long time ago."

"Well, they're very nice."

He sat down on the step beside her. She was growing, he realized, looking at her long arms and legs stretching across the porch. And she wasn't dressing as a Goth these days. Sheldon was all about a good Goth phase, but Maddie's had included stealing and a lot of self-hatred, so he wasn't sad to see her branching out. She still didn't wear many colors, so these purple pajamas were a revelation.

"You're stretching," he commented.

"I know," she said, with satisfaction in her voice. "I'm a late bloomer, I guess. We have to go buy new pants for me because they're all like an inch too short."

"Who would have guessed?" he said. "You're taller than your mom?"

"Three inches now." She lapsed into silence, holding her face over her cup and staring at a potted cactus. Sheldon knew what she was going to say before she said it.

"Do you know who my dad is, Sheldon?" Maddie glanced behind her as she whispered as if to see whether Theresa was standing over their shoulders.

I wanted to be your dad, Sheldon thought. But he smiled at her. Her elfin face was so much like Theresa's. Sheldon had searched her face over the years to see whether he see Maddie's father in the shape of her bones, but she simply looked like Theresa. This height could be an indicator. But still, all they would know was that Maddie's father was white and most likely tall. Or at least taller than Theresa.

"No," he said. "I don't. I'm sorry."

Sam came through the gate then, bounding up the steps. He stopped when he saw the two of them sitting side by side in the surprising sunshine.

"My two favorite people," he said, grinning. Then the smile slid off his face, and he frowned. "What are you doing sitting around? Back to work!"

"You're not the boss of me anymore," Maddie joked in a mock grumble, poking Sam in the ribs. When she stood and offered Sheldon a hand, though, he saw sadness in the shadows of her face.

Theresa had always insisted that Maddie was better off not knowing who her father was, but Sheldon wasn't so sure. Inside the house, Reesey sat at the kitchen table, surrounded by pieces of paper, her computer, and a few swatches of fabric. She looked up.

"Maddie! What on earth? Clothes on, kid, you're going to be late!"

Maddie sped off to get dressed, and Sheldon and Sam joined Theresa at the table. Sheldon picked up a few pieces of paper and looked over them. They were sketches of ideas, as well as a few printed pictures that Reesey must have found on the Internet.

"I'm hoping for light and breezy," she said, "with an old feel. Old barn, not old Tuscan or anything horrifying like that." Sheldon grinned at her. They shared a horror for the craze of cluttery fake Tuscan decoration. "But the tricky part is that it should function as a studio space, while still being visible from the front of the shop. So all the messy cluttery bits could be right out there in an ugly way if we don't figure out how to make it beautiful."

"That's no big deal. You're talking to someone who runs a grocery store," Sheldon said, puffing out his chest. "I understand clutter."

He placed a blank piece of paper in front of him and picked up a pencil, starting to sketch. Sam looked over his shoulder, muttering suggestions. "Nope, that wall is a structural impossibility- put it over here."

Maddie rushed out of her room and went flying down the front steps. Theresa got up to hug her goodbye and give her the lunch she had forgotten. "Don't forget you have an appointment with Faith today," she called. "Katie will drive you after school."

"She's still seeing Faith?" Sam asked, when Theresa came back, looking slightly lost. Her expression pulled on Sheldon's heart, but he tried to ignore it. He couldn't jump up every time Theresa looked sad. That would be odd.

Theresa nodded. "Maddie loves Faith, and I think therapy is helping a lot."

The morning went by quickly. They drank coffee and sketched and talked. They looked at color palettes and photos of studios. Sheldon felt contentment that he had missed for years. He was talking design with two of his favorite people in the world, all of them sitting around the table, heads together, deep in the process. There was nothing better than this. Add the butterflies that took flight in his stomach every time Reesey met his eyes, and it made for an invigorating morning. They finished with a plan that Sam promised to sketch up on his computer.

"I've started making pots already," Theresa told Sheldon as he rolled up the sleeves of his white shirt to wash the coffee cups. He ran the water, raising his eyebrows, impressed.

"You set your wheel up?"

"Yes. I put it on the veranda out back."

"It's not getting wet in the rain?" There had been a few stormy nights before this shift into sunshine. The rain was a relief because Aveline badly needed it, but Sheldon thought it might be dangerous to trust the elements and keep the wheel outside.

Theresa shrugged. "The veranda is covered, and it's been okay so far," she said. "I have a shelf for drying pots in the laundry room. Come, I'll show you."

Sheldon followed her out to the porch. Reesey's pottery wheel and an old, paint-splattered chair were under one corner of the little covered area. A bright sheet stretched across the open side, forming a quiet, secluded place for her to work. She had set a metal table against the house, and Sheldon could see she'd been wedging clay. Reesey sat down now, apparently without thought, as though she couldn't help herself. She grabbed a chunk of clay and a bucket of slip and turned the wheel on. Sheldon watched, bemused, as Reesey began to center the mound of clay, oblivious to the fact that she was splattering her dress. He looked around for a chair and found one in the kitchen, dragging it out to the porch, and sitting down to watch. Theresa glanced up.

"You need a handmade mug, I think, Tazzy," she said.

"I'm sure I do."

He pulled his phone out of his pocket and typed a few words in, scrolling until he found what he was looking for.

*"And did you get what
you wanted from this life, even so?"* he read.

Theresa glanced up. He smiled at her and kept reading.

*"I did.

And what did you want?
To call myself beloved, to feel myself
beloved on the earth."*

She smiled at him, sitting back to admire her work. A large chunky mug sat on the wheel.

"I remember," she said. "You used to read me poems while I painted."

"I did."

"Who wrote that one?"

"Raymond Carver. It's called *Late Fragment*. I think it's a perfect poem." He sighed. "I thought I would be a poet, but I turned out to be a gentleman grocer."

She laughed, using a piece of string to cut the pot away from the wheel and standing to reach a piece of cardboard. She carefully set the cup on the board and put the whole thing on the metal table.

She looked around. "You see why I need shelves," she said. "What do you think? Handle? No handle?"

"No handle," he said. "I need something to warm my lonely hands."

She gave him a skeptical, 'I know what you're trying to pull,' look, but couldn't keep herself from smiling.

Over the next weeks, Sheldon started to visit more frequently, often reading to Theresa as she worked on pots. The rhythm behind the words that Sheldon read was the sounds of hammering and sawing from Sam in Theresa's studio. Every day, Sam made progress, and their merged visions began to take form. Sheldon should have been mistrustful of this much happiness, but he accepted it all without question, as though he had never learned a thing.

CHAPTER TWENTY-THREE

Over the weeks that followed, Theresa started to adjust to the feeling of being at home in Aveline, as she slipped into a comfortable rhythm. Sam helped her score a good deal on a car, which meant that she and Maddie were able to explore the other side of the lake on weekends, walking the shores with Remus and a camera. Today was the first day Theresa would drive Maddie to her appointment with Faith in Billers, instead of Katie. Theresa couldn't tell whether Maddie was happy about this or not, but it was one more step toward their new life together.

The car was an old hatchback—something Theresa could lug pottery around in, if she wanted to, but not so big that it was hard to park. She had already fallen in love with it.

While they drove to Billers, Maddie slouched in the passenger seat, gazing out the window or fiddling with the stereo system.

"How has therapy been going for you?" Theresa asked.

"Good," Maddie said.

"Good. Anything more than that?"

The road curved through the mountains. Theresa kept her eyes on the curves, drinking in the sunshine that filtered through the trees.

"I don't know. We talk about a lot of stuff." Maddie shifted in her seat. "Can we talk about the play now? You said we could once we were driving."

Reesey let out a long breath. She counted to ten three times. "Sure," she said.

Maddie had asked her about the play over breakfast, but Theresa was so focused on getting out the door in time that she hadn't been able to hear anything Maddie was saying, and she asked her to wait.

"Sheldon wants me to be Maria," Maddie said. "He says I should audition, but I need to make sure it's okay with you."

"Sheldon wrote the play?"

"I think so," Maddie said. "But, Mom, why is this something we need to discuss? What possible reason could there be for me not being in the church play? It's the safest thing a teenager could do!"

Theresa's hands flexed on the wheel. She forced herself to breathe, to drive slowly, to resist the rising panic. Of course, Maddie couldn't understand. She didn't know anything about the unfriendly eyes.

"Who is playing José?" she asked. If only it were someone safe, that would mean a lot.

"Lewis," Maddie said. "Sheldon says Joseph would have been a lot older than Mary."

Theresa relaxed a bit. She had met Lewis a few times at

Green's, and he seemed like a kind, safe person. He was not the menace in the forest.

"And who else is in the play?" she asked.

Maddie stared at her. "George, Ingrid," she counted off, then trailed off. "Is this really necessary?" she asked. Her voice was like ice. "Do you remember how you put me on a bus by myself to cross the country and live with Grandma without even checking with her first? And then she and Sam argued back and forth about who had to take me? Do you remember that?" Maddie's voice broke, and she turned to the window and pressed her face against it.

Theresa pulled the car over to the side of the road and tugged on Maddie's jacket. Maddie resisted at first, but then she collapsed into Theresa's arms.

"I'm so sorry, baby," Theresa said. "You're right. That was a horrible thing for you to go through. But I'm trying to do better now." She gazed out at the manzanita trees beside the car, and the tall firs behind them, thinking about how much to tell Maddie. What was the proper mix of innocence and reality?

"There was this graffiti..." Theresa started. Maddie looked up.

"I know. The kids at school told me about it. One had pictures."

"Well, knowing we have someone so hateful in town makes me worry about you. If you can just tell me who is in the play, I'll know whether I can relax."

"Do you know who did it?" Maddie was looking at her with a puzzled expression.

"I just want to know if I consider the people safe."

"Okay," Maddie said. She started counting on her fingers, and Theresa pulled back onto the road. It was good that they had left early for the appointment because they had taken up a lot of time on the shoulder. Under the tall, tall trees. "Sheldon is the director, George, Lewis, Katie, Ingrid, Grandma..."

"Grandma?" Theresa broke in.

"Yes, she's one of the three wise men," Maddie said. "Katie, Lewis, a whole bunch of little kids, and Lucy. I think that's it."

Theresa was holding back tears. Panic was still imminent now that she had stumbled into the fearful place. "That sounds okay," she said, her voice almost a whisper. "A lot of those people have loved you for a long time. I'm sure you'll be safe."

The waiting area outside Faith's office was minimalistic and soothing. Maddie had run straight into the room with Faith's name on the door when they arrived, so Theresa settled herself in a comfy chair with her sketchbook, looking around. The office was located in an old house with wooden floors and framed paintings on the walls. No horrible carpet, no deathly fluorescent lights. There were dozens of potted plants, sofas, and chairs. That was about it. The wainscoted walls were cream and blue, and the sofas made of a dark weave, flecked with coral. Theresa picked up her pencil.

She wanted to make another sculpture series, but she'd been so distracted with the move that she hadn't had time to decide what the series should be about. Her agent had been begging her for another show for months. But this new life was so complicated, with a lot to do and many different roles.

Theresa was struggling to find her focus. She needed a central theme or idea that could take form in sculpture.

She started to sketch, drawing line after line, looking into her heart to see what she was feeling. The emotions she found were complicated, involving safety, love, and danger. Home.

She looked up, startled, as a voice finally broke through to her. Maddie and Faith stood in front of her. Faith smiling, Maddie scowling.

"Mom," Maddie said. "We called you seventeen times."

Faith turned to look at Maddie. "Three," Maddie corrected quickly. "We called you three times."

"'Thank you, Maddie," Faith said. "That's enough."

Theresa quickly jammed her sketchbook in her bag and stood. Faith gave her a firm hug.

"Thanks so much for your help with Maddie," Theresa said. "It feels like forever since I've seen you." She stepped back to take a look at her old friend. Faith was tall and long-limbed, with dark brown skin and a short natural haircut, a little like her mother's but cut asymmetrically. She wore long silver earrings and had a septum ring.

"Oh!" Theresa said. "You're so beautiful."

Faith smiled. "I guess you haven't seen me since before high school," she said.

Theresa nodded. "I think I left when you were still in middle school," she said.

"I was sad to hear I missed you at women's circle the other week," Faith said. "I've been so busy I haven't had time to go." She turned to Maddie. "Did you know your mom used to babysit me?" she asked.

"What?" Maddie asked, looking shocked.

"It wasn't really babysitting," Theresa said, grinning. "Faith was in charge. You dragged me around by the hand, asking me to draw things for you."

"I remember that you seemed magical," Faith said. "You could draw anything I wanted."

"That's so funny. At the time, I was still harboring the delusion that I was going to have a career in science," Theresa said. She paused, looking closely at Faith. "How are you?" she asked.

A shadow crossed Faith's face. "Can you come in and talk for a few minutes before you go?" she asked.

Theresa fought down a wriggly feeling of panic at the thought of being in an enclosed space with such an aware human being. Secrets never seemed safe around people who could look into your soul. *Don't be silly, Reesey,* she told herself. *It's just Faith, little Faith with braces, and the addiction to mint chocolate chip ice cream. She's all grown up, but she can't read* minds.

"Sure," Theresa said.

She walked into Faith's office, which was furnished in the same spacious, light way as the waiting room. Theresa settled into an armchair, and Faith sat across from her.

"The anniversary is soon, isn't it?" Theresa asked.

Faith ran her hand over her face.

"Yes. It hurts every year." Faith had lost her brother when she was twelve. "My mom has been attending a lot of protests lately," she said. "I go with her sometimes. It gives us a way to work through our grief."

Theresa nodded.

"Do you think the protests will accomplish something?"

"They have to! People are so much more aware than they used to be. I can't even think of what we'll do if they don't work. It's good that my mom is going—she has a lot to say, and she's very gifted at speaking. But I'm afraid something will happen to her. And then what would become of my father? Haven't we paid enough?"

Theresa leaned across the small table between them and grasped Faith's hand. Faith squeezed Theresa's hand for a moment, taking deep breaths. Then she looked up.

"That's not why I wanted to talk to you," she said.

Theresa sat back.

"Maddie is doing really well," Faith said. "There were some things she brought up today, though..." she leaned forward. "You have an autism diagnosis?"

Theresa nodded, and Faith smiled. "That must be a relief," she said. Theresa felt a piece of her heart soften and relax. She was so used to defending her diagnosis.

"It is," she said. "You knew me when I was younger. Does it make sense to you?"

"It doesn't have to," Faith said. "And it's not my specialty, but... yes. Are you seeing someone? Will you have any help as you go on this journey with Maddie? She's a bit angry about it."

"What else is new?" Theresa asked. "But she has a right to be angry." They smiled at each other. "Yes, I'm continuing with my therapist online," Theresa said. "It's going well. But I'm tired. Everyone reacted in strange ways when I told them. I couldn't have predicted that."

Faith shifted in her seat. "She's also pretty obsessed with her father."

Theresa sat back. "I can't tell her who her father is."

Faith played with her hands. After a moment, she spoke again, meeting Theresa's eyes straight on.

"Reesey, I know you. The autism diagnosis makes sense to me, but some of the things Maddie has told me are only possible with considerable trauma. What happened before you left? Why did you run?"

CHAPTER TWENTY-FOUR

Panic. Theresa felt her throat closing and bent half over, trying to breathe. Faith got up and came back quickly with a glass of cold water, handing it to Theresa. Theresa took it and drank, trying to steady herself, breathing slowly. After a while, her throat felt less tight. When she was able to open her eyes, she found that she was still in the chair, rocking slightly back and forth, rubbing her hands over her knees. Faith sat in the opposite chair, watching Theresa with concern in her eyes.

"I can't tell her," Theresa whispered. "I can't tell anyone. It...unravels me. Let's just say that for a long time, it was easy to take advantage of me. I'm working on that."

"Oh, Reesey." Faith's eyes were somber. "Someday you're going to have to reach into the past and deal with this. It will eat at you if you don't."

"I can't," Theresa said. "It's impossible. It's better, far better, for Maddie not to know who her father is. He's...not a nice person." Red flashed before her eyes for a moment, and she pressed her palms to her cheekbones, trying her hardest to remain here, where she was safe.

After a few minutes, she took another sip of water, then put the glass carefully on the table beside her. She stood on shaky legs. Faith stood as well, and they looked at each other.

"I'm happy for you," Theresa told Faith. "Look at you. I know I'm only a decade older than you, but I feel proud of my friend, like an old auntie."

Faith laughed. "I'm happy for you, too. My artist babysitter is famous."

Theresa flushed. "Not famous."

"Close enough. I read the New York Times."

Famous, Theresa thought, after she gave Faith a hug and left with Maddie. Fame meant that anyone could follow her, read about her, know about her. Her heart sped up again. She had been an idiot to think she could move back here. That she would be safe. That anyone was safe anywhere.

Her hands shook on the wheel.

"Where now?" Maddie asked. Theresa looked at her, a little surprised to find that her daughter was in the car with her. She had been lost in her own world. *Pull it together, Reesey,* she thought.

"We need to eat lunch," she said. "Then off to the garden shop."

"Here? Not at Sam's?" Maddie asked. "Does he know how unloyal you are?"

"Disloyal," Theresa murmured. "And he doesn't have the plants I want. Have you ever been to the nursery in Billers?"

"No," Maddie said.

"Well, you're in for a treat. But first, you need the best Mexican food in the world."

As soon as she walked into the taqueria, Theresa stopped short, and Maddie bumped into her. The taqueria was like a time machine, the smells, sounds, and decor identical to the day Theresa had last seen the small restaurant.

"Mom!"

"Sorry," Theresa murmured, forcing her legs to move as she walked to a booth. She looked at the familiar green and red salsa bottles, the plastic bananas hanging from the ceiling, the black and white photos of Frida Kahlo and Diego Rivera. She was still shaky after her talk with Faith, but this place calmed her.

"Are you ready?" she asked Maddie.

"Ready for what?"

"You've never tasted anything this good, I can promise you that."

The woman who bustled over to their table carried menus, but Theresa knew what she wanted, so she barely glanced at them. She looked closely at the woman. She had white streaks in her hair now, but Maria hadn't changed much beyond that.

"*Tia, por favor*," she started, and the woman looked at her, startled.

"¡Ay! ¡Mija, Dios Mia! Look at you! Has Sofía seen you?"

"Not yet, no. Is she here?"

"No, of course not, she works at the National Forest office."

"Oh, well, then. I can go to the Forest office to see her sometime."

Maria frowned. "She missed you, Mija. You never came to visit."

Theresa flinched. "I didn't come back to visit anyone. I'm sorry."

Maria nodded, her face smoothing out. "Well, we all have our reasons for things."

"This is my daughter. Do you remember Maddie?"

"Do I remember Maddie?"

Theresa grinned. "Sorry, of course you do."

"Oh," Maddie said. "I'm sorry, I don't remember you."

"You were very small when we came here. Maria's daughter Sofía and I were best college friends," Theresa said. "She decided to be a park ranger, and I became an artist."

"And a *mamá*," Maria said.

"And a mother," Theresa agreed. "Maria used to babysit you sometimes, Little. When Sofía and I went out."

Maddie sat back in her seat, looking around the taqueria. "That's why," she said. "I felt like I was walking into something I had dreamed of." She looked at Maria. "Did we...cook together here?"

"We did. We made churros, and you used to stuff them into your cheeks like a little *ardilla*, a squirrel."

Maddie and Maria smiled at each other, and Theresa felt a familiar twinge of guilt. She had taken Maddie away from so many people who loved her.

Maria switched her intense gaze to Theresa. "Sofía worried about why you left. She thought you might be in danger."

157

Theresa felt a flash of alarm. Maddie was listening to this. "No!" she said. "Just needed a change, that's all." She changed the subject. "We're starving, Tia. Can we get the sopa, four carne asada tacos, and a side of rice?"

Maria regarded her for a few heartbeats, then nodded and bent to kiss Theresa on the top of the head. "Of course. But I will add an order of empanadas because you are so skinny you look like you will blow away. If you need anything, you come and talk to me, and you don't ever run away again. Sofía will be very happy to know that you are back."

Theresa wasn't so sure. She had missed a lot of her friend's life. But Sofía knew better than almost anyone why Theresa had to leave. Maybe she would understand why it had taken her so long to come back.

The drive home was quiet, possibly because they were digesting the enormous amount of food they had consumed, but Theresa thought they were probably just all talked out. Her hands weren't shaking anymore, but she was thinking about the red words. They flashed into her brain at all times. Even the fact that the back of the car was filled to overflowing with plants couldn't lift Theresa's spirits.

She dropped Maddie off at home and drove straight to Green's to talk to Sheldon.

Theresa strode into the store, finding it surprisingly full, with Sheldon nowhere to be seen. Raj, the new manager, smiled at her.

"Can I help you with anything?" he asked.

"No, I'm just doing some shopping," she replied. "Why is it so busy today?"

Raj shrugged. "Everyone getting ready for the holidays, maybe?" Theresa stared at him. "Yes, maybe you're right," she said. She picked up a basket, knowing that if she stormed straight into Sheldon's office, the store would be all ears. So Theresa wandered down aisles, picking up a few things that she needed here and there until she came to one of the chalkboards.

At the slightest touch, you easily will unfold me, it read.

Theresa sighed, feeling two things simultaneously: One, a rush of longing from her head to her toes, and two, frustration that Sheldon still didn't get it. What was wrong with him?

She found him in his office. He was wearing the devastating white shirt, two top buttons undone. His hair was all mussed, and he had the tortoiseshell glasses on. She stared, and even knowing she was staring, she couldn't pull her eyes away from him, not even when he looked up and saw her there.

"Reesey?" he asked.

She dragged her eyes away from his shoulders and up to his eyes.

"Tazzy, this has to stop," she said.

"What has to stop?" he asked.

"You know! Don't act like you don't know! The signs, the poetry. I know what you're doing."

He smiled into her face, lines radiating out from the sides of his eyes. He wasn't listening to her.

"It's dangerous," she said. "Trust me."

His smile disappeared, and he took a step toward her.

"What do you mean, it's dangerous?" he asked. "Theresa, you need..."

"No. I can take care of myself," she said, stepping back as he reached for her. She felt a familiar rush of panic, like hot water filling her from head to toe. "You're not listening. You did this last time, Sheldon. You thought you could fix me, thought you could fix everything. But you can't. No one can, but especially not you."

He stood there looking at her, hands clenching and unclenching. His face was grave, and he was breathing quickly.

"Theresa, you tried to take care of it yourself, and it didn't work. Why do you think you can now? What about Maddie? We all care about her!"

"And now you want to put her in the play," Theresa said, trembling.

Sheldon frowned, looking confused. "She shouldn't be in the play? Reesey, what are you talking about? How could the play be dangerous?"

"You ask that because you don't know about the eyes," Theresa said. She realized she wasn't making sense and that she was rocking back and forth slightly. She needed to get out of here before she melted down completely.

"Maddie shouldn't be in the play because of eyes?" Sheldon asked. "What are you saying? Explain it to me."

"Yes, no. She can be in the play if she really wants to, I don't know. Just the fact that it's so simple for you shows that you don't understand. You thought you could do this last time, thought you could be her father. But you can't, because she has..." her voice was rising.

People were passing, glancing into the open door of the office. Theresa felt pressure like a hard hand squeezing her heart. It was getting hard to breathe again. Sheldon reached out to grab her, but Theresa evaded him and slipped out of the office, dropping her basket and running through the store, until she was out in the cold air, running, slipping, and running, all the way home. She didn't stop until she was under her blankets, in the dark, away from all the eyes.

CHAPTER TWENTY-FIVE

The next morning, Sheldon went through the motions of checking stock, but his head was foggy, and he was barely able to pull his thoughts together. He had not been able to stop thinking about his conversation with Theresa. What was she talking about? What did she mean—all the eyes?

He tapped his fingers on the shelf he was inspecting—beans and sauces—and bent closer to squint at a label. Was it too hard to love Theresa? Sheldon had decided to try one more time to win Reesey over and, in the meantime, to be an excellent friend. It wasn't that difficult to write poems on chalkboards or to read to Reesey while she worked on pottery.

The hard parts were the leaps of hope, the little skips in his heartbeat. He slept or did not sleep based on whether the day ended on a good note. He hadn't slept last night, so the morning wasn't going so well. His eyes felt like beds of fresh gravel. You tried to do this last time, Theresa had said. That hurt. Thought you could fix everything. Well, who wouldn't want to help Theresa Lily Grant?

His desire to help was not the problem—the terror she felt, the danger she mentioned, that was the problem! And Sheldon still didn't know what the threat was, because Reesey wouldn't tell him! Besides all that...Sheldon didn't want to fix her. He liked Theresa the way she was, and he wasn't the only one—if only she would notice—

"Sheldon?"

Sheldon jumped nearly out of his skin. Raj was directly behind his left shoulder.

"Are you having trouble reading that?" Raj asked. "You've been staring at it for five minutes."

Sheldon looked from Raj to the can in front of him, and back to Raj.

"It says black beans," Raj added helpfully.

Sheldon scowled. "Thanks," he said. "Considerate of you. But let me as you a question. Have you ever had a problem with 'eyes?'"

Raj stared at him. "Do you mean, do I need glasses? Like you might want to look into?"

"No, do you worry about eyes looking at you?"

"How else would people look at me?" Now Raj looked alarmed.

Sheldon sighed, tapping his index finger against his forehead. He had a raging headache. "Never mind. Did you have a question?"

Raj nodded, snapping his fingers. "Yes! Sorry, there's a customer here with a complaint."

"You can handle complaints now, you know," Sheldon said with another sigh.

"I tried that," Raj answered. "But he only wanted to talk to you."

Sheldon lifted an eyebrow at that. Strange. He handed Raj his clipboard and walked to the customer service desk slowly. To his surprise, the person standing there was Daniel.

"Daniel?" he asked, puzzled. "Do you have a complaint?" Only after he spoke did he see how pale Daniel was. His hands were jammed in his pockets, his light brown hair sticking up, what looked like a few days of beard growth on his face.

"A complaint? No," he said, looking confused. "I needed to talk to you, and you weren't in your office, so I asked your new manager where you were."

Sheldon turned to look at Raj, who had followed with the clipboard. He smiled, unabashed. "He said he wanted to talk to you," Raj said, "and he looked upset. I assumed it was a complaint."

Sheldon started to say something, then gave it up, shaking his head. "What do you need, Danny?" he asked. "Oh, and Raj, you can go finish counting that stock." Raj walked off, muttering about his college degree.

"Can we talk in your office?" Daniel asked. Sheldon took a closer look at him. No, Daniel was not doing well. He looked shaken.

Sheldon led the way to his office and shut the door after Daniel came in behind him. Daniel looked out of place in Sheldon's cluttered, antique-filled little office. He wore a plaid flannel shirt and a pair of Carhartt work pants, his hands were still in his pockets, and his shoulders were bunched up around his ears. Sheldon patted Daniel on the shoulder, and he flinched, hard, banging his elbow on the door.

"What's going on?" Sheldon asked. "Whatever it is, I promise we'll make it okay." You thought you could fix things, he heard Theresa say again. Did he really do that? Always? Ugh. "I mean, just tell me what's going on. It doesn't have to be okay."

"I don't think it can be okay," Daniel said. "The vandal struck again this morning. Someone spray-painted horrible, racist things on George and Mercy's office building. They used the 'n' word and called Mercy a monkey." Daniel shuddered. He looked as though he might cry.

"What?" Sheldon felt the blood drain from his face. "I have to go over there."

"I just have to finish telling you..." Daniel said. "The police came and questioned me this morning, Shel. I swear to you, I didn't do it. I would never. But they're watching me. The bank CCTV caught it. The vandal is wearing a ski mask, but he looks like me—my height and weight, and he's wearing black boots like mine. But Sheldon. It wasn't me."

Daniel's eyes were tortured, rimmed with pink, with dark shadows underneath. Sheldon reached out, and this time Daniel didn't flinch as Sheldon patted him on the arm. Sheldon changed his mind and pulled his old friend into a hug.

After a moment, he stood back and looked at him. "I believe you. We'll work this out. Right now, let's go talk to George and Mercy."

"I can't," Daniel said. Sheldon started to reassure him, but Daniel shook his head.

"No, the police say that because I'm a suspect, I can't go near the law office, or even near George and Mercy. This is a hate crime."

Sheldon's stomach dropped, and he felt as though he might throw up. George and Mercy had been through too much. How could this have happened to them?

"You go," Daniel said. "Give George my love. Tell him that I would never do this. Not in a million years."

"I will," Sheldon said. He was out the front door in a flash, jogging up Aveline's main street. The Jacksons' law office wasn't far, and soon Sheldon could see a small crowd was gathered on the sidewalk outside. His throat tightened as he felt the urgency of getting to his friends. It was another ridiculously sunny day, unsuitable for the rage that was building inside Sheldon's ribcage. Francisco, George, and Mercy stood huddled together just in front of the stairs, a little way from a cluster of policemen. Sheldon could tell that his friends were praying. As he drew near, a car squealed to a halt, swiftly parallel parked, and Faith jumped out, running straight to her parents, into their arms. Francisco stepped back to give the family a moment, and Sheldon went to stand beside him. Francisco had been crying, Sheldon could see.

"I just heard," Sheldon said.

"How?" Francisco wanted to know.

"Daniel," Sheldon told his friend. "He's rattled. The police are circling him."

"It wouldn't be the first time I've made a bad judgment

call in my desire to think the best," Francisco said. He gave Sheldon a long look. "Do you think it was him?"

Sheldon looked at Francisco, startled. "You're wondering if Daniel wrote that?" he asked, gesturing at the ugly words on the building. They were so violent, so hateful. So uncaring of what the family had gone through, losing their son, never getting justice, and the sheer volume of hate mail they'd received for attempting to press charges. "How could you ask that?"

"From what I know of Daniel, he couldn't," Francisco said. "But, I'm confused." He nodded his head toward the other end of the street. "Here comes your lady."

"My what?" And then Sheldon turned his head, and Theresa was there. As distraught as Sheldon was, she still took his breath away. He felt winded, as though he'd run a lot farther than two blocks. Her long hair was woven into two braids, and she wore red leggings and a long black coat. Her face was a mixture of rage and sorrow.

"I don't want to interrupt them," she said, not bothering with greetings, "but I really want to give them a hug."

"Give them a few minutes," Francisco said. "You're close to Daniel, right, Theresa? Do you think he would do this?"

Sheldon couldn't believe how much Theresa's face changed in just a few moments. She turned to Francisco, her small face pale and afraid, her lips pressed tight.

"I'm going to say this very, very clearly," she said. "I know with every part of me that Daniel did not do this. He would never. It wasn't him. It's wrong for you to doubt him," she looked back and forth between Sheldon and Francisco, and Sheldon wanted to protest that he hadn't doubted him, but when he looked deep inside himself, he knew it wasn't entirely true. There was a tiny part of Sheldon that wasn't sure. Theresa gazed fiercely at them for a moment longer, then walked over to Mercy, who had stepped back from hugging Faith. Mercy turned and opened her arms. Theresa walked into them and hugged her hard.

"Two things," Francisco said. "One is that I really like her, Sheldon. Look how she doesn't even hesitate to walk into a tricky situation and give a hug. The other is, how can she be that positive... unless...?"

"Unless?"

"Unless she knows who did it."

Sheldon looked at Francisco, his eyes wide.

"You think...what? You think she might know who's doing this?"

Sheldon turned to watch Theresa—his small, mighty friend who pulled and pushed at him at the same time. Sheldon's thoughts whirled. She had left Aveline so suddenly, all those years ago. She often seemed afraid.

"We're calling a town meeting," a voice said. Sheldon came back from his thoughts to see George. Sheldon clapped a hand on his friend's shoulder. He didn't know what to say. He felt like anything he did say would intrude on something he couldn't understand.

"I'm sorry, George," he said finally. "I'm sorry people are like this."

George nodded once and rubbed at his forehead. "Meet at the church at seven o'clock," he said. "Everyone should be there."

CHAPTER TWENTY-SIX

The rest of the day dragged. Sheldon tried to focus on work, but it was as though his brain cells had been muffled with a large, ugly scarf. At the same time, his mind couldn't rest. He saw the words on the Jackson's office building, Faith's pinched lips as she stepped out of the car, the way George looked as though he had been punched. He saw Theresa's pale, fierce face.

He would never. It wasn't him. How could Reesey possibly know that? Was she guessing? Or was Francisco right? Did Theresa know who was defacing the walls of Aveline with hate speech? If she did, why hadn't she told anyone?

Sheldon paced. He tried to take deep, calming breaths. Pacing and breathing did nothing to slow his thoughts. He glanced at his watch. Six o'clock. Finally. He left Raj in charge and walked up to his apartment, feeling like an old man. He had just enough time to eat before the town meeting. He sautéed vegetables with a few cubes of tofu, reheating a bowl of rice from the day before. He sat down at his table and looked at his window, already dark. All he could see was the reflection of his kitchen and his tired face, pale in the light of the pendant lamp above his table.

You did this last time. Thought you could fix it.

It was too hard to love Theresa. He ate without tasting his food, washed his dishes, and went to the coat rack by his front door. He pulled down a dark brown pea coat and herringbone scarf. He flipped the pea coat so that it flared out as he put it on, tied the scarf around his neck, and gently pulled a fedora onto his aching head. At the last minute, he added a walking stick. He didn't know why he was arming himself with accessories. He only knew that he had to if he was going to make it to the meeting.

A memory, a whiff of remembrance.

Sheldon was around seven or eight. Sitting on the floor of the shelter with his dad, crying. His father talking.

"Mom is very, very sick," he said. "That's why she's in the hospital."

"Was it her sickness that made her scream?" he asked his dad.

"Yes," his dad said. "It was."

When they got their apartment, years later, the rooms were bare. At first, Sheldon and his dad didn't even have chairs. When they did get chairs, there were only two, and they didn't match. Sheldon slept on a stack of blankets on the floor. His dad was worn out at night when he finally got home from work. They didn't talk about Sheldon's mom much anymore. Sheldon read library books on his pile of blankets in the long, lonely evenings. One bright day, Sheldon's dad told him that he had got a job in a nearby town called Aveline.

"We're going to move there," he said. "I'll be the janitor at the university."

"Will we have furniture?" Sheldon wanted to know.

"Is that really your first question?" his dad asked, laughing, reaching out to ruffle Sheldon's hair.

Sheldon looked down at his hands.

"You want furniture pretty badly, don't you?" Sheldon's dad asked softly.

"Yes," Sheldon said simply. He couldn't explain what was in his heart, which was that his mother had made pillows into a nest for Sheldon, for him to read beside her on the couch every night before she had got so sick and started screaming and pulling her hair out and set a fire, and the police had taken her away that night.

Sheldon liked the new town. He liked their new apartment. And he loved the lake.

One night his dad woke him up, late. "Come on, kid. We're going to get some furniture."

As they drove down to the university, Sheldon got worried. "Why are we getting furniture in the middle of the night? We're not stealing it, are we?"

His dad laughed. "Of course not, silly," he said. "All the students are leaving for the summer, and they throw their stuff out, so they don't have to move it. We're doing a good deed if we rescue a few unwanted things and give them a home." He parked the truck and got out.

Sheldon flinched at the idea of people just throwing their possessions away. He ran to keep up with his dad.

They found a lot of great stuff—nearly perfect things that took Sheldon's breath away. They piled the furniture into their pickup, moving quietly, so no one would wake up and say, "Hey, why are you stealing our trash?"

They found two beanbag chairs, perfect for making nests. A small table. (Like it was made for us, Sheldon's dad said.) Two wooden chairs. The chairs matched. Dishes. And best of all, a bookshelf.

On second thought, Sheldon thought, standing in front of his coat rack, he wanted his silver-tipped walking stick, the one he only used for special occasions.

He went to fetch it from his bedroom and looked around at his apartment, filled with things he had rescued. Maybe Theresa was right. Maybe he was always trying to fix things. And maybe it would never work.

Sheldon was conscious of a tight pain around his sternum as he jogged toward the church, a little late now. The memory had nearly wiped him out.

The sanctuary was nearly full, and it smelled like incense. Sheldon looked around, and though he saw Sam, Katie, Dorothy, and Maddie, he didn't see Theresa. He sat beside Maddie at the end of the pew.

"Where's your mom?" he whispered.

Maddie shrugged. "She wasn't having a very good night," she said. "So, she stayed home to throw pots." Maddie shot him a look. "Stuff like this is hard for her. Meetings and scary things like racism."

"Yeah," Sheldon told her, "but she was the first one today to give Mercy a hug. After Faith, of course. She runs straight into scary things sometimes, which is very brave."

Maddie's face cleared, and she dabbed at her eyes quickly with the backs of her hands.

"Maybe you should tell Sam that," she said. "He was pretty hard on her for not coming."

Looking along the pew, Sheldon could see that Katie's arms were crossed over her chest, and Sam's jaw was clenched. "Oh, dear," Sheldon said. Maddie shifted, a half-smile on her face.

Then Francisco stood up and began to speak.

CHAPTER TWENTY-SEVEN

"All right, friends," the reverend said from his place behind the pulpit. "We have serious work ahead of us. Something insidious has taken up residence in our town," he said. "Something that wants to threaten the haven this place has become."

"Well, it's to be expected, isn't it?" called a man in the back row. "With your big plans for this place."

Sheldon groaned.

"Thanks, Rich, we all know your opinion on immigrants," Sam shouted, half rising out of his seat, and Sheldon leaned forward and popped his eyes at his friend. *What on earth?* Sam knew better than to feed trolls. Katie put a hand on Sam's arm. Sheldon peered back at Rich, who was sitting next to Lenny. The two of them slouched in the pew, arms crossed over their chests, body language saying that they didn't feel they needed to be there.

"We know who did it," said Cam, from his spot across the aisle from Sheldon. "It's that creepy postal worker. He's always been a weirdo, and we let him continue looking through our mail, hands all over our stuff. We need to get rid of him."

Sheldon was surprised at Cam. He'd never heard him talk this way before. "Cam," he said, "first of all, Daniel's not creepy. But more importantly, innocent until proven guilty, right?"

"What else do we need?" Rich asked. "We have footage."

"We have footage of a person wearing a ski mask!" Sam shouted.

Oh my, Sam was in a shouty mood tonight.

George stood. "We're getting ahead of ourselves." He took a breath. "I'm not even sure that identifying the perpetrator is the main thing right now. I feel that most of all, we need to recognize that this evil thing, the racism that has dogged our steps for hundreds of years, is with us today. And it will *continue* to be with us unless we *eradicate* it." He had fallen into his lilting tone, half pastor, half lawyer, and the people in the church were silent, transfixed. "What does that mean for us? What does it mean for the people we are inviting to live here with us? What does it mean for the most vulnerable among us?"

George was middle-aged, not very tall, and wore his hair shaved close to his head to disguise his balding. But he looked fierce and powerful as he faced them.

"Perhaps our family was mistaken to think we were coming somewhere safer than the place we left. Or that the memories of Zion's death would be less painful here. But I don't think we were wrong to assume that in this place we can form a shelter of agreement. That we can support each other. Maybe if we can start by admitting the wrong in ourselves, we can rid ourselves of this evil." He smoothed his left hand over his shirt, a gesture Sheldon had seen him make hundreds of times. Sheldon had tears in his eyes. "I want to tell you, my friends, that if you are under any delusion that this is the exception, that this has nothing to do with you, you are wrong. The evil of racism has stirred against my brothers and sisters since the beginning of this country. It has never ceased biting at our heels, and we are tired. We need you. We need our dear friends to help us."

He blinked, seeming to come back to himself. He grinned. "Sorry," he said, "You can take the man out of the courtroom, but you can't take the courtroom out of the man."

There was laughter in the room and then cheers, mostly from Sheldon's pew and Carlo, who was always loud, everywhere. A few of Aveline's other black citizens called out, "Thank you!" and "Amen!"

Francisco gave George a hug. Sheldon sat in his pew and thought about his own casual belief that racism couldn't touch them here. "Look at us!" he had thought to himself. "We have a Salvadorian pastor, a pair of black lawyers, and a hundred professors of different races."

And yet, here it was. Hate building up, reaching out to strike at them all. Sheldon felt a sudden wave of exhaustion, but then he looked up and caught Mercy's tired, traumatized eyes. She gave him a slight smile and shake of her head, and he dipped his head, remembering.

Faith was twelve years younger than her brother, Zion. When Zion was killed in a police shooting at a mall, the family had packed their things, moving to Aveline. At the time, Mercy was traumatized and not functioning. She had professor friends who lived in Aveline, and suggested that it would be a good change for the family— a place to live out of the city but continue their practice in L.A., as well as opening up for work in Billers and Aveline. Mercy had been unable to make a decision, but George, scared by the effects of PTSD on his wife, made the decision for them. They moved.

The people of Aveline did their best to come around the family and welcome them. Dorothy especially had kicked into overdrive. She and Mercy had started the women's group that continued to this day. The group that had made Francisco jealous enough, when he eventually moved to Aveline, that he started backyard night. Theresa had become Faith's babysitter as the new law firm got off the ground. And Sheldon had watched it all, still feeling like an outsider—a kid who grew up in shelters and lost his mom to an undignified death in a mental institution.

Sheldon was eighteen when he first met Mercy. He hired her as his lawyer when he came into a sudden inheritance from a grandfather he had never met.

"You don't know how to deal with this," she had told him.

"It's not a bad thing to deal with," he told her. "But I can't help wishing he had used his money to help my mother before she died. He disowned her and then gave it all to me. If he had helped her, maybe I would have actually had a mother." His throat hurt like he was going to cry. He cleared it and dabbed at his eyes.

Mercy had given him a moment, looking over the paperwork. After a while, she looked up, folding her hands carefully in front of her. "Sheldon, we don't get to pick. But don't think of this as an easy thing. You have some thinking to do. What do you want? What do you see around you? You need to find a place to put this money- somewhere to invest, or it will disappear. I've seen it again and again during my career. A kid who never had anything and suddenly comes into money needs a plan."

"Did this happen to you?" he asked her.

"No," she said, her voice clipped. "I grew up with plenty of money. George too. But that didn't save us. There are no guarantees. All you get is now, what you have in front of you. And even that can be taken. What can never be taken is invisible, you know that, right, Sheldon? You are a child of God, and that can never be taken, even if your son gets taken, and the man who kills him goes free."

She sat back and pressed her hands to her face, then sat up and looked at him with a fierce, determined expression.

"So, what will you do?"

Mercy had the same look on her face as she looked at Sheldon in the church. He sat straighter and shook the self-pity away. All you get is now, what you have in front of you. No feeling sorry for yourself because the town of your dreams isn't as perfect as you believed it to be.

CHAPTER TWENTY-EIGHT

"Go with your strength, Reesey," Theresa whispered to herself. She was scrambling a mess of eggs, tomatoes, and kale.

The morning had started out quietly enough, but Theresa's thoughts were racing. Maddie and Sam had filled her in on the contents of the meeting, and Theresa's heart broke as she thought of how courageous George had been. Not that it was strange for him. George had always been brave. He had never, ever ceased to be brave.

Theresa didn't even have enough courage to go to a town meeting. She felt a brief pang of self-loathing, then shook her head and turned off the burner. She scooped the vegetable scramble onto two plates, then poured green smoothie from the blender into two glasses. Theresa had been letting Maddie make breakfast for herself, but she'd noticed lately that Maddie rarely ate more than a piece of toast with jam. Not enough for a teenage girl.

What were Theresa's strengths? When she was living in

her weakness, she often forgot. What use was it to the world if Theresa could make pottery? There were amazing people out there like George and Mercy who overcame incredible odds to be strong, and there was tiny, fragile Theresa who made sculptures. Ugh.

But she knew that comparison would kill her. She thought of how God was the one who formed her, including all the unusual things about her. *He made you to be you, strange mind and all. He made you to throw pots.* Okay. Theresa would throw pots. She would sculpt and be a good mother to Maddie, and being a good mother to Maddie included staying away from town meetings because Theresa would be a basket case for a week after a town meeting. It didn't matter if people—including her own brother—judged her for not going. None of that mattered. No one else knew what it was like to be Theresa. She needed to figure out her own strengths and work from them, not from the expectations of others.

"Maddie!" she called. No answer. She went to Maddie's door and knocked.

"Yeah?" she heard. She opened the door.

"Are you not up yet? You're going to be late."

It appeared that there was no one in the room, but a lump stirred under the covers. The lump groaned. Theresa smiled and went to talk to it.

"Come on, Little," she said. "I made you breakfast. Did you stay up too late again?"

Maddie took the covers off her head and squinted at Theresa. Theresa felt a jolt of love so strong it rocked her backward. Her daughter's little ears poking out of her black hair, her fierce squint.

"Biology exam," she said, yawning. "I was studying. I'll come, just give me a minute."

Theresa bent and kissed her daughter's forehead.

"Okay," she said. "Come quick, though—it will get cold."

She went back out to the kitchen and sat down with her scramble and smoothie. She lifted her mug hopefully, but the coffee was long gone. Theresa had been up for hours, thinking about strength and fragility, sketching ideas. She took a gulp of green smoothie and put her pencil back on the page.

Maddie came out of the room, finally, rubbing her eyes. She was dressed but looked sleepy.

"You made breakfast?" she asked. "Cool."

"No problem," Theresa said. "But eat quickly, you'll be late."

"I'll take my bicycle."

"Did you get the brakes fixed?" Theresa asked, looking up from her work.

"Yes," Maddie answered. "Sam helped me."

Theresa looked back down at her sketchbook and drew line after line. The panic had been so intense the other day. Would her new sculpture series be about panic? That could be good. But Theresa was already mostly recovered from the fear. She was more resilient than she had believed. No, that wasn't entirely true. Theresa was more resilient than she had been ten years ago, and the memory of how she was then and how she was now was always a paradox in her mind. This town carried the physical imprint of her terror, the rapid beat of her heart when she saw the oak tree on the corner, or the way she had run, her heart pounding, pounding, straight down the middle of the street.

"Mom!"

Theresa looked up. Maddie was staring at her.

"What?"

"I've been calling you!"

"Oh, sorry, kiddo. I was far away."

"I can see that," Maddie said, pointing at the paper in front of Theresa. Whoops. Theresa saw that her drawing had left the sheet of paper entirely, wandering around the table. Shapes, lots of them. Some angular, some curved. All hollow in the middle, as though you could use them to hold water or something like it. Oil?

"Mom, I was saying that I have rehearsal tomorrow night. Is that okay?"

Theresa put her pencil down and looked straight into Maddie's eyes. "It is okay if you are very, very careful," she said. "You have to understand that there is a monster on the loose. The person who would write words of hatred on George and Mercy's walls is a person incapable of feeling compassion. If he had compassion, he would know that they are the last people on earth who should be seeing a message like that. Those are hateful, evil words, and that person is in our town."

"Mom, do you know who it is?"

Theresa stood and accidentally knocked her green smoothie over, causing it to cascade across her papers, ruining her sketches. Maddie yelped and jumped up to get a towel, but Theresa just stood and stared at the goo obliterating everything she had done.

Later, when Maddie was gone, Theresa threw some easy pots and thought about ice fishing. When she had first started ice fishing, she thought she could never ever get used to the cold. But there were so many things you could get used to. You could get used to fear or not being able to breathe very well. You could get used to kindness. You could get used to knowing things no one should know.

She should tell Francisco what she knew. There was no guarantee that Theresa was right, she was only guessing, but she felt it, the same way she felt the physical imprint of hands on her when she turned certain corners. She was terrified to tell anyone her thoughts, but she was also terrified that if she didn't, someone would get hurt. There was nothing for it. She would have to go to the church. The tall reverend with the kind eyes was the right person to tell.

Theresa put a warm coat and scarf on and called Remus. He came quickly, and she touched his gray nose and put her face very close to his. He whined a little and licked her face.

"It's okay," she told him, "we're just taking a walk to the church."

CHAPTER TWENTY-NINE

The air outside was brisk with a stinging wind. The unseasonably warm days had come and gone. Some winters in Aveline barely got cold enough to qualify as winter, but this one was shaping up to be frigid. Theresa swung her arms to keep warm. Remus sniffed at trees and occasionally lifted a leg to pee. Oak leaves crunched under Theresa's feet, and the clouds in the blue sky looked like popcorn.

There wasn't enough distance between her house and the church, and when Theresa got there, she felt utterly unprepared. She looked up at the old stone building, admiring its shape against the sky, feeling sick to her stomach, trying to bring herself back to the present. She tied Remus to the bike rack and told him to sit. He did. He was a remarkably well-behaved dog, Theresa thought, and her stomachache eased a little.

She walked up the stairs, through the dark foyer, and into the sanctuary. At the front of the church, she saw the shape of the pulpit with a few lit prayer candles to one side. Theresa knew that Francisco had taken some flack for introducing prayer candles, but he insisted that they were helpful. A small ritual like lighting a candle, he said, was a good reminder that in prayer, a real interaction had occurred. Something has happened. You have spoken to God, and he has listened well because that is what he does.

Theresa walked to the front of the church. She looked at the candles in their glasses, thinking about containers. Every person was some kind of vessel, made to hold what he or she could offer. Theresa's vessel seemed so damaged, sometimes. She picked up a candle, bringing it to her nose to inhale its scent. It didn't smell like anything but wax. She picked up the lighter and bent her head.

I'm so lost, she told God. *And I think I know too much, and I don't know what to do with what I know.*

She lit the candle and waited. She knelt and smelled warm wax and the fragrance of old wood. She, as a vessel, held a complex mix of things. Confusion, cowardice, hurt, misunderstanding. But she also held other things, like creativity, some bravery, and so much love. What was God asking her to pour out? Had she come back to settle this score, finally, after all these years? Or was it something else? What did she really know? By telling what she thought she knew, she might be ruining an innocent person's life.

And then there was the danger. To herself, yes, but again, Theresa thought of Maddie, of the threats they had received without Maddie's knowledge, all these years, and Theresa realized she couldn't do it. Her vessel simply wasn't big enough.

God, she prayed. *Help me know what is next. I can't. I can't.*

As she sat there with her head bowed, she felt peace flow into the hurt places in her heart. After a while, she could take an easy breath again. She saw her own cracked cup, and she saw the pottery she made. It was all she could really do. She would never be some spectacular mother, some great world-changer. But she could make pottery. She thought of her friend, Faith. Faith was a magnificent vessel. Francisco, too. And then she smiled. She knew what her next sculpture series would be.

She stood, feeling stiff. *Thank you,* she said. When she turned to go, she nearly bumped into Francisco at the end of the aisle. He was so tall, she had to tip her head back to look at him. She pressed a hand to her heart.

"Sorry," he said. "I was trying to figure out a way to announce my presence without scaring you. It's the average reverend's biggest problem. We're always walking around quietly, trying not to startle people while they're praying."

She smiled at him.

"Did you have something you wanted to talk about?" he asked.

"No," she said. "Well. I did. But I don't think I can. But I have answers I didn't think I would find in a church, so that's good."

"It happens more than you'd think. But Theresa, if there's anything—well, you know I'm here, right?"

"I do," Theresa said. "I know." She couldn't hold eye contact, so she spoke to his left shoulder. "But anyway, I have to go. I'll see you later!"

Francisco patted her on the shoulder, and she made her escape, bursting out into the cold fresh air, untying her dog and running with him down the street. Now that Theresa knew her next steps, she couldn't bear to wait any longer.

At home, Theresa fed Remus and put her coveralls on. She tied her hair up in a scarf and turned a Feist album way, way up. Theresa would start with Faith. Faith was the sculpture Reesey imagined, not how she really looked, but how her vessel looked—what she could hold and what she could do. Faith's sculpture would be tall, with strong, curved sides. Big enough to hold all the strength and love she had poured out since she was a twelve-year-old helping her grieving parents.

Theresa rolled large slabs and used slip clay to mold the edges together. She would build layer by layer, knowing this sculpture would be large, but that she would shape it in segments, so that the first part was partially dry before she added the next.

Bent over her table, engrossed in the smells of clay and sounds of loud music, Theresa almost didn't hear Sheldon at all. Eventually, he stepped on a creaky floorboard, and Theresa straightened to look at him. She was flushed with the brilliance of a new idea, the exhilaration of knowing exactly what she was meant to do. The hope of a new project always hit her like a few glasses of wine, and in that state, seeing Sheldon was like missing a step walking down the stairs.

He wore a fitted black shirt, with suspenders and funky tan pants, brown boots laced up. He walked to Theresa quickly, and she saw that he was wearing the glasses she loved. He hadn't shaved. She stared at his face, thinking that maybe he was starting to grow a beard. A beard! Her Tazzy!

He spoke before she could say a word.

"Don't go far off, not even for a day, because --
because -- I don't know how to say it: a day is long
and I will be waiting for you, as in an empty station
when the trains are parked off somewhere else, asleep."

She stared at him. "Did you write that?"

He laughed a little. "No, that's Neruda."

"Are you growing a beard, Tazzy?" she asked finally. His eyes were burning into hers. To distract herself, she reached up toward his face and ran her hand over his cheek. Stubbly. She touched the beautiful line of his jaw, the dimple in his cheek, the top of his cheekbone. He grabbed her hand, and she looked up at his eyes again. His eyelashes, so dark. There were nebulas in his blue eyes, like the posters in Daniel's post office. She was drunk on creativity and sculpture. Theresa knew she needed to move away, but Sheldon turned her hand over and kissed her palm. His breath and lips on her skin startled her. What was she doing? Sheldon was not a sculpture that she could touch at whim, though he was so very beautiful, and the dark hairs on his forearms made her feel slightly weak. She pulled her hand away gently and stepped back, feeling her heart racing away, heat rising to her cheeks.

He let her go, his eyes never leaving her face.

"I'm not sure how I feel about a beard," she said, putting her hands under her arms so she couldn't touch him again.

Sheldon smiled, those new lines spreading from his eyes, creases forming deep in his cheeks.

"We'll just have to see then, Reesey, won't we?" he asked.

And Theresa nodded, feeling dazed.

CHAPTER THIRTY

Sheldon watched from the front pew as his actors clustered on the stage for a rehearsal. They ran through the first scenes once while he watched, making notes for feedback.

"Maddie!" he called, cupping his hands around his mouth. "Give yourself more room! You shouldn't be hiding behind Lewis! Make your circle."

Maddie flashed Sheldon a look, but stepped away from the other actors and did as he told her, spreading her arms out and turning in a circle. He gave her an exaggerated thumbs-up, and Maddie turned away so he wouldn't see her smile. He still saw it.

Sheldon was ecstatic that Theresa had agreed to let Maddie be in the play. Maddie was the perfect teenaged Maria—a little freaked out by the idea of pregnancy, clinging to her older husband, slightly bewildered as they were turned away by shelters and seedy hotels.

And Sheldon was proud of the play he had written. Imagining the holy family as flotsam drifting in the chaos of modern times helped Sheldon to think about his own past. Unwanted, wandering, looking for a place to make a nest.

Sheldon's mother had contracted an infection and died not long after she entered a minimum-security prison. A judge convicted her of arson, with the caveat that she was mentally unwell, so she spent her last days living in the psychiatric ward, where her burns apparently weren't treated with appropriate care. Sheldon's mother's slide into instability had seemed instantaneous to him, as though one day she had been making him sandwiches and reading with him on the sofa, and the next, she was being arrested for purposely setting several houses on fire. It wasn't until many years later, when Sheldon was a teenager, that his dad told him about the drugs.

Sheldon's mother had grown up in a home full of violence, and she had fought a heroin addiction on and off throughout her teen years. "She was clean when we met, and other than one relapse, she stayed clean during our relationship. She did especially well when you were born, Sheldon. She loved you so much."

Sheldon had sobbed when his father told him this. For years Sheldon had carried around the thought that something he did had caused his mother to burn those houses. He thought he had sent her to prison. He wished he had always known that the burning, the insanity, was the sad end to a long story, rather than his fault.

The short version was that when Sheldon was eight years old, his mother had started using again. Sheldon's father didn't know why. She kept it from her husband for a long time, until one day, suspicious; he searched her bags and discovered a used syringe. They fought about it, and Sheldon's mother promised not to use anymore. Sheldon's father went as far as to threaten her dealer. One day, though, she injected heroin she had bought from an unknown dealer, a substance that turned out to have been mixed with methamphetamines. This cocktail had a disastrous effect on Sheldon's mother, leading to a manic spree of insanity and setting fires.

Sheldon's father used his meager savings to appeal the verdict, based on her need for help. That appeal was overturned, and Sheldon and his father were homeless for many years. They drifted from shelter to shelter while Sheldon's father fought to overcome the deep depression caused by the conviction— and eventually, the death— of his wife.

A long-ago sad story, Sheldon told himself, pulling his fedora farther down on his head. But it explained a lot about him for anyone who wanted to know. He knew that a person could just disappear and that society would not care about their disappearance, no matter how much that person was loved. He knew that possessions helped to anchor a person, though they were temporary. And he knew that people were more than their disorders. His mother had been one of the loveliest people he knew. To this day, she had told him more truths than anyone else in his life, besides *maybe* Theresa. He'd had eight beautiful years with her. And then she was taken from him by an illness that most people didn't want to say aloud. Words that were whispered in alleys.

When he first had come to church with Sam, Francisco had taught on Mary Magdalene. "What kind eyes Jesus had."

Frankie had said. "Eyes that saw past the whispers around her, into the truth of who she was beyond her sickness." Sheldon had listened with his whole self. And then he had come back the next Sunday.

The pews were mostly empty during play rehearsal, but there were a few spectators. Sheldon didn't like it. He wanted the actors to have a distraction-free environment. Lewis and Maddie performed the scene where they wandered from motel to park bench to shelter, looking for a place to stay, and Sheldon needed to watch, but instead, he kept glancing back at the people in the pews. Some people needed to be there— actors waiting their turn, choir members—and there were harmless spectators, like the church janitor and a woman Sheldon had never met before. But then there were Lenny, Rich, and Cam.

Sheldon hadn't exactly *liked* Cam before the town meeting, but he hadn't had a real problem with him. Since that night, though, he was looking at him sideways, especially since he was hanging out with Lenny and Rich, who were outspoken about their dislike of Francisco. Was this how hateful ideas spread?

What were they doing here? It was nerve-wracking. Sheldon couldn't help thinking of Theresa's warning to keep the rehearsals safe for Maddie. At the time, Sheldon hadn't understood, but with this crowd lurking around and a vandal still on the loose, he was starting to see.

He stood and walked to the side of the stage, where Francisco stood chatting with Mercy and Dorothy.

"Can we do anything about these guys?" Sheldon asked. They didn't even need to ask who Sheldon was talking about.

Dorothy's eyes swiveled in the direction of the three men, while Mercy and Francisco looked at Sheldon.

"You want me to kick people out of the church?" Francisco asked, raising an eyebrow.

"You know they're only here to make us feel uncomfortable," Sheldon said.

"I don't know that. They haven't said anything. Maybe your play is changing Lenny's mind about these things. That would be good, wouldn't it?"

"*That man*," Dorothy said. "Lenny has never been good for much."

Francisco choked, and Sheldon grinned. Dorothy always said exactly what she thought, reminding Sheldon of Theresa.

"I don't know why Cam's been hanging out with those two," Mercy added. "He's always been a decent guy."

Dorothy glanced at her. "You think?"

"Why, you don't think so? He was friends with Sam for ages, right?"

Dorothy considered. "He's polite. But I don't really know anything about him, and he and Sam haven't been friends for a long time."

"Was Lenny friends with Sam?" Mercy asked.

Sheldon was already shaking his head. "Lenny was a bad seed all the way back in high school," he said. "And Cam and I were never friends. He always avoided me, for some reason, but he's always been polite. I agree—it's weird that Cam puts up with Lenny."

Francisco spoke in a low voice. "Lenny is my top suspect for the graffiti."

Sheldon considered. Yes, Lenny was the right height and shape.

"So why are you letting him sit in your pew?" Dorothy said.

"Innocent until proven guilty," Mercy said, though her face was stiff and sad as she spoke.

"I can't throw them out for sitting there. Or, rather, I won't. If they cause a disturbance, I'll do something, okay?"

"Who is the new lady? In the back?" Sheldon asked.

A huge smile transformed Francisco's face. "That's Ani. She's the consultant who's going to help our refugees make their homes here. She's getting to know the town so she can be ready to help them."

"She's from Syria?"

"No, from Iran."

"She doesn't feel uncomfortable in a church?"

All three of them looked at Sheldon like he was stupid. "She's a Christian, Sheldon," Dorothy said. "Don't make assumptions."

Sheldon held up his hands and shot one curious look at Ani, then went back to watching the actors through the scene, thinking about Lenny and the possibility that he was the vandal. It was disturbing to imagine such hateful thoughts simmering close by. What was Lenny thinking as he sat watching the actors rehearsing their lines, and the choir sing the songs about young Maria?

"All right, everyone!" Sheldon called after the choir's last song. "That's it for today. You did great!"

He checked his watch. It was getting late. He would walk Maddie home and hopefully get to talk to Theresa. He packed up the scripts and locked the prop closet. By the time he went outside, Maddie was in front of the church in a little group that included the new woman, Francisco and his daughter, Rosa, Mercy, Lenny, and Cam. Rich was nowhere to be seen. Everyone seemed tense.

Sheldon felt a sudden rush of anger. What was happening to his town? Aveline had been a good place for Sheldon for so many years. A safe place, after the worry of living from day-to-day.

When Sheldon reached the others, he heard Rosa introducing Ani to the different people in the circle.

"And this is Sheldon," she finished up. "Sheldon, this is Ani."

"Hi," Sheldon said, taking her hand and shaking it. "It's nice to meet you." Sheldon was surprised by how firm her grip was. Ani was slight of build, with large, dark eyes and a sweet face. She looked young but had a surprising gray streak in her hair.

"Nice to meet you, too," she said. She had a slight accent. "Rosa has been telling me about you."

"Oh dear," Sheldon said, making a face at the little girl, and Ani laughed. Sheldon glanced back and forth between Ani and Francisco, thinking fast. Francisco saw him and gave an almost imperceptible shake of his head. Well, they would be spending a lot of time together, wouldn't they? And it seemed that Rosa was already a fan of the woman.

"Francisco says you're from Iran?" Sheldon asked.

Ani nodded. "I am. But I am Armenian-Iranian, so I speak a lot of languages and have a lot of cultures inside me, vying for my attention." She smiled.

Sheldon didn't like the way Lenny and Cam were eying Ani. Why didn't they just leave?

"Been well lately?" Francisco asked Lenny.

"All right," Lenny said. "Having trouble finding work." Every word was loaded.

Francisco nodded. "Well, I hope you find something soon." It was not clear to everyone else who didn't know Francisco well, but Sheldon could tell that it was a dismissal. Lenny, however, didn't get the memo. Cam turned to Maddie.

"How's your mom?" he asked.

"My mom?" Maddie asked.

"Yeah, I knew her in school."

"Oh," said Maddie politely. "She's doing well."

This was excruciating. Sheldon needed to pull away from this brutal small talk circle.

"Are you ready to go, Maddie?" he asked.

"Are we going somewhere?"

"I told your mom I would walk you home."

Lenny and Cam turned to look at him. Lenny held an unlit cigarette in one hand and looked at Sheldon with what seemed like hatred. Sheldon felt the impact of it, even while he wondered what he had done to deserve such a look. Yes, this could be a man who had tagged Sheldon's store with rude words. Cam was looking at Sheldon, too, but his face was smooth, relaxed. Sheldon grabbed for anything.

"Cam," Sheldon said. "How are you?"

"Can't complain," Cam said. "Ready, Lenny?"

"Yes, the reverend says we can't smoke on the grounds, so we'd better go find a place for our dirty habit."

"Just not on the stairs," Francisco said. "Feel free to smoke on the grass."

The two gave little waves and walked down the stairs. Beside Sheldon, Mercy let out a long breath, and Sheldon felt his shoulders relax. He realized he had been preparing himself for some sort of altercation. In front of Francisco's church? It felt as though they had all entered a strange alternate world. Surely this wasn't Aveline.

CHAPTER THIRTY-ONE

"Should I have asked him about the graffiti?" Sheldon asked Mercy as they watched the men walk away. "Was it wrong to just sit there and chat with him?"

Mercy smiled and patted his arm. "I could have asked him myself if I wanted to. I know you have my back. But it would have been interfering with an investigation. Better to let the police do their work."

Francisco nodded. His face was thoughtful.

"I just wish I knew why they were baiting us," he said.

"You know why they're baiting us, Frankie," Mercy said. "You *know*. You challenge them. They've clung to some belief that their world wouldn't change, and they've been listening to rhetoric from videos online, and here you are. Pastoring their church, bringing refugees in. It worries them. Either they'll prove to be good seeds and come around, or this will push them farther into their fear."

Beside her, Ani was nodding. "This is all part of it," she said softly. "We need the grace of God to help us."

Sheldon was deep in thought as he walked Maddie home. He roused himself to pay attention to the girl next to him. Maddie was humming slightly, giving a little skip at every other step. She was still such a kid, though he knew better than to say it to her.

"Maddie, were you uncomfortable when Cam was talking to you?" he asked.

"Not so much," she said, "but I didn't understand how he knows my mom."

Sheldon thought about that. He remembered that Cam was friends with Sam in high school. Had he known Theresa back then?

"I'm not sure," he said, "but I do know that those are the kind of people that your mom is asking you to steer clear of as we do this rehearsal. I'm not sure why she's worried about you, but there's been a lot of hatred in our town lately. I think as we go forward with the investigation, the play, and our new families, we're going to see more of what it means to try to unravel hatred."

"Unravel hatred?" Maddie asked, looking over at him. Her face was open, though Sheldon could see anxiety in a slight tightening around her eyes. Worry for her mother, he would guess. For her fragility.

The sun had set. Twilight fell quickly. Dead leaves lay scattered on the ground, crunching under their feet. Sheldon looked up and saw the feathery black tips of a single redwood tree against the violet sky. It stretched almost higher than he could see.

Maddie stopped and looked at it with him.

"It's so tall," she said.

Sheldon nodded. How should he put this? "The thing about hatred," he said, "Is that when you take all the rage away, it mainly resembles fear. But that fear fuels self-pity and self-pity fuels blame. Suddenly people divide over trivial things, and they can't see from any perspective besides their own."

"So, what do you do about it?"

"I don't know. I hate that this kind of division has come to our town. I thought our town would always be free from it."

Maddie nodded slowly. They started walking again. The moon had already risen, and wispy clouds drifted along in front of it. Sheldon hoped Theresa wouldn't worry. He pulled out his phone and sent a quick text.

On our way. Almost there.

Absorbed in his phone, it took him a minute to hear what Maddie said.

"Sorry, what?" he asked, slipping his phone into his back pocket.

"I wonder what Faith would say about that?" she said. "Would she think Aveline was free of racism before now?"

Sheldon thought about that, watching the fourteen-year-old in his peripheral vision. Grown or no, she still had the same adorable, stompy walk that he remembered from when she was little. It reminded Sheldon of Theresa.

He thought about Maddie's words and frowned, watching their feet, never quite in sync, walking through the smatterings of leaves over the sidewalk, under the bright moon. How was it that he had never asked Faith or even Mercy or George what Aveline was like for them? Sheldon had always thought of their life as having a distinct *before* and *after*. *Before* being hard and scary. *After* being Aveline, with friendly neighbors, police who knew them well, the sun on the lake, the oaks and jacarandas sheltering nearly every street from the burning sun. But that was how Aveline was for Sheldon. Was it stupid to imagine that Aveline was the same place for everyone? His stomach twisted as he realized it was.

He thought about Ani, about what her job would be over the next weeks and months. Her work was not stocking grocery shelves. Her work was helping traumatized people from a war-torn country settle in a place where 29% of the people had voted not to have them come.

Or what life was like for Theresa, for that matter. She lived with a disorder in a place where— as she said—it had been easy to take advantage of her. Something terrible had happened to her here, severe enough that she left. These streets must hold a story of very mixed experiences for her.

And with that, Sheldon was back to thinking about Theresa. Lately, he couldn't hold himself away from thoughts of her. He thought of her face the other evening, the night he had come to read the poem to her. Flushed with excitement over her work, her coveralls splattered with clay. The way her eyes lit on him, suddenly, focusing so intently on him in that way she had. Sheldon knew the look on Reesey's face. It was the feverish look of creating something she thought was going to work. Sheldon loved her for that look, for the obsession in the bones of her wrists, the way she trained herself onto the thing in front of her with the eyes of an owl, diving in with every cell. He was starting to see how life was for her. If she could exist in that space forever, she would be fine. Reesey thrived in a clear liminal space where she plucked ideas from the air and transformed her thoughts into shapes that could be held and seen by people. This she did effortlessly, gracefully, with power that surprised even Sheldon, who knew this part of her well. It was the rest of life that was such an uphill climb for her.

And now the moment he kept flashing back to. Reesey's face, this one for him, after he had read the Neruda poem. When she had walked to him and touched his face with her hand.

Sheldon had never had the easiest time understanding God through conventional means. Maybe that was why he connected so well with Theresa. She had always expressed something to him that reminded him of the Eternal One, the Creator. Sheldon understood God through the smell of old wood in church, the sheen of tomatoes, and the carving on an antique cabinet a man had made for his wife. And there was something in Theresa's level gaze that told Sheldon things he wouldn't be able to know about God if she didn't exist. That was why it had hurt him so badly when she had gone. She was not the sum total of her difficulty in interacting with people. She was more, so much more. She was beyond words. She was spirit and possibility and a closeness to God as effortless as her art. And it made him want to be closer to her, because with her he felt that it might be possible for him to feel closer to God, too.

Sheldon had marked the poem in his book of poems by Pablo Neruda long ago, knowing it was for Theresa. He wanted to read it to her at their wedding. When she disappeared, he had stored the book out of sight on his highest shelf.

But Theresa had come back, and Sheldon had pulled his Pablo Neruda book off the shelf and dusted it off. He had read the poem and watched as her face changed, a new blazing intensity just for him as she zeroed in on him, walking closer while he held his breath.

When she touched his face, it had taken every bit of self-restraint that he had to kiss her hand and walk away. But Sheldon knew Reesey. She was like a bird or a deer in the forest. She would startle at even the hint of a threat. He would walk softly, quietly toward her. He also knew, after that look, after the feeling of her clay-covered palm against his lips, that his question was answered— he would continue to approach her. She was worth everything to him.

CHAPTER THIRTY-TWO

Maddie nudged Sheldon, bringing him back to the present yet again. They had reached the house. Sheldon followed Maddie as she walked under the bougainvillea-covered arch and up to the door. To his surprise, Sheldon heard the sound of hammering around the back of the house, coming from the studio.

"It's late," he said to Maddie, as she opened the front door. "What's she doing?"

Maddie shrugged, slipping her shoes off. "It's probably Sam," she said. "He gets obsessed with his projects."

Sheldon considered this. She wasn't wrong.

"Let's go see," he said.

Maddie sighed dramatically but followed him down the garden pathway to the studio. They found Sam at the front of the studio, working on one of the floor-to-ceiling shelving units. Sheldon stood back for a minute to admire the effect of the work on the room. Sam and his team had transformed the small building—essentially a shed—into a light-filled storefront with a workshop in the back. They had expanded the front half until it was twice its original size, with large windows forming the whole front wall. There were delicate stair step shelves to show off Theresa's smaller-sized ceramics, as well as floor stands for larger works, and a wood and glass cabinet. In the middle of the room, there was a shift from display to workplace, with long concrete countertops and paint-splattered walls. The workshop opened to the add-on drying and firing room.

Sam removed his headphones. "Hey guys," he said. "Rehearsal over?"

"No, it's still going on," Maddie said, her voice dripping with sarcasm.

"Hey," Sheldon said. "Don't be hard on him. He's old."

Sam raised his eyebrows. "Both of you are sassy as ever, I see." He spread his arms to either side, showing off his work. "What do you think?"

"Looks great," Sheldon answered. "You guys are quick."

"Have to be. Reesey wants her opening to be before Christmas."

Sheldon felt his jaw drop. "What?"

Sam shrugged, turning back to his work. "She's crazy. But she says that missing the Christmas season would be the worst."

"Do you know where she is?" Sheldon tried to keep his voice casual, but to his annoyance, it cracked.

Sam turned back, raising an eyebrow at Maddie. She crossed her arms and shook her head. "Don't encourage him," she said, but she was smiling.

They found Theresa at her makeshift work area on the

back veranda. Theresa's chair was under the awning, but even so, she had a leaf caught in her braid. She wore clay-spattered coveralls and sat before an enormous pot. It looked like a giant vase, though Sheldon didn't know what you would put in something like that. It was twisted and curved, the sides sloping upward and then flaring out in unexpected ways, almost feminine in shape.

While Sheldon held back, watching her, Theresa picked up a long rope of clay and dipped her fingers in water, smoothing the water over the pot and then holding the rope to the wet spot and pushing the edges in with her fingertips. She had a fierce look of concentration on her face, and after a moment, she leaned back to look at the effect, noticing them as she did so.

"Oh, it's you two," she said, smiling at Maddie. "How did rehearsal go?"

Sheldon could see the concern in her eyes. Should he tell her about Cam and Lenny? "Your daughter is wonderful," he said simply.

Beside him, Maddie blushed and elbowed him. "Thanks," she said. "I can't say the same for you, though. Mom. Sheldon is a monster as a director. You should be glad you're not in the play. He drives us to exhaustion."

"Hey," Sheldon protested, laughing.

"It's not hard to make you exhausted, lazy daughter," Theresa said, raising an eyebrow at Maddie.

Sheldon smiled at her, but he didn't know what to do. Theresa seemed like she was in a good mood. He could stay and talk with her more, or he could leave it like this. What would help the shy deer walk forward? Maybe it was enough.

He had delivered her daughter safely. He would walk away, not push his luck.

"I'll see you tomorrow," he said, as Maddie went through the patio door and into the house.

Theresa looked surprised. Did she also look disappointed? Sheldon couldn't tell, as much as he wanted to imagine that she did.

"You don't want to stay for a while?" Theresa asked. "I have a bottle of wine."

"No," Sheldon said, "you look busy, and I have enough to do tonight. I'll take a rain check."

"Oh," she said. "Okay, see you tomorrow." He definitely wasn't imagining the disappointment in her voice. He lifted a hand and waved, walking away, feeling a little smug. She wanted him to stay. The moon was stunning as he walked home. He wondered if it had ever looked so beautiful. Halfway back to his apartment above his store, Sheldon realized that he hadn't told Theresa about the guys at the church. It didn't matter. He was probably overthinking it anyway.

CHAPTER THIRTY-THREE

Theresa walked home from Green's, soaking in the feel of sunshine on her face and arms and legs. Remus trotted at her heels, stopping to sniff every tree.

"I don't think anything has changed since the last time you checked, Pup," Theresa said, wrinkling her nose at him.

The weather had turned for good as the December days passed, with leaves falling and the house chilly every morning. Theresa felt like she was often cold, especially when she worked with clay. Her hands grew stiff, and she needed to take breaks to run them under hot water. Minnesota had been much, much colder than Aveline, but in Minnesota, Theresa had a woodstove in her studio. At the moment, she was working on her back veranda. So yes, she was cold. She moved between small pottery and her new series, and on warm days she moved her worktable out into the sunshine to warm up a bit. Under the bay tree, her veranda didn't get much sunlight.

It was nice to walk in the sunshine, thinking about not

much at all, a string grocery bag in each hand, full of colorful vegetables. Theresa had plans for soup and homemade bread for dinner, with the loaves already rising at home.

At the gate, Theresa paused and called Remus, smiling at his funny crooked run as he bounded ahead of her and up to the house where he first kissed his stuffed elephant and then went to his water bowl.

Theresa heaved the bags of groceries onto the kitchen counter and went to shut the front door. She could smell the dough rising, and it gave her a little thrill of happiness. Theresa loved this house. She loved the studio that was nearly finished. She loved getting to know Maddie again and seeing how much her daughter had relaxed, how good Katie and Sam were for Maddie. All of them, really. Lucy, Faith, Francisco, and of course, Sheldon. All of them giving Theresa's daughter the love she needed. Theresa and Maddie had been alone for so long.

Just yesterday, Maddie had asked Theresa if she could *have a friend over*. Theresa had stared at her for nearly a minute before gulping and saying, "Yes, of course you can, yes!" at which Maddie narrowed her eyes, and Theresa realized she had overdone it. She tried to hide her reaction by walking to the sink and getting a drink of water, but then she choked, and Maddie had to pat her on the back until she could breathe again, muttering, "Okay, Mom, be cool, calm down."

Maddie had a friend. The two of them had a home, a family, and *friends*. Theresa hadn't allowed herself to believe something like this could happen, not for a very long time.

She was humming to herself, swinging the door closed,

when she saw the envelope lying on the front porch, half-hidden under the doormat.

Theresa stared at it, and her heart seemed to stutter to a stop before it jolted back into action at high speed. She put a hand to her throat. It was probably nothing. Probably junk mail or a bill. A note from Sam? A poem from Sheldon, or an invitation to women's group, or something from Frankie about church. Still, Theresa couldn't make herself pick it up.

She was frozen, and as she finally bent to pick the envelope off the ground, her hand seemed removed from her body, and her heart felt as though it would pound itself out of her chest. Her name was written on the front of the envelope in tiny, careful block letters. Now Theresa's skin was hot and cold by turns. She was going to throw up. She backed into the house quickly, slamming the door and locking it, her hands shaking.

Her body wanted to get as far away from the envelope as possible. It felt like the flu, like falling from an airplane, like drowning.

She threw the note on the ground and walked around the house, closing her curtains. The problem was, she didn't have as many curtains as she should. Theresa had thought it was nice to have a clear view of the garden and had left many windows bare. She had been *stupid*.

Maddie was still at school. Theresa couldn't breathe. She walked back to where she had thrown the envelope on the ground and stared at it, wrapping her arms around her ribs. Should she open it? She didn't want to—felt sick at the thought of opening it. How could this be happening? How was Theresa back in this nightmare?

She bent and picked up the envelope with two fingers, staring around her with wide, dry eyes. Everything in her house looked different than it had just five minutes earlier. The shock of seeing those tiny block letters reverberated through her whole being until Theresa felt as though she had been punched, shaken, and scraped raw.

She went to the swing chair in the living room—she had been so happy to finally have one—and sat down gingerly. She used her fingernail to get a piece of the envelope open, then pulled her hand across clumsily, ripping the paper and giving herself a cut in the process. As she pulled her finger to her mouth, a dozen tiny leaves fell onto her lap. Each one was different. They were leaves from the trees in her garden, carefully collected, and placed in the white envelope.

Theresa thought she would faint. She knew who had done this. He always did things like this. Now she hurried. She had to read what it said. She pulled a letter out and unfolded it with shaking hands.

Dear Theresa, the note said. *I saw Maddie yesterday. I talked to her. She's beautiful but not as beautiful as you. You can't keep avoiding me, I don't want you talking to him. Stay away from him. You have always belonged to me I'm not done with you. Stay away from him. You've seen what I can do when I'm angry.*

The letter wasn't signed.

Theresa jumped out of the swing chair, crying out when she twisted her ankle. She stumbled into the kitchen and put the letter in the sink, turning the tap on it, then shoving it into the garbage disposal and turning the switch on. The roaring sound of the garbage disposal sickened her. She was going to have a heart attack. Something was happening to her vision. Everything felt slow, oily, prickly.

Theresa pushed her palms into her forehead and then raised them and smacked herself hard, on the forehead one, two, three times. She realized she was rocking, humming, and it wasn't helping. She hit her head harder. She needed to get out of her skin; it was going to smother her. Panic.

She was powerless. She had always been powerless against people who wanted to harm her. It felt like there was fire in her chest. Her heart was beating so hard. She put her fingernails against her head. She needed to scratch the fear out—no. No more scratching. She had promised. She half ran, half stumbled to the bathroom, tearing her clothes off and climbing into the shower. She turned the water on as hot as she could stand and she let it run over her face and hair, over her head.

She couldn't do this.

It hurt so much. The brutality of the world. The ugliness. After the bad thing had happened, Theresa thought she would die. And then baby Maddie came, and then Sheldon carefully came closer and closer to her, and Theresa thought maybe things would be okay. But the menace in the cruel forest had closed in on her all those years ago. She had done the only thing she could do. She had run.

Why had Theresa thought she could come back? Good things weren't for people like her. Nightmares always found her.

The words. Those words. Suddenly Theresa was crying, and then she was squatting under the water, rocking back and forth on her heels, wailing. The sounds that came out of her would have been terrifying if anyone had heard them. Theresa cried until her voice got crunchy with it, and then her crying slowed, and then it stopped.

Her breath came slower. She found that she was sitting on the floor of the shower, leaning against the wall. The water ran over her, slowly calming her until the panic started to fade.

Feeling ancient and spent, Theresa stood and took a bottle of frankincense oil from the windowsill. She shook a few drops into one hand and then rubbed her hands together, wiping them on her face and neck, and as the hot water warmed the oil, the smell of frankincense filled the room. Theresa took a deep, shuddering breath, breathing the beautiful scent, coming back to her body. She tapped lightly on her collarbone and temples.

Okay, Reesey, she told herself. *Hey. Hi. It's okay. You're still here.* If she thought of the note, though, her eyes welled with tears, and her heart started racing again.

She never, ever wanted Maddie to know about the notes. She needed to keep the menace in the cruel forest far, far away from Maddie. What was Theresa going to do? She stared into her pruney hands and realized that she had absolutely no idea.

CHAPTER THIRTY-FOUR

Finally, after what seemed like hours, Theresa turned off the shower, grabbed a towel, and pulled it tightly around her. She walked out of the bathroom to find that she wasn't alone in the house.

Sheldon was in her kitchen. First, Theresa jumped half a foot, her senses already jangling, then she felt heat rush to her face as she realized she was only in a towel.

"How did you get in?" she asked, her voice still scratchy and sore.

Sheldon was red in the face. "I'm sorry," he said. "You forgot one of your bags of oranges, so I brought it when I got a chance, and your door was open. I came in to put it on the counter, and then I heard you crying."

He started to walk toward her, but she held a hand out. She could feel how she looked, how swollen her eyes would be, how red her forehead from hitting it. She didn't want him close to her. He stopped and put his hands in his armpits, rocking back and forth a little, chewing on his lip.

"Reesey," he said, his voice low. "What's wrong? Tell me, please. I want to help."

She looked at him, so exhausted that she felt as though she could sleep for a month.

"Give me five minutes," she said. In her room, Theresa pulled on a pair of warm pajama pants and a T-shirt, then pulled a blanket off her bed and wrapped it around her. She took a few breaths and walked back out to the kitchen, suddenly glad that Sheldon was here. Theresa did not want to be alone at all.

Sheldon was putting Theresa's groceries away. He had wiped the counters and washed the few dishes that had been in the sink. Sheldon was so, so beautiful and so comforting, standing there. He had heard the worst part of Theresa as she wailed in the shower, and he had not run away.

If she told him about the letter, maybe he could help. He had gone through many hard things in his life. He had taken the crap his childhood had given him and grown from it. He was smart and kind.

But Theresa's cruel forest would eat him alive. There had been letters in the past. *I'll cut his face and hands.* She knew the menace would do it. She touched the scars on her left arm. People always assumed she had done it to herself. She had never told anyone the truth.

Right now, though, all Theresa wanted was Sheldon. So she went to him. She walked very close, and after a moment, she put her arms around his waist and leaned her face on his chest. His arms came around her, and the weight of them was the last piece she needed to drive the panic away. She stood there, breathing more and more slowly, listening to his heart.

"Reesey," he said, his voice a rumble. "What's wrong?"

"I can't tell you that," she said.

"I won't tell anyone. You know I can keep a secret. I'll keep you safe."

Tazzy's heartbeat beneath her cheek was like the feeling she had when she was under the covers during a storm. He smelled like linen and sunshine. If only she could tell him, share this horrible thing, so it wasn't sitting on her alone. If only Theresa could let Sheldon take care of her. If she could be with him again, she would be the happiest woman alive.

Theresa remembered the horrible, tearing feeling when she had been forced to flee. It had been so hard to walk away from her curly-haired boy, this man who had taught her how to be free.

She pulled away and looked up into his eyes. He touched her face gently with his hands, smoothing away the tears that were still spilling out of her eyes.

"No one can keep me safe," she said. "I can't have this kind of relationship, Sheldon. That's all I can say. I'm not allowed. If I try, the people I love will be in danger."

His eyes were very soft, but his eyebrows drew together in a frown. "Is someone threatening you?" he asked. "Is that what this is about, Reesey? I always thought you meant you couldn't be with me because of something inside you that kept you from being able to stay. Are you saying that someone made you leave?"

She looked back at him, flooded with every bit of longing she had ever felt for him over the years. What could she tell him? She had missed him like a limb. There were parts of her that could never even be alive if he wasn't around. Jokes that she could never share. Wildness she kept locked away. How could he think it was something inside her that made her leave? But she had never told him. How could he know? She felt panic again. She didn't know how to keep this perfect person safe. Her boy. Her friend, who didn't find her too weird or make her feel stupid for not understanding the social world.

She was powerless again. She couldn't control what would happen or keep Sheldon or Maddie safe. She couldn't stop the hate or vandalism. She felt one tiny thread of her guard start to unravel, and she nodded and said.

"Yes. I left because someone made me leave."

He drew in a breath. His face changed so many times that she couldn't keep up with it. He pressed his lips briefly to her forehead, some kind of tension rushing out of him, and then pulled back and asked another question.

"Was the someone Maddie's father?"

Every muscle in Theresa's body seemed to freeze and then scream. She couldn't hold eye contact and flicked her eyes away from Sheldon's. She needed to run. She pressed her palms into her cheeks and then began to tap her forehead with her fingers. Tap, tap, tap, tap. Sheldon didn't move to stop her. A small part of her brain remembered her mother or her brother pulling her hands away from her head, telling her to stop tapping. Sheldon didn't. Maybe that was why she answered him. Maybe that was why, in the tiniest voice, she whispered, "Yes."

Theresa heard Sheldon take a breath, and then he drew Theresa back into the circle of his arms. They stood there for a long time, rocking slightly back and forth. Her head was on his chest, listening to his heart as it sped up and then slowed. He was warm and strong, and Theresa felt safe. She knew it was only a feeling, that even now the menace of the cruel forest could eat them both, but she was so relieved to feel safe that she let it be. She stood there leaning on Sheldon, imagining that it could last forever.

CHAPTER THIRTY-FIVE

Sheldon woke with a start, opening his eyes and sitting upright in his bed. His heart was pounding. His dreams had been tortured and full of anxiety. Theresa slipping off a cliff and Sheldon reaching for her only to accidentally let go. Driving down a steep hill in a car with no brakes, Theresa in the passenger seat.

Sheldon was coming to the slow, horrible realization that he'd had it wrong all these years. Theresa wasn't worried, fickle, or hard to please. She hadn't even left because anything that Sheldon had done or not done. Theresa wasn't *safe*. And Theresa not being safe felt unbearable to Sheldon.

He sat on the edge of his bed, trying to calm his rapid heartbeat. After a moment, he stood up and walked over to the window, pulling up the shade to look at the scene below. It wasn't yet dawn— the street was dark. Sheldon checked his watch. Only four o'clock in the morning. His heart was still beating fast. He remembered another part of the dream.

Theresa had been talking to someone. A man. Sheldon couldn't quite see his face. Theresa was afraid, cowering, and as the man shouted at her, she sank onto the ground, holding her hands over her head. The man got angrier, screaming until he was shaking, and when Sheldon finally broke out of paralysis and grabbed the man by the elbow, he turned, and Sheldon saw that it was Daniel.

Sheldon shook his head to clear it now, looking at the line of light that was just beginning to show between the clouds and trees in the distance. It couldn't be Daniel. Theresa had said it wasn't. She wouldn't lie to protect him, would she? Because he had a disorder like hers?

The birds weren't even awake yet, and the whole town had that pre-dawn hush.

It wasn't Daniel, Sheldon realized with relief. Theresa didn't have the capability to act naturally around people she didn't like. Sheldon remembered how Reesey had run from that agent, all those years ago. Whoever had hurt Theresa couldn't be someone she spent time with regularly.

Was it Lenny, with his anger problems and harsh opinions? Rich? Cam? Or someone he hadn't thought of? What about the old man who lived on the other side of the lake? Parents often told their children to steer clear of that man's house. There was no proof that he was dangerous, but he wasn't in his right mind. Or the man on the edge of town who had been pulled in for domestic abuse, more than once?

Theresa had barely told him anything. Sheldon needed to know more, but Theresa was too afraid to say. Sheldon was horrified by the thought that none of them had caught this. That they had blamed her for taking off to Minnesota and never coming to visit. *Sheldon* had blamed her. How could he have done such a thing? He *knew* Theresa. Why had Sheldon assumed that everything revolved around him? That she had left because of him?

He began to pace. He needed to get back to sleep. Work would start early in the morning. He shivered. The weather was colder than usual for central California, and Sheldon's unheated apartment was chilly.

He got back under the covers, thinking of Theresa burrowing into his chest as if Sheldon could hide her from every terror. But if Sheldon wanted to help her, he would have to know who or what the threat was. He needed to try to find out. It was his last thought before he drifted back to sleep.

Later, Sheldon knocked loudly on Katie and Sam's front door. Sam opened it, looking sleepy and annoyed. It was still early. Sheldon couldn't care less.

"I need to talk to you," he said, pushing past his friend into the house, walking back to the kitchen. Katie was usually in the kitchen, and Sheldon wanted to talk to her, too.

"Come on, Sheldon, give us some warning before you bust in like this," Sam grumbled behind him. "It's our day off."

Katie *was* in the kitchen, as Sheldon had hoped. She was chopping vegetables at the kitchen counter, and she looked up as he entered, her face startled. She was more of a morning person and managed to look happier to see him than Sam had.

"Shel? What's up? Is everything okay?" she asked.

"Have you talked to Reesey lately?" Sheldon asked. He

didn't know what to do with his hands or where to be. He ended up leaning against the island, crossing his arms in front of him.

"Depends what you mean by recently," Sam said. "I talked to her yesterday, tying up some loose ends before the opening."

"Why, Sheldon?" Katie asked. "What's going on?"

"She got some sort of threat," Sheldon said. "I don't know if we should go through with the opening."

Katie carefully put her knife down on the counter and wiped her hands on a towel. Wordlessly, she beckoned for Sam and Sheldon to follow her. She walked out to the sunroom and sat down.

Sam had built the little room off the back of the house just before the wedding, so the two of them would have a place just for them on the ground floor. It was furnished with colorful old couches Katie had found at the flea market, as well as armchairs, blankets, and pillows. The space was a welcome sight for Sheldon's tired eyes. He sank onto one of the couches, feeling exhaustion sweep over him, all the way into his bones.

"Okay," Katie said as Sam sat beside her on the other couch. "Explain. You know we can't call off the opening without Theresa's approval."

"I'm not suggesting we do that," Sheldon said. "That's nuts. I'm wondering if you or Sam could ask Theresa about it. She acted like someone threatened her yesterday. She was terrified, and I don't think this is the first time something like this has happened. Maybe she should lay low for a while and not invite the whole town to her house."

Katie's hair was tied back in a scarf, giving Sheldon a clear view of her eyes and the look of compassion on her face. Sam studied Sheldon, chewing on his bottom lip. They both looked at him for a long time.

"What?" he finally asked, irritated by their silence. Didn't they understand what he was saying?

"You really love her still, don't you?" Sam said.

Sheldon gaped at his friend. "Are you for real?" he asked. "Do you know me at all? How could you have missed that I have never for one day stopped loving your sister or even looked at another woman? In ten years, Sam! My love for Theresa has never been in question. The question has always been why she ran so far and fast to get away from me."

Katie and Sam were quiet, listening. Encouraged, he continued, sitting back and lowering his voice a little.

"I assumed that she left because of me, but I'm starting to wonder if it might be someone else that she's running from. And not a relationship. A threat. Do you see what I'm saying?"

"I think so–" Sam said, but Sheldon interrupted.

"What this means is that maybe we assumed Reesey was running from love, or consolation, or companionship, because of the hard time she has socially. It fit our assumptions, Sam, to think that, but maybe she has been in actual danger from an external threat, and we never knew. I'm trying to tell you that I think Theresa is in actual danger. If that's true, Sammy, we failed her."

Sam got to his feet, his face troubled. "I don't understand. You think she's been threatened, and she never told us?"

"Do you know who Maddie's father is?" Sheldon asked.

Sam frowned. "You know I don't. It's true now, just like the last million times you asked me."

"Well, does anyone know who Maddie's father is?" Sheldon asked, his voice breaking. "Don't you think it's a little strange that we don't know?" Katie and Sam were silent. Sam sat back down.

"Haven't you ever wondered why no one knows who Maddie's father is? Surely if she came from a one-night stand or just a bad breakup, Theresa would have told someone. One of us, Sam. We're her closest friends. But what if there was something traumatic about whatever happened with Maddie's father?"

"Are you saying that Maddie might have come from an act of violence?" Katie asked. "Are you talking about rape?"

Sheldon winced. He felt like he wanted to cry at the word. At the thought. "I don't know what I'm saying. All I know is that I think we've attributed a lot of Theresa's behavior to just Theresa being different, and maybe we've missed signs of something important, something that could put her in danger."

CHAPTER THIRTY-SIX

S heldon went to work. It was all he could do, though he couldn't concentrate. He piled stock, went over lists, called his dairy supplier, and got involved in the most irritating conversation with one of his cashiers about the difference between a real smile and a sarcastic smile. She claimed to be having a hard time differentiating between the two. Sheldon was reasonably sure that the cashier, Janelle, just didn't like people very much.

"Like this," Raj said helpfully, offering a toothy grin.

The cashier frowned at him, and Sheldon did too because the smile was terrifying.

"I've never seen you smile like that before," he told Raj.

"Sure you have," Raj said, through his teeth. "I smile like this all the time."

"No, you don't," Sheldon said, pinching his nose. "Because if you did, I would fire you. Listen, Janelle, just don't openly mock the customers, okay? That lady was only talking about the weather because it is a common, polite thing to do."

"A pointless thing to do," Janelle replied.

"Be that as it may," Sheldon said, turning to leave, "it's your job to be polite. That's your last warning."

"Just try," Raj added.

"Thanks, Raj," Sheldon said, heaving a huge sigh.

He straightened a rack of reusable bags on his way back to the office, wondering when he would get time to talk with Theresa. But when Sheldon got to his office door, Reesey was already in there, sitting in his beach chair. He did a double take.

"How did you get in here?" he asked.

She tilted her head to one side. "I walked, Taz. You were too busy demonstrating your smile."

"You saw that?" he asked, picking up a paperweight on his desk in an attempt to be casual. He wanted to hug her. Reesey was pale, with shadows under her eyes. Today her hair was loose under a beanie, curling around her shoulders. She looked small and vulnerable.

"Yes, you should teach lessons," she said. "I know I could use them."

"You already have a beautiful smile," he said.

"I seem to use it at the wrong times," she said.

It was true. Theresa had always trusted people without question and seemed surprised when they didn't live up to her firm idea of goodness. Sheldon had noticed the pattern when they were younger. Now he understood why she grew confused in social contexts and why she got herself into difficult situations. It was as though she was missing cynicism or wariness, a hefty portion of what it took to be in the world as a human. Sheldon knew that this lack was balanced by her directness, but her naivety made her vulnerable in a way that seemed unbearable to Sheldon. He felt terrible about not seeing it before now.

Sheldon pulled a chair close to the beach chair and held out his hands to Theresa. After a moment, she put her small, cold hands into his. He pressed them close to his chest, trying to warm her up. She kept her eyes on his face.

"How do you feel today?" he asked.

"I don't know," Theresa said. "Tired, I guess. But I feel stronger today. I had a lot of time to think on my walk this morning."

It was a good lead-in to what he wanted to ask her, but before he could speak, she continued.

"I came because I need to buy a bunch of stuff for the studio opening. Katie's going to cater, but I'll handle the drinks, and maybe we could have some fruit for people who don't want to eat a lot."

"Can't Katie handle fruit and drinks if she's catering?" He winced. It wasn't what he really wanted to ask. He wanted to ask her to postpone the opening. But he needed to work up to it.

"She's tired lately. Have you noticed? I don't want her to work too hard."

"Do you think...?" he asked, startled.

"She's pregnant? Maybe." She smiled. "Maybe it's too early for them to tell us."

"Or maybe they don't know."

"Or maybe she's got a touch of the flu, and we're over-thinking." They grinned at each other.

She looked cute in his beach chair, bundled in a sweater, the beanie pulled down over her forehead. Every time he thought she couldn't get more beautiful, she proved him wrong. She was lovely, strong, and resilient. Not the quitter he had assumed for a long time. He had to say something.

"I need to ask you something," he said, "but don't respond until you've heard me out, okay?"

"Okay..." she said slowly, narrowing her eyes. "But maybe I know what you're going to say."

He took a deep breath, clutching onto his stone paper-weight. "I think you should postpone the opening."

"Yup, that's what I thought you were going to say," she said. She looked up at the ceiling.

"Theresa, please listen to me. Don't block me out."

"I'm listening."

"Yesterday was crazy. I've never seen you so upset."

"Yesterday was part of what it means to be me."

"But you know what I'm trying to say. Are you safe? Is it safe to have a bunch of people at your house for an opening? Why won't you tell me more?"

She ran her hands up and down her cordoroys. "Who is ever safe?" she asked.

He sighed. "But will the danger you fear...show itself at your opening?"

"How could I know that?" Reesey asked, finally meeting his eyes. When he would have spoken again, she held up a hand. "No, listen. You're just now hearing this. I've been *living it* for a decade and a half. I'm tired of letting fear run my life. If I allow this...danger...to change me, it's winning." Her voice caught, and he reached for her hand again.

Theresa pulled away. "I will never have a *life* if that happens," she whispered. "I need to have a life, Taz. I need to be able to open my shop and do my work, to sell my pottery in my community."

Sheldon's heart was beating fast with conflicting emotions. The need to protect, the need to support.

"What do I do to help keep you safe?" he whispered.

"I don't know," she answered. "But this is my dream, and I don't want to lose it because of one terrible person." Her voice broke. It tormented him to hear her so sad.

"Okay," he said. "Okay, Reesey. I get it." She turned and laid her face on his arm, and the tenderness in his heart threatened to break him open.

CHAPTER THIRTY-SEVEN

The sound of the on-going construction was comforting to Theresa, even though she was certain it was louder than it needed to be. Honestly, how could just a few people make so much noise? But the hammering, sawing, and clattering meant that Theresa wasn't alone at the house. The presence of the workers comforted her when her heart raced with fear.

Theresa had made the decision to go ahead with life in Aveline, to hold her studio opening, and to emerge as an artist publicly. This was what she wanted, and she was through with running.

But terror still followed Theresa, lurking in the corners of her mind, waiting until she let down her guard and relaxed enough to joke around with Sam or Sheldon. Then, she felt the sudden spike of terror, making her heart race and her hands shake. Fear waited for Theresa in the wee hours of the morning, when she woke from nightmares of the menace of the cruel forest watching her, always watching.

Theresa did everything she knew to fight the fear. She watered her garden and pulled weeds, sitting in the grass, inhaling the fragrance of compost and rich earth. She threw pots and painted on glazes. She sewed curtains and put them up in the living room. It made her feel safer, and she could pull them open if she wanted to see the garden outside. She tinkered in the studio, setting up her supplies, while Sam oversaw the last of the construction. She saw Maddie off to school each day, sending her with lunch and a hug.

But deep inside, Theresa was afraid. Not only that—she was angry. Through every minute that she worked to keep fear at bay, Theresa burned with slow rage because she still couldn't relax, and this life she wanted so badly felt temporary, as though it would all be stolen from her. She hadn't even talked to Sofía yet, afraid of what she would hear. She knew the reason she was still unable to talk to Sofía. Sofía knew everything, and she always wanted Theresa to tell. Theresa couldn't do that, and it wasn't good enough for Sofía. All Theresa wanted was a peaceful life.

Why did it feel unavailable to her? Theresa wanted a life with her family, in the town where she was born. She wanted to make art and sell it. What was it about Theresa that kept her from living in a way that seemed natural for other people? Theresa knew she had Aspergers Syndrome, but that couldn't be all of it. She had learned to manage her ASD, at least enough that it didn't incapacitate her during day-to-day life. She had found ways to live from her strengths and rest after she did things that exhausted her.

The menace in the forest. Why was Theresa hounded the way she was? Why did she always have to deflect unwanted attention? She had driven all the way to Minnesota to get away from unwanted attention, and still, she had received unwanted letters. She thought of that heartbreaking first year, of putting Maddie into school and trying to adapt to the icy winters, trying to adjust to loneliness.

Theresa had learned her way around her disorder in Minnesota. She had learned not to hate herself for being a person with ASD, to stop belittling herself, or wishing she were different. The time in Minnesota hadn't been wasted. But Theresa wanted to move on. She longed to stay in Aveline, to have a life here, with the women's group and the church, her family, and most of all, with Sheldon. She wanted it so badly, her teeth ached with the yearning.

One morning, Theresa was making a cup of coffee when Remus started acting strangely, scratching at the inside of the front door and whining. After watching him do this for a moment or two, Theresa wiped her hands on her pants and went to see what he wanted. She opened the door and looked around. No one was there, but after a moment, Theresa noticed that the bougainvillea was knocked askew on the arbor, one side swinging drunkenly. She walked down the steps to fix it, propping it the vine back up and snapping off a sprig of the fuchsia blossoms to bring back to the house.

As she climbed the porch steps, Theresa caught a glimpse of white and froze. Another note was lying tucked under the doormat, the corner of it a glaring contrast to the red tiles. She stood staring at it for several minutes before picking it up between two fingers and carrying it into the house.

At first, Theresa dropped the note onto the countertop. She laid the bougainvillea blossoms on the white tiles of the island and paced through the rooms of her house. She felt a stinging sensation on the side of her index finger and looked at it, surprised by drops of blood. Theresa must have scraped herself on one of the bougainvillea thorns. She went to the bathroom sink and ran her hand under the tap, gazing at her pale face in the mirror. The note didn't mean anything. Theresa didn't want to open it—didn't want any thoughts of the menace in her own thoughts right now. She hadn't asked for his presence.

She put the note in a drawer and closed it without reading a word.

The next morning Theresa placed a green smoothie on the table in front of a sleepy Maddie, who thanked her and then went back to her book. Theresa pulled onions, tomatoes, and bell peppers out of the fridge. She sliced the onions into tiny chunks, and then diced the bell peppers and tomatoes, using her favorite knife. She heated olive oil in a pan, then added the onions and sautéed them until they were soft and translucent, adding the bell peppers and breathing in the scent. She tossed in the tomatoes last, then beat eggs and added them to the mix. She spooned the scramble onto two of her favorite plates, topping it with ground pepper and a sprinkle of grated Swiss cheese. Maddie was still deep in her book.

Theresa sat down, setting a plate and fork in front of her daughter. Maddie looked up and made an 'O' with her mouth.

"What's the occasion?" she asked.

There was no occasion. Theresa simply knew that one of the ways you handled fear was to slow everything down and focus on each small thing. Making good food. Sitting in the morning sunlight with her beautiful daughter. Savoring each mouthful. She smiled at Maddie.

"No occasion," she said. "I just felt like cooking."

After Maddie left for school, Theresa picked up a large painting she had recently had framed and walked over to the studio. She found Sam installing the final shelves with one of the other workers. He had finished the large wall behind the shelves: white plaster and partially exposed brick. Theresa loved the result. The shelves Sam was finishing now stretched from the floor to the ceiling, with different heights for different sizes of pots and displays. In front of the large windows at the front of the shop, there were several floor pedestals, for Theresa's most substantial pieces.

"I brought you this," she told her brother, indicating the painting. It was meant for the one blank space on the front wall.

He glanced up and nodded, then went back to drilling.

Theresa wandered around the studio, looking out at the shadows the midday sun made in between the trees. She went to the workshop at the back of the studio and spent some time organizing her tools into the drawers under the wide concrete countertops Sam had built. It was all so much. Theresa was used to working in a shed in the back yard.

She stared out at the oak tree, lost in thought, yelping in surprise when Sam touched her arm.

"What's wrong?" Sam asked. "You're chewing your lip as though you want to eat it."

"Sorry, I was daydreaming." She turned and looked at the

studio, gesturing with one hand. "This is just so perfect. It's overwhelming."

The light in the workshop changed throughout the day. In the late afternoon, the streaming sunlight was like a gentle touch on every surface, making Theresa feel as though she were traveling in places only unlocked in her imagination. At night, the whole studio was lit with warmth, glowing in the garden. It was lovely at every moment of the day.

"Are you sure you're okay, little sister?" Sam asked. "Sheldon was worried about you the other day. He didn't want you to do the opening."

Theresa looked at him and smiled, giving him a big hug. She pulled away after a moment.

"I'm totally fine," she said. "And Sheldon is being over-protective. But thank you for everything. For making this so beautiful, for loving Maddie, and for looking out for me. You're a good big brother." It was their joke. She was a year older than Sam, but he had outgrown her when they were still very young. She had always been smaller and less substantial. Her smile faded. Maybe that was why she was an easy target. She banished the thought, knowing that Sam was much better at reading her than she was at knowing his thoughts.

"What about you guys?" she asked, forcing a smile. "Do you have any news for us?"

Sam looked blank. Theresa shook her head at him. He was sufficiently distracted, and after frowning at her for a moment, he went back to his shelves and Theresa went back to fiercely staring out the window, determined not to let anyone force her to flee again.

CHAPTER THIRTY-EIGHT

Later that day, Theresa carried a few orders to the post office. She had listed her older mugs and bowls, clearing out space and testing her online selling ability. The listings had sold out on the first day. Over the last year, Theresa had been playing with photography and social media, just little bits here and there, and she had gained thousands of followers. Apparently, her followers were excited to buy what she sold.

She kicked at little heaps of fallen leaves, enjoying the contrast of the color against the gray concrete.

Remus trotted along in front of her. The dog occasionally turned to wait, eyes trained on Theresa, as though making sure she was still with him. For a moment, Theresa squatted to pet him, leaning her forehead against the dog's neck. His short fur was soft and smelled good after the bath Maddie's had given him yesterday. It was pure pleasure to have a warm, furry animal to hug under the trees and the blue sky. Remus loved her without complication and was always happy that she was there. Theresa didn't need to figure out what he was thinking or make sure she didn't say something too outrageous in his presence.

This is good, she told herself, *and it's normal*. I don't have to think about the forest menace, or about eyes watching me. It's okay to be happy and to love my dog. For a single moment, it truly broke through to her, just how guarded she had always been, and how lovely it was to be here now, learning what she had. She straightened and kept walking, enjoying the feeling of afternoon sunshine warming the top of her head. The night would be chilly when the sun went down, and Theresa would burrow under her down blanket. In the distance, she could see the glimmer of the lake. Soon she would open her studio. It was a whole new chapter of life. She thought of how she had believed this could never happen for her, and she smiled at her younger, sadder self.

Daniel was counting boxes at the front of the post office, absorbed in his work. Not wanting to interrupt, Theresa paused to look at one of his posters of a nebula. The colors were so brilliant, an explosion of warmth in a faraway place. She thought of how these were things they could never see up close, or even at the time they occurred. Before they'd had strong enough lenses to see stars and planets that far away, only God had known how beautiful they were. It was such extravagant beauty.

Daniel finished his counting and looked up.

"Reesey," he said. "I've been wondering when I would see you again."

He came and gave her a quick, tight hug. She smiled into his face, but after a moment, her smile faded. Daniel didn't look so good. His shoulders were tense and hitched up high, and he had several weeks of beard growth on his face, and shadows under his eyes.

"Hey," Theresa said. "Are you doing okay? They're not still bothering you about the hate crime stuff, are they?"

She chewed her lip, wondering for the millionth time whether she should tell what she knew. She would, Theresa thought, if the only concern was her own safety. But the menace had threatened Maddie, and Sheldon, and well, everyone Theresa loved.

"I had good news this morning," he said. "The police are dropping me as a suspect. George spoke up for me and told them he didn't think I did it. He told them he didn't want them to focus on me anymore because it was distracting from the real investigation."

Relief flowed through Theresa. She wouldn't have to tell.

"That's wonderful," she said. But Daniel's face didn't change. "Isn't it wonderful?" she asked, feeling suddenly unsure.

He shifted from foot to foot. "In a way, it's great," he said. "But I feel as though suspicion is drifting along behind me wherever I go. All I really want is work and music, science and maybe some good food now and then. A walk to the lake. Spending time with you and Sheldon. Friendship with the guys at backyard night." His eyes had drifted to the window as he spoke. Theresa's throat started to sting. Daniel was describing something similar to what she wished she had for herself. "But there's this thing that follows me," he went on. "People look at me strangely, and even George isn't sure about me anymore."

His face was so sad. Even Theresa could see that. Her stomach ached, and she put a hand on his arm.

Daniel spoke very quietly. "Do you think you should tell?"

Theresa looked up so quickly she got a crick in her neck. She winced at the pain, absently putting one hand to the spot and taking a step back.

"What?" Her voice was hoarse.

"Never mind," Daniel said. "I'm sure there's a reason you haven't said anything. I've seen his...violent tendencies."

She stared at him. Daniel mouthed a name to her, and Theresa drew in a shaky breath. For a moment, she felt as though she might fall over. She could see the cruel forest, see the eyes emerging from it. Daniel grabbed her hand, and the menace cleared from her vision.

"How long have you known?" she whispered.

"I think I've always known. I just know you too well, and I spend a lot of time trying to figure people out. Before you left, I could see how you changed when his name came up or if he walked down the street." He squeezed her hand, then let it drop gently. "I remember everything, and I know too many details. It gets me in trouble. I would rather not know because I wouldn't always be wondering about whether you can help me."

Theresa's eyes flooded with tears. "I would..." she couldn't finish the sentence. Her throat was starting to close, and she reached up to rub at her forehead.

"It's Maddie, isn't it?" Daniel asked. "She the one you're protecting."

Theresa pressed her palms into her eyes. She had to make

him understand. It wasn't a lack of love. Theresa looked at her dear friend, willing him to understand.

"Since this all started, so many years ago," Theresa told him, "I have never gone a day without wondering if I would die or my daughter would be hurt that day."

Daniel stared at her. "No one should live like that," he said. "You need to go to the authorities."

"I tried," she told him. "In the very beginning. He hasn't always been the way he is now. He used to be well-respected, and the policeman I spoke to told me it would be my word against his. I had already been categorized as unstable because of public meltdowns before my diagnosis. I thought I could just be better, try harder, not be victimized or weak. But he got worse and worse until I finally left."

Daniel looked at her for a long moment, and then gave her another hug. She let herself relax against him. He pulled away and looked at her.

"I trust you," he said. "I know you'll do as much as you can. And I can deal with a bit of suspicion if it keeps you safe."

Theresa cried all the way home. All the optimism from the walk to the post office was gone. She was not strong enough to face this again. She should never have come back. Remus pushed his nose into her hand, worried about her. When she got to her house, she went straight inside, closed all the curtains, and sat on the couch. Maddie was at Dorothy's, so there was nothing to make her get up from that spot. That was where Sheldon found her that evening.

"I thought you might be making pots, and I could read to you," he said gently.

She just looked at him. "It's been a rough day."

"I'll just read to you, then," he said.

She burrowed into the sofa while he read.

"It's by Wendell Berry," he told her.

"Oh, I love Wendell Berry," she said.

"It's called The Real Work.

It may be that when we no longer know what to do,
We have come to our real work,
And that when we no longer know which way to go,
We have come to our real journey.

THE MIND that is not baffled is not employed.

THE IMPEDED STREAM is the one that sings."

She turned her head and looked at his beautiful face, lit by the lamp beside him. His kind eyes, black hair. His long bones. "Do you want to look at the stars like we used to?" she asked.

Sheldon's face was very still.

"Down at the lake?" he asked.

"I think we could just lie in the backyard," she said. "There aren't many streetlights around here. We can bring blankets."

"That sounds good," he said. He reached one hand over and touched the inside of Theresa's wrist. She shivered.

She boiled water and made them hot lemon, rum, and honey, while Sheldon carried blankets and a speaker out to the grass. They lay back and looked at the stars, and the sounds of Vivaldi's *Four Seasons* swelled around them.

Theresa thought of the galaxy in Daniel's office, of how he traveled through the universe, and saw so many details, how he had memorized the way Theresa's eyes widened or closed when the menace was near. Of how he knew more than he wanted to. She thought of all the tiny post stamps he lined up perfectly on each package he mailed.

She turned her head to the side and found that Sheldon was already looking at her. If she were Daniel, she could maybe deduce what Sheldon's eyes meant, but Theresa thought she could guess. Underneath the blanket, Sheldon's hand found hers, and the feel of it was so familiar that tears leaked from Theresa's eyes, wetting the cloth beneath her head.

Every impossible thing rose up before her, but she was holding Sheldon's hand, and it made her feel as though everything would be all right. And Daniel was willing to keep her secret.

I can do this, she thought. *We don't have to leave. We can keep Maddie safe. Surely there are enough of us that love her. We can keep her safe.*

CHAPTER THIRTY-NINE

Sheldon stood in front of his armoire, looking through suit choices. Tonight was the dress rehearsal of the play, and as director and writer, he needed to dress for the play's success. Which suit, though? The baby blue forties-style with stovepipe pants? He even had a baby blue fedora to match. Or should he wear the embroidered purple suit he had worn to Sam's wedding? No, it was too soon to wear that one again.

He flipped through his clothes, enjoying the clack of the hangers along the dowel. He needed the perfect thing. *Ah.* Maybe this.

Sheldon had spent a brief time traveling after he received his inheritance from the grandfather he had never met. He wandered through India, Nepal, and China, before making his way to Greece, Morocco, and Egypt. The caftan Sheldon held in his hands was from Morocco, proof that he had once spent time browsing Moroccan *souks* before he came back to Aveline and bought the nearly defunct grocery store that he transformed into Green's. It was a rich woven black with colorful embroidery on the front panel and sleeves.

Sheldon put the caftan on. It fell to his ankles. He found a *fez* to go with it, blowing the dust off the hat and setting it on his head. Sheldon examined himself in the mirror. It would do. He picked up his walking stick and left the apartment.

The caftan drew a lot of attention as Sheldon made his way to the church. He got a catcall or two, and a "Well, hello, Sheldon!" from a woman on the corner. Sheldon shook his head. People in this town were far too excitable.

He ran into Francisco in the church foyer. The reverend looked Sheldon up and down with raised eyebrows.

"I like it," he said. "Wow, Shel, you really went all out. Any reason in particular?"

Sheldon thought about the question. "Do I need a reason to dress up?" he asked.

Frankie shook his head. "No," he said. "You don't. But you've been quiet in your wardrobe choices lately. I wondered if anything had changed."

Sheldon crossed his arms over his chest and looked at his friend. There was so much more to Frankie than met the eye, like the way he had sussed out that clothing meant more to Sheldon than most people. Clothing for Sheldon could signal a need or an emotional shift, and over the last days, there had been a lot of momentum in his emotional state.

"I did get to talk to Daniel," he told Frankie. "It went really well."

Sheldon had decided to talk to his friend because of Theresa. She had been brittle, like a delicate sculpture, tension ricocheting off the walls when he was around her. She seemed to know something, but she wouldn't talk, and after Sheldon had intercepted a few glances between Daniel and Reesey, he thought Daniel might have some answers for him. So he showed up at the post office around closing time. Daniel took one look at him, then heaved a sigh.

"All right, give me a minute to lock up, and then we can go for a walk."

They walked down to the lake, the stones clattering under their feet. The air was chilly, and Sheldon pulled his jacket tight around him as he walked.

"You want to know if I know who the vandal is," Daniel said.

Sheldon glanced at Daniel, surprised.

Daniel snorted. "You," he said, "are particularly easy to read. I learned your tells a long time ago. Plus, Theresa was by a few days ago, and I figure that if you've been around her at all, you've seen how tense she is. This is all that is on everyone's minds. But I don't have anything I can tell you."

Sheldon frowned out at the water. That was an odd way to put it.

"What do you mean," he asked slowly, "you don't have anything you can tell me? That doesn't mean the same thing as, 'I don't know anything, Sheldon, so it's no use asking me.'"

Daniel laughed without humor. He looked at the ground, rocking back and forth slightly on the balls of his feet. After a moment, he bent to pick up a large, smooth stone, holding it in the palm of his hand while he turned it over, looking at the continuous stripe down the center of the stone.

"Being different doesn't make me a vandal with violent, racist thoughts," he said, finally.

Sheldon was shocked. "Is that what you think I'm asking?" he asked. "If you did it?"

Daniel looked up. "Are you?"

"No! You've been cleared of suspicion," Sheldon said.

"I can recite every known planet and moon in the universe," Daniel told him. "I can remember dates and addresses so that if you ask me when Dorothy last sold something from her boutique online, I can tell you when and where she sent it. This is why I'm an excellent postal worker, Shel. I am shy, and I have only ever opened up to a handful of people. You and Theresa are two of those people. I was just beginning to open up to George, but I can tell that he is no longer sure of me. Just because I'm reclusive doesn't mean I would ever harm or threaten anyone."

"I know you wouldn't—" Sheldon started to say, but Daniel held up a hand to stop him, his fingers closing around the stone in his hand.

"I can't tell you who has been doing these things. There is more in the balance than you, or me, or George, or anyone. And so even though I desperately want to tell the whole world that I am not the monster they think I am, my lips are sealed. You need to leave this alone. Let it lie. The graffiti has stopped. I've got my eye on the situation."

Sheldon held his breath. This was insane. Theresa knew something. Daniel knew something. And Sheldon was supposed to just...what had Daniel said. *Let it lie?*

Daniel turned suddenly and flung the stone he had gathered into the lake. It fell with a gentle, anticlimactic plop, and when Daniel looked back at Sheldon, Sheldon saw genuine pain in his friend's eyes. He reached out and put a hand on Daniel's shoulder, and after a while, the two men walked back into town in silence. Sheldon had no more clarity. All he knew was that he was supposed to *let it lie.*

But he was more certain than ever that Daniel had nothing to do with the graffiti.

There had been a few peaceful days after his visit to the post office. Sheldon, Daniel, and Theresa had gone for a long, lazy lunch at the Aveline Cafe and talked about an anime show that Daniel and Theresa were both obsessed with. While they were there, Theresa had noticed Ani eating by herself and called her over to join them. It was such a purely Reesey thing to do, so effortless and open that Sheldon relaxed even more.

He went over to Theresa's house nearly every evening. She threw pots if she had the energy, or they played cards if she didn't. Sheldon attempted to keep himself from staring at Theresa, but it was nearly impossible. She caught him at it sometimes, and he tried to laugh it off.

All of this went through his mind as he stood talking to Frankie in the church foyer, and he wasn't exactly sure how to communicate any of it to his friend.

"Well," he said. "It's a dress rehearsal, isn't it? And I want it to go well."

Frankie shook his head, smiling. "Dress rehearsal, Sheldon," he said, "means the actors do their parts while dressed in their costumes so the rest of us can see the full effect before the actual event of the play."

Sheldon grinned. "Heaven help your narrow thinking,"

he said. Francisco burst out laughing, and they walked into the sanctuary together.

The room was buzzing with activity— actors in costume hurrying around, set building in progress, the choir practicing in the corner. Sheldon spotted Theresa and waved, but didn't dare go near her. He knew he wouldn't be able to pull himself away from her if he started talking to her. It was bad enough trying to concentrate with Theresa in the audience. She was there for Maddie anyway. Not for him. Still, he couldn't help noticing that whenever he glanced over, she was looking back at him. And he couldn't help how warm that made him feel.

CHAPTER FORTY

Sheldon walked backstage to the actors' dressing room—a converted coffee room—and gathered the cast around him.

"Are you ready?" he asked. Most of them nodded, although a couple cast members muttered, 'No.' "Do you feel good in your costumes?" he asked. Same response. Sheldon smiled, looking from person to person, from Lewis to Maddie, George, Dorothy, Ingrid, Lucy, and all the others. "Well, you look great. Let's start at the top and go all the way through without interruption. I will only stop you if I absolutely have to, and I'm hoping it will be a quick run, and we can all go home! Let's make the most of this!" They put their hands in the middle of a circle like a basketball team, and Sheldon gave the call, "Modern nativity!" and everyone broke apart, laughing.

Sheldon took a seat in one of the front pews to observe, but only after noting exactly where Theresa was sitting. He was very aware of her behind him and struggled to keep his attention on the play. *Get yourself together, Kid,* he told himself.

Maddie looked excellent in her costume: ripped up jeans and a dirty T-shirt. Her hair was up in a ponytail that Lucy had oiled and rubbed to look greasy and matted. Lewis depicted José as a little shy, and he acted with a natural quality that was perfect. Lewis and Maddie, as José and a very pregnant Maria, trudged along, thumbs out as they tried to hitch a ride to a nearby town to go to Maria's immigration hearing, Sheldon's version of the census. Sheldon thought about the story from the Bible as he watched, knowing he had taken liberties with his modern version of the story. But they had all heard the story too many times to truly take it in: the couple on the road, the census, the stable, and the flight to Egypt. None of it would have been easy, and none of his beginnings would have recommended Jesus to the people in charge.

Being in costume did something amazing for Maddie, and she played her role better than she ever had in rehearsal. She shone. Sheldon felt some emotion that was a mix of love, loss, and pride well up inside him. He glanced over his shoulder to see Theresa watching her daughter avidly, sitting forward in her pew, her face open and delighted. Down the aisle from Sheldon, Rosa sat with her Lupe, swinging her legs and offering a running commentary.

"I wish we had a donkey," she stage whispered to Lupe at one point, and Sheldon exchanged a look with the older woman. "You want a donkey?" Sheldon heard Lupe ask. "I will get you a donkey for your sixteenth birthday. We will import one from El Salvador."

Sheldon was momentarily distracted by this, but he pulled his focus back to the play. He glanced back when he heard a noise, and saw that Theresa had gotten to her feet. "Over there," she called, pointing to the shelter that was open for the night, the place where Maria would have her baby. Maddie gave her mother a look, and Theresa sat back down. Sheldon chuckled to himself. Theresa always talked to the characters in movies, as well.

When the run through of the play was finished, he jumped up and applauded. He hadn't had to stop them at all.

"You're ready," he told the cast from his seat. "That's that, then. Rest up, we have one more week until the real thing."

Theresa was talking to Francisco, so Sheldon found Maddie and gave her a big hug. She squeezed him back, her eyes glowing.

"Thank you for letting me be Maria," she said. "I feel so much closer to understanding the mother of Jesus now."

He smiled down at her. "You are killing it," he said.

"So why are you all dressed up?" she asked.

He looked down at the caftan and was going to give her the same answer he had given Frankie, but she was looking at him with raised eyebrows, so he was honest.

"I'm walking your mother home," he said. "And I wanted to look nice."

She nodded as if that was what she had figured. "So you're still working on the plan, are you?"

He drew his head back and gave her a look. "How do you know about the plan?" he asked.

"Sam told me you used to always have some kind of plan to get my mom to notice you."

"Ah. Well, that's true. It worked back then, but I'm not sure about now. Do you have any ideas?"

She laughed out loud. "You want me to help you get my mom to notice you?"

"More than *notice* me," he said. "I want to convince your mom that I am the only one for her."

Maddie cocked her head to one side. "Well, I don't know how you can convince her," she said, "but I do know that the two things she needs most are for life to be exciting, and to feel safe. And I think you're doing a good job of both of those things."

Sheldon smiled at the short spunky girl who had first caught his heart a dozen years ago. "Thanks," he said.

He went to find Theresa, trying to ignore his nerves. Reesey stood in the foyer, watching a conversation that was happening a little way away with a dreamy smile on her face. Frankie, Rosa, and Lupe were talking rapidly, switching between Spanish and English, discussing the donkey and whether or not it was possible to import donkeys from El Salvador.

When Sheldon looked back at Theresa, her eyes were on his. She wore a long purple dress that made her look queenly. When Sheldon got close, she lifted a piece of the fabric up to his caftan.

"It matches some of your embroidery," she said.

"True," he answered. His mouth was dry, and his palms were sweaty.

"I like your dress," she said.

"You know it's not a dress," he replied.

One corner of her mouth quirked up. "Of course," she

said. "I remember this. You got it in Morocco. Don't we have a date?" She switched the topic so fast his head swam.

He cleared his throat. "Are we calling it a date?"

"If a boy walks a girl home, it's a date, isn't it? But I suppose I wouldn't really know. I've never really dated. It was only ever you."

A shadow crossed her face as she spoke, and she ducked her head. Sheldon knew what she was thinking because he was thinking the same thing: It had only ever been him and the man she would never talk about, the one who hurt her. Maddie's father. He couldn't ask her that question again, and he didn't want to. He didn't want the shadow of that encounter to come anywhere near this evening, this walk together.

"You seem particularly bright and beautiful today," he told her, taking her arm as they left the church. "Is it because of your studio opening tomorrow?"

"Let's go sit by the lake," Theresa said in response.

Going to the lake with Reesey was very different from going to the lake with Daniel, Sheldon thought. He wasn't incapacitated by Daniel's mere presence, to the point where he barely noticed the lake or the stars. And why was Sheldon thinking about Daniel? Sheldon's brain was scrambled by Theresa, and he had the strangest rabbit trails going on in his mind because he couldn't focus properly. Everything was a distant backdrop for her until it seemed to all be her eyes, her face, her smell, her mouth. She was a painting, and not a Picasso, but she was more than a painting because he could feel her beside him.

"I feel bright around you, Tazzy," she said, after they had

been sitting for a few minutes in silence. "That's why I seem brighter today."

The words seemed to drift like smoke between them, unlocking something that had been shut away. Sheldon leaned very close to Theresa, pressing his lips gently to hers, breathing her in. She moved closer to him and kissed him back, and they were kissing, and it was happening, and Sheldon couldn't believe the feeling of home that clicked back into place in his heart. Reesey pulled away after a few moments and stared at him, her large dark eyes moving from his chin to his mouth, his mouth to his hair. She reached up and combed her fingers through the hair on his temple. Then she smiled the biggest, sweetest smile and leaned in for another kiss. He could have kissed her forever, but she moved back again, putting her hands on his chest, running one finger over the embroidery. He made a small sound.

"You feel so familiar," she whispered. "You feel so wonderful. How can you still want this?"

He sighed and sat back. "How can I convince you that you are the only thing I want, forever?" He searched for words to tell her, not wanting the moment to end or for her to push him away. "How can I convince you of how beautiful you are? Not your face, or the things everyone sees, but you. Everything about you. You are perfectly beautiful to me."

She kept her eyes on his face for a long moment, and then looked back out to the lake, inky black in the darkness.

"I think, just a little bit," she started, then broke off. She took a deep breath. "I think I'm starting to believe you."

CHAPTER FORTY-ONE

Early on opening day, Mercy, Zoe, and Ingrid showed up on Theresa's doorstep. They rang the doorbell, and Theresa ignored her little jolt of fear, going to the window to see who it was. When she saw the three women, she swung the door open.

"What's going on?" she asked. "Did I forget something?"

"Nothing at all," Mercy said. "We're here to take you out for breakfast."

"Oh?" Theresa stared at Mercy. "Did I miss a text?"

After a moment, Theresa realized with a jolt that the women were still standing on the front porch, so she moved to one side to let them in.

"No, it's a surprise," Ingrid said, as she stepped into the terracotta-tiled house. "Surprise!"

"Oh, this is nice," Zoe said. "What a gorgeous house."

"Thank you," Theresa said, but her mind was whirling. She had about a million more things to do before she was ready for the opening. She really didn't have time for breakfast, but she thought that maybe this was something that friends did, and she shouldn't tell them about how she didn't like surprises.

"Do you want some water?" she asked, walking to the kitchen to fill some glasses, giving herself time to think.

"Water would be nice," Mercy said, "but we really need to get to the café. And your mother said not to worry, because she will help you with all the things you need to do later. Just come."

Theresa smiled. Her mother knew her well, as much as Theresa hated to admit it.

"We came to get you because we thought it would be nice to walk in together," Ingrid said.

Theresa looked at each of them in turn. "Well, okay," she said. "Let me get my boots and coat."

It was nice, actually, to walk along the street in a group. The other women were funny and pointed things out about the houses that Theresa hadn't known before.

"That house is a heritage house, and the lady who lives there is so proud of it that she is unbearable."

"The couple in that house have been married for fifty years, and he told me he still takes tea to her every single morning."

They stood in front of Francisco's house for a moment, until Ingrid urged them on with a giggle. "Do you think he'll ever remarry?" Theresa asked Mercy.

"Francisco? No," Mercy said. "I've never seen a man who loved his wife more."

"Ah, it's too bad," Zoe said.

Then they were at the café, and Theresa saw the real

reason for the silliness and secrets. A whole corner of the wide wraparound porch had been festooned with flowers and ribbons, and a sign that said, "Congratulations, Reesey!"

Theresa stopped and put a hand on her heart. "Wow," she said. "But, you guys," she turned to the women, "I'm already throwing a party for myself tonight!"

They burst out laughing. "We know that," Zoe said. "There's a difference between a party you throw for yourself and a party your friends throw for you."

"Yes, I guess there is," Theresa murmured, turning back to look at the porch, following slowly as the others made their way up the walk. She looked to see who else was here. Lucy was standing in the doorway. Maddie and Katie must be somewhere. There was her mother at the table, sitting with— who was...was that...? And then Theresa was running, pushing past the others, as the woman jumped up from the table and met her halfway along the porch, and they were in each other's arms and then had fallen on the ground, laughing and weeping. *Sofía.*

After some time had passed and both Theresa and Sofía were calmer, and Theresa had stopped touching Sofía's face and saying, "It's really you," Theresa found herself sitting at the table like a normal human being, not like someone who had found a friend who had once been a star in her galaxy, a friend she thought she had lost forever.

"So," Katie said. "Do the rest of us get to know what this is all about?"

Mercy smiled. "I forget, sometimes, that you're so new."

Katie stared at her. "How could you ever forget that? I'm like an infant in Aveline."

Mercy shrugged, laughing. "I guess you fit in."

"And I knew your grandmother," Dorothy said.

"Let's not talk about me," Katie said. "I want to hear about Theresa and Sofía."

Theresa kept shooting glances at Sofía. She looked so much the same, and yet so different. Sofía had long black hair like always, but now there were threads of gray in it. She had the same deep brown eyes and light brown skin, but now there were lines at the corners of her eyes. She was less skinny, softer, more beautiful. Theresa remembered something her therapist had told her.

"Women with ASD often find a single, grounding friendship that means more to them than any usual friendship. It is identity-forming, affirming, and gives them an anchor in a social world they don't understand."

It had taken Theresa hearing this to understand her friendship with Sofía and how it had broken her when the friendship ended. *Sofía.* They had been friends in high school, but even better friends once they got to college. Theresa could close her eyes and hear Sofía's laugh, or her voice when she was angry at something on television. Sofía had brought the best out of Theresa. She had only ever wanted to work with animals and trees. She danced when she walked, and she pushed Theresa to do things she never would have done without a friend beside her.

Theresa cleared her throat. "Sofía is my best friend," she said. "But I haven't seen her for a long time." She couldn't stop the tears. Sofía drew near and leaned her head on Theresa's shoulder. She spoke, and her voice was the last piece in a puzzle that had once included Theresa, Sofía, and Sam.

They had all been such good friends. Sofía was a better friend to Theresa than Sam was, and a better friend to Sam than Theresa. She had glued them together.

"We disagreed," Sofía said. "And I did the stupidest thing I could ever have done. I took my friendship away because I thought what we disagreed over was more important than remaining friends."

Theresa just sat there, feeling the familiar weight of her friend's head on her shoulder, trying not to remember the day when Sofía had left. Sofía was the only person on earth who knew what had happened on the night of the cruel forest. She was the one who had pulled tiny stones out of cuts on Theresa's arms and face, who had whispered over her and cleaned her up. Sofía had lied and told everyone that Theresa had a terrible case of the flu, that she couldn't come to class because she was too sick.

And the whole time, Sofía had pushed Theresa to tell. She had even accompanied Theresa to the police station the one time she tried to tell. Sofía had been horrified when Theresa refused to go back again. She had urged Theresa to report it, again and again, until Theresa screamed at her to stop. She couldn't. She couldn't do it.

It was the first thing in their friendship that had divided them. Sofía felt that she had tried to be understanding for a long time, but after a while, she felt that Theresa was being irresponsible. That the bad thing could happen to someone else because Theresa wouldn't tell. Theresa didn't think it was likely. The only person the menace cared about was her.

They were already losing their friendship when Theresa found out she was pregnant with Maddie. And by that time,

Theresa was so low, so unable to rouse herself from the stupor her life had become, that she didn't tell anyone about the pregnancy, which she hadn't discovered until she was six months along. She stayed at home in her mother's house, wearing baggy clothes until it was too late to hide her shape anymore.

Hiding the pregnancy was a blow to Sofía and Theresa's friendship, but Sofía did her best to recover from the hurt she felt because Theresa had withheld something so huge. She moved away to take on a National Park internship for a year, but when she came back, she and Theresa got together as often as they could, with Dorothy or Sofía's mother, Maria, watching Maddie. And then came the day Theresa had left. Sofía had been so angry. She wanted Theresa to fight to stay. But Theresa couldn't do it. Slowly, the phone calls and letters stopped. But Theresa had never stopped missing her friend.

But now here she was. Theresa pulled her head back to smile at her friend. Sofía wrinkled her nose and snorted.

"Welp!" she said. "We sure know how to make a party awkward. We've always been amazing at that, haven't we Reesey?"

Reesey only smiled.

Breakfast was rather quiet, with small spurts of catching up between courses. Mercy asked after Sofía's sister. Sofía asked Katie how she had met Sam. When Theresa finally felt that she couldn't wait any longer, she excused herself to prepare for the opening.

"Can I walk home with you?" Sofía asked.

"Sure," Theresa said. "I'd love that."

They walked in the old way, Theresa, with her focused stride, and Sofía with the little hop she had as she kept up.

"It's good to see you," Sofía said.

"You too. So, your mom told you I was back?"

"She did. You didn't call."

"I tried! The number I had didn't work."

"You didn't come back to the restaurant."

"Sofie..."

"No, I won't lecture you, but I think I know why you didn't come back."

Theresa knew too. She didn't have to say it. She still didn't want to talk about it.

"Has he threatened you again?"

Theresa didn't answer, so Sofía got in front of her and turned around, stopping Theresa in her tracks. "Theresa Lily Grace. Has that man threatened you again? Since you've been back?"

"The menace," Theresa murmured, not meeting Sofía's eyes.

"What?"

"I call him the menace."

Sofía waited, folding her arms over her chest.

"Sofie, I don't want to do this again."

"Just answer the question."

"Yes, okay. He left a couple of notes."

Sofía turned red with fury. "You know this isn't okay, right? It's not normal, it's not okay, and it shouldn't be your life."

Theresa met her friend's eyes. She was surprised to see that Sofía was crying, and then she was surprised to find that her own cheeks were wet as well. Theresa kept looking at Sofía's eyes, so Sofie would know she was serious.

"I can't do this right before my opening, okay? Let me get this party out of the way, and then we will talk about what you think I should do. I'm open to ideas."

Sofía stared at Theresa for a long moment and then nodded. "Okay, Reesey," she said. "Thank you."

CHAPTER FORTY-TWO

On the night of her opening party, Theresa eyed her reflection in the mirror in her room. She wore a sparkling tulle skirt, a black button-up shirt, and a fedora that Sheldon had loaned her. Theresa fastened on a red coral necklace, applied a touch of lipstick, and was as ready as humanly possible. She leaned close to look herself in the eyes.

"You've got this, Reesey," she said. "Just one day of talking to everyone, and then you can go back to being quiet, being in your own home with your work. This is just for the opening." Theresa tried not to think of what she had promised Sofía.

"Talking to yourself, Mom?"

Theresa turned quickly and saw Maddie standing in her doorway.

"Wow," Maddie said. "You look amazing." She slipped into the room and gave Theresa a hug. Theresa pulled back to look at her. Maddie was wearing a long black dress and a tiara in her hair.

"You look beautiful, too, Little," she said. "Actually, I can't believe you're wearing a dress," she said. "What's gotten into you?"

"Katie bought it specifically for the opening," Maddie said. "So don't get your hopes up, okay?"

"I see." Theresa smiled at her daughter. Maddie looked back at her.

"I'm so glad we moved here, Mom," Maddie said softly, her eyes filling with tears. "You seem happy here, and I love Aveline so much."

Theresa used a finger to wipe one tear away from her daughter's cheek. She didn't say anything, but she squeezed Maddie a little tighter.

"Let's go," she said.

It was worth it, she thought, as they walked out of the room together. It was worth it to be here, even though Theresa didn't know what was going to happen, how she could keep the torn edges of her life together, or keep the menace at bay. Was Sofía right? Was Theresa making things worse for others by not confessing what she knew? She hadn't even told Sofía about the vandalism. Even the idea made Theresa's legs shake, and she reached out and grabbed onto the doorframe nearby.

Was Theresa enabling the menace of the cruel forest by not telling anyone? Was she the unwitting cause of racist vandalism in Aveline? Theresa walked to the living room window and pressed her face to it to look out on her garden. She had chosen to have the party at night to show off the lovely lighting in the studio, and the garden looked welcoming and soft, twinkle lights strung through the trees in the deepening twilight. There were paper lanterns that

Katie and Theresa had hung from the trees or placed on tables.

Looking out on the beauty of her garden, Theresa knew with a sudden certainty that the ugliness of the menace would not disappear on its own. That kind of evil lived in hidden places. To make it go away, Theresa needed to expose it to sunlight. And she was so afraid of what that meant.

Theresa closed her fists and stood taller, calling on the memory everything in her life that made her feel stronger. She thought about Sheldon, and about the peace she had felt as she prayed in the quiet church, the way she was learning to be loved by God without having to be someone else. She thought of evenings of poetry with Sheldon, of the women's circle, and of Maddie, so loved and blooming into someone Theresa barely recognized. Theresa would always find life hard, and she couldn't always trust her mind, but somehow, she had still managed to make a life.

She needed to throw the doors open on this hidden thing, or she would never have the peace she needed here. George and Mercy deserved to know about the menace—if Theresa was right about the menace and the racist vandal being one and the same, that is.

After the opening, then, like Sofía said. After the opening, Theresa would ask Sheldon to help her talk to Francisco. She and Sheldon could find a way together through the residue of all the years of fear, through that twisted threat in the shadows. Theresa didn't have to hold it all on her own. Could it be?

It was as though someone had lifted an enormous weight off of her. The thought of opening up and allowing someone else to take the secret from her was like a window opening in a musty place, letting sweet outdoor air to rush in.

She felt someone beside her.

"Ready?"

Theresa turned and saw Sheldon, her lovely, beautiful, patient Sheldon, the one who had waited for her all these years and written her poetry and been his quirky, wonderful self. Sheldon had not changed. He had been a good friend to Maddie even though Theresa had been terrible to him.

She stood on tiptoe to kiss him, and he bent his head to meet her. His lips brushed hers ever so softly. She made a happy little sound, and he laughed softly, a low rumble.

He stood back and looked at her.

"Wow," he said.

"What?" she asked him.

"I know you don't like to hear this," he said, "but you are so absolutely beautiful that you make everything else in the entire world look dull in comparison. I've never seen anything or anyone as lovely as you."

Theresa felt heat rise to her face and felt a powerful thud in her chest. She thought for a minute and realized that these weren't bad feelings.

"I don't think I mind when you say it, Tazzy," she said. "It's just the rest of the world that I don't want looking at me."

"You're going to have to let them look at you for just a little while longer," he said.

"Yes," she said.

"And then back to pottery and poetry."

"We could also listen to music," she said. "You don't always have to read to me. It must make you tired."

"There are so many things we could do," he said. "We'll do them all."

She grinned at him, and he stole one more kiss. "Let's go open the doors," she said. "Katie should be here in a minute with the food." She felt the smile slide off her face. "And Tazzy?" she said, "I have something... well, in the next few days, I'd love to talk to you and Francisco."

Theresa saw his face change, but she couldn't read the expression.

"Is this about the vandal?" he asked.

"Yes," she said. "And...other things."

"Okay," he said. "Is there anything you want to tell me now?"

Theresa opened her mouth to speak.

"Lovebirds!"

She turned. Sam had walked into the kitchen. "Oh my," he said.

Theresa realized that she was standing very close to Sheldon, and he had his arms around her.

"I mean, wow," Sam said. "I'm certainly supportive, but you realize we have a party to put on right now, right? Or should we reschedule and do it again at your convenience?"

Theresa scowled at her brother and squeezed Sheldon's hands in apology. She took a deep breath, picked up a sheaf of flyers from the table, and squared her shoulders.

"No, no postponing anything," she said. "I'm ready."

CHAPTER FORTY-THREE

I t was easy to see very quickly that the party was a success. There was a path of lights from the garden door back to the little shop, and through the window, all of Theresa's shelves of bowls, plates, and cups were visible. The studio looked warm and inviting, and Theresa was burning her favorite scented candles. Katie had made finger foods for snacks, and there was hot rum for the adults and hot chocolate for the kids.

Theresa grew alarmed as the evening went on, and she sold almost everything she had. She was going to have to work for ages to replenish the shelves, and she wanted to focus on her big project. But it was not a bad problem to have, and Theresa could see that Sheldon thought so too. He kept grinning whenever he caught her eye. Theresa talked and talked, meeting the people who had come to the opening, smiling until her face hurt. She was relieved whenever she ran into someone she knew well. Sofía squeezed her hand, Francisco gave her a hug and said, "Courage," and Daniel winked at her, which perfectly communicated that he wasn't angry with her.

"Theresa!" Lucy called. "Did you order a pizza?"

"What?" Katie shouted. "How dare you?"

The people around them laughed, but Theresa shook her head. She walked over to the doorway, where Lucy and Katie stood.

"Of course I didn't order a pizza. I don't even eat pizza."

"No, wait, sorry. This guy says it's a clay delivery."

"Well, that sounds more likely," Theresa said, "but why at night?"

"I don't know," Lucy shrugged. "But he's adamant that he needs you to sign for it. He's at the gate."

Theresa sighed. "They always become sticklers when it's least convenient," she said, already walking out to the garden gate. When Theresa got there, though, she didn't find anyone. She looked down the street and saw the delivery truck parked a few spaces away. She squinted. The delivery guy was standing behind the truck, already pulling the roll-up door open.

"Sorry," he called. "I tried calling earlier but couldn't reach you. And there's no parking closer to the house."

"What is it?" she called.

He looked down at something. "Looks like something from Clay...I can't make out the second word. Clay Emporium?"

Ooh, that was exciting, Theresa thought. It must be the new batch—the one she had ordered for the sculpture series.

Theresa walked to the back of the truck, and the only

warning she got was a faint prickling on her arms before she felt a sudden pain, and everything went dark.

THERESA WOKE WITH AN AGONIZING HEADACHE, like a snake curled around one eye. She groaned and rolled over, then went rigid with panic when she opened her eyes. Her surroundings were black, without even a sliver of light, and she could feel the rumbling of wheels under her head. She felt the painful area over her temple and gasped as she touched a sticky gash over one eyebrow. What had happened? Where was she? Theresa felt panic washing over her like icy water and felt around to try to get a sense of where she was, but she could only feel bare metal, and she could see nothing. She faded into darkness again.

A little while later, Theresa's senses seemed to revive, and her mind cleared enough for her to think. This was it. The menace from the cruel forest had come for her, right before Theresa had made a move to destroy it. There was no other explanation for where she was and why she would be here.

Waves of panic. Theresa tried to breathe through the fear and keep the meltdown at bay, but her body and mind betrayed her. The switch had been triggered, and she lost it, crying and banging her hands on the walls. Theresa rocked back and forth, her arms wrapping around her knees, weeping, and the tears wouldn't stop. She hit her head, hard, to try to stop the panic. She scratched at her forehead and banged the walls of the truck again, but there was no response, and she couldn't hear anything from the cab, except for loud music. Slowly, slowly, the panic ebbed. Her head throbbed harder, and in addition to the wound above her temple, Theresa knew that now she had scratch marks on her forehead. Her breathing began to slow. Her mind threatened to check out again, to let her fade into oblivion, but she forced it back, listening to the music, trying to hear it.

When she finally figured out what it was, she wrapped her arms tighter around her.

She couldn't believe he would be so cruel.

Cam had been sweet to Theresa at first. He was Sam's friend in high school and college. Younger than Theresa, and always kind, even when her brother was acting like a jerk. Theresa was young and naive. She didn't yet know about the pitfalls of her neurological condition—she didn't even know that she had one. Theresa only knew that things that seemed simple for other people were hard for her.

She didn't yet know that she needed to be wary, and she thought Cam was nice, even though Sofía had never liked him. Sofía had gone on a few dates with Cam and declared him a weirdo. But Theresa thought he was sweet.

Theresa took a gap year after high school, so she, Cam, and Sam entered university at the same time, attending the State University in Aveline. Theresa had trouble adjusting to the new environment, and Cam helped her with things like talking to her professors about late assignments. He grew a little possessive of Theresa at times, even though they weren't dating. He hated it when she hung out with Sofía, and started asking her where she had been whenever she went somewhere without him. After a few intense talks with Sofía, who was very worried, Theresa tried to make some boundaries, asking for a bit of space.

Cam didn't want space. He followed Theresa everywhere. He left notes on her walls, or in her pockets. He pleaded with her to stop going to social events, to end her friendship with Sofía. He said Sofía was getting between them. Theresa started to feel scared, but she didn't know what to do.

Then came the dreadful night, in the forest near the university. First, the oak tree in town, where Cam slammed her against the wood when she wouldn't get in his car. Then the drive, the music blaring, the cruel forest. Pain that she wouldn't have believed. He spoke words of hate and love twisted together, telling her she was ugly but beautiful to him. She was terrible, a horrible person. But he loved her. When she finally got away, she had run and run, aching, bruised, and bleeding.

Sofía wept and helped Theresa into the shower. She whispered the word. "Rape."

Theresa faded in and out of wakefulness for days.

Cam had told Theresa he would kill her if she told anyone. She didn't want to tell anyone, besides Sofía, who she couldn't have avoided telling.

Sofía and Theresa argued about it. Theresa wanted to forget it. Cam avoided her after that night, so there was no need to revisit the cruel forest, which was what Theresa began calling it in her head. She constructed a strong barrier around the night and its events.

Eventually, Sofía convinced Theresa to go to the police with her. They sat in the station in Billers and told about the night, only to hear that it would be a long, messy process for anything to happen. Theresa was so overwhelmed that she left halfway through the interview, and nothing Sofía said could convince her to go back.

Cam was wealthy and well connected. Maybe no one would ever have listened to her. In the years since the event, more than one therapist had told Theresa that this happened to many women. They couldn't talk about what had happened to them. They felt like saying it made them complicit. They got tangled up in the murky boundaries of the body, the way that something that was supposed to happen between two people was forced onto one person. It took a solid delineation of personhood to avoid feeling shame for actions that were imposed upon your own body.

Learning about ASD had taught Theresa that these barriers were always confusing to her, so it made sense that she had not wanted to tell. Theresa had always felt that if she talked about it, she would end up back in that cruel forest, and she never wanted to be there again. She and Sofía were never able to agree on how Theresa had decided to handle the event.

Theresa hadn't even realized she was pregnant until she was six months along. That was how naive she had been.

And then there was Sheldon. Theresa began to fall for him when Maddie was two years old. She had known him before. He had been there—on the fringes of their life—since they were in high school, but after he traveled, he came back into her life so sweetly. Theresa was so scared to have a relationship, but Sheldon got past all of that by being the best friend that ever existed.

Sometimes, during those years, she got threatening letters from Cam. The letters said she would be exposed for what she was, what they had done in the forest. They stated that Cam would hurt her. Theresa tried to ignore them, but she grew more and more paranoid, and it began to be hard for her to do even the simplest tasks. She started drinking, just to numb the fear. Sheldon was worried about Theresa's increasing jumpiness, and he wanted her to get therapy, to figure out what was going on.

He asked her to marry him anyway. Even though she was a mess. She said yes, and they started preparations for the wedding. She was so happy with Sheldon, and he was going to be Maddie's father.

Then came the worst day. Theresa got another letter from Cam. In his tiny, block letter writing, he threatened to kill Sheldon. Theresa couldn't stop crying after she got the letter. She told Sofía she was leaving, and they had the biggest argument they had ever had. Sofía was adamant that Theresa should stay and fight. Theresa was too scared. So she packed up Maddie and all their belongings and left Aveline, driving as far as her car would take her. Theresa sent Cam a letter of her own, saying that she would tell all she knew if he followed her. She told him she would not marry or be with Sheldon anymore, but that he had to leave her alone. It was as though she finally dared to push back. Cam listened. He had sent her creepy letters over the years, but he had left her alone. He had left Sheldon alone.

And then, all these years later, Theresa had come back and fallen in love with Sheldon again.

Stupid, stupid girl.

CHAPTER FORTY-FOUR

Sheldon had watched the gallery owner for a while, knowing at once that this was someone different. The man walked around, picking pieces of pottery up, gauging their weight in his hands, and peering at the seams. In one corner of the room was a display of the newest sculpture series that Theresa was working on, clearly labeled "Series in Progress," and "Not For Sale."

The man spent the longest time there, then looked around and, seeing Sheldon's eyes on him, approached.

"Where is the artist or her agent?" he asked immediately. "I'd love to talk to one of them about a show in Los Angeles."

"Theresa Grant is here, though her agent didn't come out for the opening," Sheldon said, trying not to sound overeager. "I'll find Theresa, for you. Just for curiosity's sake, how did you find out that this was happening?"

"I was at her last show, in Minneapolis," the man said. "And heard she had relocated. She put the opening on her website."

Clever girl, Sheldon thought to himself. Theresa might prefer actually drawing or working with clay over anything else, but really, she was an excellent businesswoman.

He was excited to find her and tell her about the gallery owner. But then he couldn't find her. He walked around, searching the house and yard.

"Katie, have you seen Theresa?" he asked.

"Last I saw, she was talking with a customer," Katie said.

"Maddie, what about you?"

"I haven't seen her in a while."

It took Sheldon a few rounds of the house and the yard to start to worry, but as he did, his heart began to beat faster. This didn't make any sense. Reesey wouldn't take off in the middle of her show. Or would she? She wasn't having a meltdown somewhere, was she?

"Last I saw, she was picking up a delivery from the truck outside," Lucy said.

"Whoa, wait," Sheldon said, holding up a hand. "There was a delivery truck here at nine o'clock at night? That doesn't make any sense."

Lucy looked flummoxed. "No, I guess it doesn't," she said. "He was insistent that he needed Theresa specifically and that he had a large shipment of clay."

Sheldon went outside. Nothing. No truck, no Reesey. His stomach started to hurt.

He went back inside. Francisco and Daniel found him walking around the kitchen, opening and closing drawers.

"What's going on?" Francisco asked. "You're tearing around this place like it's a mini track meet."

"I can't find Theresa," Sheldon said. "Lucy said something about a delivery truck needing a signature, and now Theresa's just gone." He looked up. "Daniel, you need to tell us what you know."

Daniel was pale and tight-lipped. He gripped his elbows. "I don't know if I can."

Sheldon went back to opening and shutting drawers, filled with rage like nothing he had ever experienced. How could Daniel continue to withhold information?

"Are you crazy?" Francisco asked. "What are you doing?"

Sheldon didn't answer. He picked up an envelope that was shoved in a drawer, addressed to Theresa in tiny block letters. He tore it open and stared at the note, feeling the blood drain out of his face.

If you date him again, I will kill him. And then I will kill you and Maddie. Don't even think about it. You promised.

It was like someone had kicked the air out of Sheldon's lungs. His heart lunged into double time. Silently, he handed the letter to Daniel.

"Who is it?" he asked, his voice hoarse. "Tell us, please, Daniel. Is it Lenny? I'll kill him!"

Daniel stared at the letter. Francisco's face was horrified.

"It's Cam," he said.

CHAPTER FORTY-FIVE

The van stopped, and then the engine cut off.

Theresa had moved from panic to resignation, but now she felt something completely different beginning inside her body. She prepared herself, still rocking for comfort, but now using the momentum to gain strength. Reesey was not the same woman she had been, nearly sixteen years previously. *Today*, she thought. I wanted to wait until after the opening, but today is the day I get my life back. How long have I lived under this fear? How long have I let him control me?

Nearly half her life, she realized with growing anger. What did Cam think he was going to do to her out here? Rape her again, like he had in the cruel forest? She could think the word now. She could even say it out loud. Theresa had lived her adult life in fear of someone who took freedom and safety from her.

For a long time, the power Cam held over her was the fear that he would tell Maddie she was a child of rape. Theresa had never wanted her daughter to know it. She had not even planned to keep Maddie. She had been considering adoption, but she was so confused that she hadn't gone through with it, and then she had fallen in love with her baby. Maddie was light and love, and Theresa never wanted her daughter to know about the violence that had been part of her origins. Maddie was not the child of that violence. She was the child of a quiet hospital, a kind nurse, and the daughter of Sheldon and Theresa's new love, as they walked with the toddler on the lakeshore.

The roll-up door screeched open suddenly, and light flooded in. Cam had stopped the truck in a large store parking lot. *You idiot*, Theresa thought. *This is so public.*

He had the upper hand, at first, though, as Theresa was blinded by the streetlights. Cam grabbed her by the wrist and hauled her out of the van. Tears streamed down his face as the motion jolted her head again.

"I didn't want to have to hurt you," he hissed at her. "You made me hit you."

"You're crazy," she spit at him.

"You're the crazy one," he said, growling and bending her wrist until she nearly cried out. "I told you not to date him. I told you I would kill all of you. I love you, Theresa, and I would do anything for you."

"Cam!" Theresa cried. "This is not love! The violence, the threats. How can you even think you love me? This is nothing like love."

"You drive me to it, you sorry-faced witch. I saw you kissing him through the window. Are you forgetting that you are mine? You promised me, Theresa. I've been following her every day, did you know that? I watch my beautiful daughter all the time."

A hot torrent of anger rushed through Theresa. Oh, no, no, no, she thought. This is enough.

"Do you think I'm still the weak girl you brainwashed and raped?" she rasped, trying to get her wrist at a better angle, so she could break away. Cam backhanded her, and Theresa tasted blood. He hit her again and again. She nearly passed out from the pain but forced herself to stay awake, clinging to consciousness with both hands. She needed to end this now. Maddie being safe was the most important thing in the world, and Maddie would never be safe if Cam continued to follow her around. Theresa glared up at Cam. He had made a mistake when he let go of her wrist. "Didn't you realize I would spend my life learning how to fight bullies like you?"

Theresa got the leverage she needed and delivered a hard kick to Cam's knee. She heard a horrible pop, and he collapsed, screaming. Theresa punched him once, hard, in the temple, and he was fell silent so suddenly that her ears rang.

Theresa called 911 and wiped the blood from her mouth. She was shaking so violently that she nearly dropped the phone, but she managed to tell the operator her location and that there had been an attack. Then she hung up and started to walk home.

CHAPTER FORTY-SIX

Sheldon, Sofía, Daniel, and George got into George's car to look for Theresa. Sam stayed with Katie and his mother, who were both frantic. Francisco stayed back, not wanting to fight, but wholly supportive of the others if it came to it. Daniel drove because George said he wanted to be ready to jump out if he needed to, and he was on the phone with the police.

He hung up. "Not sure if they'll do anything yet," he said. "Reesey hasn't been missing long enough, and there's no record of previous danger."

Beside Sheldon, Sofía sighed, muttering to herself. She had tears streaming down her cheeks.

Sheldon felt like he could cry, too, but for now, he kept himself fiercely dry-eyed. He was filled with self-recrimination after reading the note. Why hadn't he realized how much trouble Reesey was in? And now maybe it was too late.

Oh, Lord, it couldn't be too late. What was Cam capable of? Sheldon couldn't bear it. He moaned and put his head in his hands.

"I think we should pray," Daniel said suddenly from the driver's seat.

Sheldon looked up. Daniel was still so new in his faith journey. Sheldon would have expected that he or George would remember to pray, not Daniel. But Sheldon had forgotten about prayer completely, almost as if he thought he was in charge of the world. As though God didn't care about Theresa more than Sheldon did.

George nodded. "You'd better be the one to do it because I'm not feeling merciful thoughts," he said.

"He nearly ruined my life," Daniel said. "And I couldn't say anything because he would have exposed Theresa and Maddie."

"What would be so bad about that?" Sheldon asked. "I don't understand why you couldn't say anything, or Reesey either. Why did your life need to be ruined? Why did she need to run away?"

"He raped her," Sofía said softly. "Reesey didn't want Maddie to ever find out."

Sheldon felt rage so hot and terrible that it nearly picked him up. He pounded his fists into his knees.

"I truly am going to kill him," he said. "Cam! Cam has been living among us all this time. He comes to my shop. I smile at him. He hurt Theresa! He's Maddie's..." He couldn't finish the sentence.

"Do you see?" Daniel said softly. Sheldon looked over

and saw tears running down his face. "He's Maddie's father? How do you think she will react to that?"

George spoke. "Nearly all of us have rapists in our genealogies," he said quietly.

"Us?" Sheldon said, stupidly, before he thought.

"Descendants of the enslaved," George said. "My great, great grandfather was a white slave-owner who raped my great, great grandmother. Mercy has violence in her ancestral line, as well. We aren't strangers to violence in our family lines. We can talk to Maddie about what that's like."

Sheldon didn't have words. He reached back and grabbed George's hand, gripped it tightly and took a deep breath. Then Sheldon began to pray. He prayed that they would find Theresa and that she would be okay. It was all Sheldon could pray, over and over. He could hear Sofía's quiet prayers going on next to him, and still, he continued to pray.

"What's that?" George asked, interrupting Sheldon.

"What?" Sheldon asked.

"A truck and police car there in the parking lot," George said, pointing through a row of trees.

"Go, go!" Sheldon cried.

"I'm already going," Daniel said, crossing three lanes to enter the Target parking lot, pulling up to the police car.

"Carefully," George said. "Don't get out."

"It's Bruce," Sheldon said. He rolled his window down.

"Bruce," he called. "What's happening?" He could see a shape in the back of the cop car, but he couldn't quite make out who it was.

"Cam has been attacked," Bruce said. "I'm just holding him until the ambulance gets here. He has a dislocated, or maybe even a broken knee, and scratch marks on his arms, so I'm not sure what kind of fight it's been."

"Bruce," George said, leaning out of the window to talk to the officer.

"Oh, hey, George," Bruce said.

"You know better than that," George said. "Scratch marks? Better cuff him. He kidnapped Theresa Grant tonight, and it looks like he has a history of violence toward her. Stalking and rape."

"What? Theresa Grant?" Bruce's face paled.

"Is she here?" Sheldon asked.

"No, I arrived after someone called 911 and found Cam with a dislocated knee. He's hurt bad."

"She's not here?" Sofía repeated. "Do you mean she beat Cam up and left?"

Bruce shrugged. "I have as much information as you do."

Sheldon couldn't have said what he felt at that moment, but later, he identified it as a sort of fierce, proud joy, mixed with continuing worry. Daniel let out a sigh, and the four of them looked at each other, smiling tentatively. Sheldon would have liked to have words with Cam, but there were more important things to do. They had to find Theresa.

"All right, Bruce," George said, shifting into lawyer mode. "We'll go find our girl and bring her in for a report. I advise you to cuff Cam until we know more, okay?"

"Right," Bruce said. "I'll do that. Little Theresa Grant, that's despicable."

"Apparently she's little and mighty," Sheldon said. "She got away."

They drove the road toward home, and it wasn't long at

all before they saw her marching down the street. Daniel stopped the car, but Sheldon was outside before the car even stopped moving. He sprinted to her, calling her name.

She spun, wild-eyed, but slumped in relief when she saw him.

"Tazzy," she said, her voice broken.

"Don't worry, sweetness," he said, reaching her and pulling her close. He spoke into her hair. "Daniel told us everything, or at least what he knows."

She pulled away and looked at him, her eyes haunted. "There's more than he knows, so much more," she said.

"I can't believe you've been carrying this all by yourself," Sheldon said.

"He threatened to kill you," she said.

He saw her lovely pale face with a cut over one temple, bruises already beginning to show along her jaw. He felt such intense love, such fierce anger that he groaned aloud again.

"He couldn't kill me," he said. "I can't be taken from you. Anyway, the police have him now. And we need to go to the station to give a report."

"I can't…"

Sofía, George, and Daniel arrived beside them, and George reached out carefully and touched Theresa's face, turning it so they could see the bruises in the streetlight. Sofía reached out for Theresa's hand and held it.

"You got away," George said. "You left him there, unable to walk. You can do it. I'll be with you if you want me as your lawyer. Or, I can be there tonight, and you can hire another lawyer. We need to nail this bastard. He can't do this again, to you or anyone else."

Theresa gazed at George for a long minute, then at Sofía. She looked at Daniel, then at Sheldon.

"Okay," she said. "Let's go to the police station. And I want Sofía to come with me. But no offense, George."

George started to lift his hands, but Theresa kept talking. "I want Mercy as my lawyer," she said. "Have you seen her in court?"

Sheldon felt a grin spread across his face and saw answering smiles on the faces of the others.

Together they walked to the car, and as they drove to the police station, Sheldon said one more repeating prayer. *Thank you, thank you, thank you.*

CHAPTER FORTY-SEVEN

M ercy turned out to be the perfect lawyer for Theresa. The older woman did not let Theresa get away with a single reason for going easy on Cam or moving away from prosecution.

"I totally understand," she told Theresa. "You have a disorder, and you were threatened and afraid back then. It makes sense that you didn't press charges before now. But fifteen years is long enough, and that man needs to be in prison. He needs restraining orders whenever he gets out of prison. He needs to never come near Aveline again." She paused. "And we are definitely pressing hate crime charges." Cam had confessed to the vandalism, though he still insisted he and Theresa were only friends. It would be a long road to justice for Theresa.

Just two days after the kidnapping, Theresa and Maddie drove to Faith's office for a joint counseling session. With help from Faith, Theresa told Maddie who her father was. It was nearly as horrible as Theresa had always dreaded, with one surprising difference.

Maddie was somehow okay. The information did not unravel her in the way Theresa had feared. After Theresa finished telling Maddie, in the simplest terms, what had happened, Faith spoke. She talked to Maddie about having violence in one's history—how to process it, grieve over it, and move on. She told Maddie that it could take many years. Maddie listened quietly, now and then wiping a tear away. Then they waited for Maddie to speak. The fourteen-year-old sat in silence for a long time, then finally she said something.

"I'm glad I'm finding out now," she said. "I don't think I could have handled this when Mom and I were still alone. But we have so many other people around us. I don't think this will overwhelm my feelings about family. We have Sam and George and Sheldon. I want them to be the father-y people in my life. Not Cam."

She stood up suddenly, flinging herself at Theresa.

"Mom!" she said through tears. "I'm only hearing about this, but you had to *live* it! Knowing this, I can't believe you agreed to come back when I asked you to. You're so brave. I can't believe you did so well, making our life safe, all these years."

Theresa couldn't speak for a few minutes. "You made it all worth it," she said when she could trust her voice. "You have always been beauty and safety amid the hard places. God kept us, somehow, all this time."

Theresa had another session with Faith the next day, on her own. Faith had studied up on ASD, and they talked together about how it had affected Theresa, both in good ways and bad, in the trauma of her life. The ability to just keep going had helped, and the naivety had hurt her.

"I read that people with Asperger's are some of the most resilient in the world, despite meltdowns and all that comes with the disorder."

Theresa smiled faintly. "That's nice to hear," she said.

"Do you think you can tell the difference between a safe and unsafe person now?"

Theresa smiled. "Your mom asked me the same thing, recently." She frowned, looking at her hands. "I think in some ways, I have made a firm rule, rather than understanding the difference. I said to myself that it was just that everyone was unsafe. People were unsafe. Rather than seeing that the truth is that some people are trustworthy..."

"To a point," Faith interrupted.

"Yes, to a point. And some people should never be trusted."

Faith nodded.

Theresa looked off into the distance through the window. She thought of Sheldon, how he had automatically received the same distant treatment as every other man, many times, simply because she could not trust. She thought of the day after the kidnapping when he had come to visit her.

"I love you," he told her, standing on her porch with flowers, tears in his eyes. "I have always known it, but yesterday I couldn't bear the fact that I hadn't yet told you. If you had been hurt in a worse way..." he put his hand over his face.

"Tazzy," she said softly. He looked up and began to step forward, but she put a hand out to stop him. "Taz, I can't...

I'm not ready. Can you give me some time to think about everything?"

She saw his face, how it twisted and bent. She saw his fists clench and his brief nod. He handed her the flowers, touched her hair briefly, and left.

She saw it again as though for the first time. Sheldon always listened when she asked him to leave. How had she not seen it? Theresa told him no. She had already kissed him and snuggled with him, given him reason to believe they would get back together, and then she had turned away his profession of love, again. She had to turn him away, she had to get her head together. But he had *listened* to her. He always did.

Driving home after the session, Theresa took in the colored lights up on the houses. It was nearly Christmas, and the play would happen in just a few days. Theresa sipped at her thermos of tea as she drove the curves, memories flitting through her mind.

Sheldon sitting with her at the edge of the lake, toddler Maddie in his arms.

"Who is her father?" he had asked, slipping his hand into Theresa's.

"I can't tell you," she had said. "I can never tell you."

He had looked at her for a long moment, then looked back at the tiny, sleeping girl.

"Okay," he said.

Holding her hand. Reading her poetry. Finding the things she loved best for the shop. Bringing her a perfectly ripe tomato. Sheldon gave and gave, demanding nothing.

Theresa pulled the car over and got out. She stood on the

side of the hill, looking down into the valley around Aveline, the lake like a jewel on one side, the houses clustered up into the hillsides. This was Theresa's town again. The menace was gone. He would never be able to come back. Theresa felt as though she could actually fully live in her body again—stretch her limbs, walk with her head up, not worried that the wrong person was watching. It would take some practice, though.

"Let's talk about beauty," Faith had said that day, watching Theresa closely.

"What about it?" Theresa had asked.

"Why won't you accept your own beauty?"

"Do you find it easy to accept your own?" Theresa asked.

"I'm the therapist here, not the client," Faith said, grinning. "But sometimes I can, sometimes I can't. I'm not exactly accepted as universally beautiful, the way you are, so it's different."

"What?" Theresa was horrified. "You look like a painting. You are the most beautiful person I know."

Faith laughed. "Oh, Reesey, I remember that you always told me that. I just mean that I get stares for a lot of reasons, and not always because men think I'm pretty. But really, this is your session. It's not time to talk about me. Why don't you like to be beautiful?"

Theresa stared at her friend, still slightly horrified by the thought that she, Theresa, had some sort of universal beauty that Faith didn't. But it came to her, as Faith must have known it would have, that she had always associated beauty with attention from Cam. Of course.

"I don't know that I can untangle it all and tell it to you easily."

"I just want to suggest that you love beauty. You are an artist. Maybe you can start inhabiting yourself as you would put love into making a pot. Maybe you can look at yourself as a piece of art, rather than thinking of all the ways people have tried to make your beauty theirs. It doesn't belong to them. It belongs to you."

On the hillside, Theresa held her hands out and looked at them. Her own body. Her own self that belonged only to her. Theresa had imagined that if she hated herself and the attention she got, she could avoid Cam's jealousy and scrutiny. Theresa had never wanted it.

But this was herself. Theresa's body. God had made her, just like he made the lake in the distance, that body of water that she loved so much. God had made her beautiful, and he had never forced her to be with him, just as Sheldon had never forced her. Theresa felt shaky and exhausted, but somehow, very hopeful. Things were shifting inside of her.

She remembered Sheldon again, one day when they had gone out onto his boat. Lying in the prow on a long summer afternoon, his curly hair sticking up from the wind. Looking over at her, smiling.

"What?" Theresa had asked. She and Sheldon had been dating for about six months by then, and Maddie was with Dorothy for the day.

"I'm wondering if you have any idea how lovely you are," Sheldon said.

Theresa felt the instant inner retreat that happened when anyone called her beautiful, the feeling that she wanted to go inside and lock the door. But she forced herself to keep looking at Sheldon. He was the beautiful one, she thought, with his gentle eyes and full eyelashes, and the way he seemed to hold himself very still.

"You make me think of the sunrise," he said. "The way the whole world seems colorless without the sun. That's like the before, before you come into a room. And then the sun comes closer and closer to the horizon, and immediately color makes the whole world beautiful. That's you in a room. Your beauty doesn't make other people less beautiful. Somehow everyone seems more radiant when you are around. They want to reach for you. It's what I love most about you."

She reached her hand out and touched his face, and he smiled at her, dimples flashing in his cheeks. He caught her hand and kissed her palm.

She shivered now, thinking of it. Then she got back in her truck and drove down the hill into town. She had an idea.

CHAPTER FORTY-EIGHT

That evening, Theresa was covered in clay, caught in a feverish whirlwind of creation. Thinking about light had overtaken her as she finished the drive from Billers. By this time, Theresa had sculpted many of the pieces for her show. She wouldn't name them, of course, but they took after people in her life. Vessels. All of them meant to carry different types and different amounts of liquid, the way people were all different, with different capabilities. She thought she would actually fill them all with something different when she held her show.

Yet, as she had carried out her work, she had been increasingly distressed by her own vessel. It seemed too damaged to hold anything, with huge swathes of structure missing.

At the viewpoint, looking over Aveline, though, Theresa had remembered the light. Sunlight revealed the colors and beautiful shadows of each object in the world. Theresa's vessel did not hold the same sea as her mother's with its wide and generous basin. Or Katie's with her deep channels, or George's vast reservoir, which seemed to be as large as a bathtub.

No, Theresa's vessel was more of a jar. Yes, it was broken, but it held *light*, like the lanterns in the garden, or the lamps in her home. It was made to contain a lot of light.

She was rolling slabs for the light jar when the doorbell rang. Theresa froze, reminded herself that Cam was in jail, and left it for Maddie to answer. Hearing voices, she turned as Sam, Katie, Sofía, and Dorothy walked into the yard, arguing as they came.

"You're already back at work?" Sam said. "I thought you were resting. And what have you done to Sheldon?"

"I know we talked about this already, but I'm still struggling, Reesey," Dorothy said with a hoarse voice. She sounded as though she'd been crying again. "How could you keep this from me?"

Theresa sighed. "Listen, let me wash up, and I'll meet you in the kitchen. Help yourselves to tea or snacks, if you can find them."

Theresa took her time washing her hands, trying to shift from creating mode to socializing mode in her mind. When she made her way into the kitchen, Theresa found Sam and Dorothy sitting at the island while Katie rummaged through the tea drawer, holding up choices, and Sofía searched the cupboards for snacks.

"Cold care? Does anyone have a cold? Peppermint? Oh yes, that sounds perfect..." she held the tea bag up to her nose and sniffed it. "Never mind; actually, that doesn't smell good at all."

"I'll make a pot of rooibos," Theresa said, taking the tea basket from her. "That'll be easier, and then these angry pants won't have to choose."

"Yes," Katie said, and went to sit beside Sam on one of the kitchen island stools.

Theresa warmed the pot and eyed her family. Maddie snuck through the room behind them, widening her eyes at Theresa before shutting her bedroom door behind her without a sound. So much for solidarity, Theresa thought. She couldn't guess what Sam or Katie were thinking, but the look on Theresa's mother's face was easy to interpret. Her mother was furious. Theresa had no idea why. Sofia seemed fine, humming to herself while she shook some crackers onto a plate.

"Easy question first," Theresa said. "I'm working because I feel inspired and because it helps me to rest."

"You can't possibly rest if you're tired out from making stuff. And you repainted that wall I worked so hard on..." Sam started to protest, throwing his arms out. But he closed his mouth when Katie put a hand on his arm. Sam muttered a bunch of words that Theresa couldn't hear, then shrugged. "Okay, it's your life," he said.

"Nice of you to remember it," Theresa said, smiling despite herself. Katie grinned at her. Maybe there was a little solidarity left in the world.

"Mom," Theresa went on. "I'm not sure what to tell you. I don't know why I didn't say anything. I should have told you." Tears started slipping down Dorothy's cheeks, and Theresa walked around the table and gave her mother a hug.

"I was bound up by fear. I'm sorry that I didn't know what to do."

Her mother cried, and though Theresa was dry-eyed, she ached with deep sorrow. She didn't know if she was capable of opening up about the hardest things. It didn't come naturally to her, and she realized that her mother had never experienced the kind of confidences that perhaps she had dreamed of. Dorothy wept and then accepted a tissue from Katie and blew her nose loudly.

"I'm sorry, too," she said when she had pulled herself together. "I should have pushed harder. I knew there was something odd about the pregnancy, but I figured you were just ashamed of a one-night stand or something."

Theresa held herself by the rib cage. Sofía caught her eye. Theresa knew what she was thinking. There was a world of difference between a little shame over a one-night stand and abject terror over being stalked and raped.

"It's hard for you to communicate very difficult things, isn't it?" Katie asked softly. "Just like it's hard for you to express happiness over very, very good things, like the studio."

Theresa glanced at Sam and saw a strange expression creep over his face.

"Sam, did I not tell you how much I love my studio?" She suddenly saw. Her mother was upset because she felt as though she wasn't a good enough mother to tell. Her brother was cranky because he thought she didn't value his hard work. And Katie? Katie seemed fine. She was sitting peacefully, holding her hand gently against her belly.

"Sam, the studio is the most beautiful thing that I have ever, ever had in my whole life. I wish I could show you how much I love it. Me not knowing how to tell you that has nothing to do with you. It has to do with me and my differences. Mom, the same goes for not being able to tell you about the... rape." She said the last word very softly, and her mother reached out and caught her hand. "It has nothing to do with you not being a good mother. You have been such a good mother to me. I see it more and more now that I'm the mother of a teenage girl."

"As for Sheldon. I'm in love with him. But I'm terrified, and I don't know how to tell him. I needed time to figure out my thoughts, but I understand them now. I want to be with him forever. I'm going to show him somehow. And as for you, Katie... what do you have to tell us?"

Katie blinked at her for a moment, then grinned and said. "We're going to have a baby."

Dorothy screamed so loud that Maddie came skidding out of her room looking scared, then annoyed as she saw everyone laughing and hugging each other. Sofía and Theresa did a little dance around the kitchen island, pulling Maddie into it.

"What?" Maddie kept saying. "What?"

And when Katie finally took pity and told her, she was ecstatic, in her old mild, Maddie way.

"Finally," she said. "I've been waiting forever to have a cousin."

Sofía had come along because she was going to a different national forest for a while. Theresa stared at her, embarrassed and sad.

"We didn't talk about you," she said. "Everything was about me and my stalker, my art show..."

Sofía burst out laughing. "That's hilarious," she said. "Well, keep your phone charged, because I'm going to tell you *everything*. You'll be sick of how much I tell you by the time I'm done."

Theresa grabbed her friend in a hug. "I'm so happy to hear it," she said. She had not even dared to dream that she could have Sofía back like old times. They had argued so much about what to do about the night of the forest menace, and Theresa had started to believe they could never get past it. And now it seemed that just like that, they were back to the days before Cam. Life was becoming something that Theresa could only barely recognize, because it made her so happy.

CHAPTER FORTY-NINE

When the doorbell rang, Sheldon left what he was doing and ran downstairs, nearly slipping down the steps in his hurry.

Calm down, he told himself. *She told you she needed time, this is just dinner as friends."*

It was hard to be calm.

Theresa had agreed to come over for dinner at Sheldon's apartment. It was the long-awaited baby blue suit dinner that she had bargained with, back when Sheldon showed up at her house to work in the garden, and Theresa told him to go home and change. And they needed to celebrate. Despite the chaos of the opening evening, the gallery owner from L.A. had decided to feature Theresa's new show. Theresa's art agent was over the moon. The gallery was highly sought after, and the agent could hardly believe Theresa had landed the gig on her own.

"So what does that mean," Sheldon had asked Theresa as she sat cross-legged on the studio countertop.

"It means I have to make more than twenty sculptures for the show, which is in March," she had told him. "That's a lot of pieces. But I'm excited."

That was when Sheldon had invited Theresa over to celebrate and fulfill their baby blue suit agreement. "The night before the Christmas play starts," he had suggested. To his shock, she agreed.

Sheldon paused on the stairs and wiped his clammy hands on his suit lining where marks wouldn't be visible. Then he slowly opened the door, trying to keep calm and collected, to show a demeanor as poised as a man in a shampoo commercial.

This lasted for about two seconds.

Theresa stood outside the door to his upstairs apartment, looking glorious, but cold. Sheldon stammered as he invited her in, and she followed him up the stairs. His apartment was warm from being in the sun all day, so Theresa pulled her jacket off. He took it from her, his mouth falling open. Theresa wore an ankle-length red dress and had her hair up in a knot on top of her head. She was wearing the slightest hints of makeup around her eyes, and she had a long beaded necklace on. She was the most exquisite creature he had ever seen.

"Can I say it?" he asked.

She wrinkled her nose but nodded. "Yes," she said. "I've been working on this."

It took him a minute to realize she was talking about receiving compliments.

"You are stunning beyond belief," he said. "You are more

beautiful than a pod of dolphins. You look as though you could heal nations. You..."

She held up a hand, laughing. "Thanks, Tazzy," she said. "I've never been a big believer in immersion therapy, though." Her face was bright red. "You don't look too bad yourself," she went on. "I like that suit. A lot."

"Thanks," he said, trying not to blush at the phrase, 'a lot.' "Are you hungry? The food is ready. We can eat."

"Sure," she said, "but first, can I have a tour of your apartment?"

"Haven't you been here before?" he asked, the picture of nonchalance. He knew very well that Theresa had never been there before. Her presence in his apartment would have changed it for good, as it was doing right now. When they dated, Sheldon had still been living in a friend's basement suite.

He led Theresa through the apartment, and she admired his treasures, picking them up gently, bringing them to her nose to smell, the way she always did, smoothing her hand across the tapestries.

"You're so good at collecting things," she said. "Why do you think that is?"

He shrugged.

"Do you think it has something to do with being homeless when you were a kid?" she asked.

Sheldon grinned at her. He loved the way she was always so blunt.

"Yes, probably. I felt like I had to do an actual study on what a home was, and how to make one."

"Have you figured it out?" she asked softly, looking into

his eyes. He couldn't help himself— he had to brush the line of her jaw with his fingers. Theresa's eyes drifted shut, and she drew closer to him.

"I've figured it out halfway," he said. "There's also the matter of the people who make a home."

Her eyes flew up to his face. Very gently, he leaned forward and put his lips against hers. She pressed into him, making a soft sound in her throat. Sheldon pulled away, and Theresa blinked at him. "Let's eat," he said.

He led her to the little table he had set for two in the dining area. Music played softly in the background. Reesey listened for a minute, then grinned at him.

"Is this The Cure?" she asked. "Are you trying to evoke old memories?"

"I live old memories," he said. "I don't need to evoke them. I just thought you might appreciate an old favorite."

She picked up the glass of wine he poured for her and swirled it, sniffing appreciatively. She took a sip and made another soft moan.

"I could get used to life with you," she said. Sheldon froze. Her eyes were on the wine, but then she shot him a devilish glance. "Wine, good music, amazing collections of fine objects from around the world. What else do you offer?"

"Don't toy with me," Sheldon said, his voice hoarse.

"Oh, I'm not," she said. "Just appreciating you."

He brought the food out, taking a moment around the corner in the kitchen to press his hand to his sternum and take several deep breaths. What was Theresa saying? Sheldon picked the plates up from the counter and carried them to the table.

"Tazzy!" Theresa exclaimed as he set her dish in front of her. "Did you make this?"

There were mint-infused potatoes, a tomato coulee, and pork medallions, arranged beautifully on the plate.

"No," Sheldon said, grinning at Reesey's expression of shock. "I'm a pretty good cook, but I wanted us to *celebrate* today. So I hired Katie to cater for us."

"Wow," Theresa said softly. "She's amazing."

"Looks delicious, doesn't it?"

Theresa sighed happily as she took bites of her food. Sheldon felt that he would be perfectly happy to eat across the table from Theresa forever, but he wanted to wait for her to be sure. He wondered for a second, whether he would ever be entirely sure of her, or if she would make him wait forever. She wouldn't, would she?

He gazed at her, her dark hair tied messily on the top of her head. He thought of how this delicate, precious person fought to understand the world, and how every day was an effort for her. She had been stalked and threatened for years without anyone knowing.

Sheldon could wait for her to be ready. He bent to eat.

"Where do you get all this stuff?" Theresa asked, suddenly. When he looked up, she was gazing around his apartment. He had collections of masks, clay bowls from around the world, carpets, and art. Lots and lots of art. His apartment was almost entirely open plan, with tall shelving units creating divisions if needed, so she could see a lot of his collections from where they sat.

"I follow small trails," he told her. "I find where the most interesting handicraft trails are, and I take a trip every year to find new things." He took a sip of water. "I also go to a lot of flea markets."

She smiled at him.

"I've been meaning to travel," she said. "I need to see more pottery from around the world."

Sheldon stood abruptly to fetch dessert from the kitchen. This had been a mistake. How could he go on without knowing whether they would ever be together? When she said she wanted to travel, he immediately imagined the two of the in Istanbul, but maybe it was a pipe dream.

Sheldon turned at the sound of a footstep behind him, and suddenly Theresa was right there, her arms tight around his waist, her face pressed into his chest. She hugged him tight and didn't let go for several minutes, and when she did, it was only to stand on tiptoe and kiss him. He sighed, feeling the ache of tears behind his eyes. His heart beat fast at the feel of her in his arms, her warm lips on his. They kissed for a long while, and at one point, Sheldon opened his eyes to find that they were on his sofa, Theresa curled into him like she never wanted to let him go.

"That feels better," Theresa said, and he smiled at her. His Reesey had come back. Nothing better had happened to him, yet he was tortured by not knowing. Would she come back to him, finally? Would he get another chance to have a family?

She gazed into his eyes, and Sheldon felt lightheaded from her beauty, removed from him for so many years and now suddenly before him, sitting right here with him. Would he wake up and find that it was all a dream?

"I won't keep you waiting long, Taz," she said. "Thank

you for tonight. Part of my .... taking time... is needing to know if the spark is still there."

He tipped his head back and laughed. "Is it still there?" he asked.

"It's very much there," she said, touching the side of his face. He shook his head at her when she reached to kiss him again. "Nope," he said. "I'm drawing my own lines now. I know the spark is there. It's a roaring fire, actually. But I need to know, Reesey, before I commit more of my heart and kissing power to this. Let's have dessert, beautiful temptress. We should clear our heads and have some sensible discourse. You can tell me how much you're looking forward to seeing my play tomorrow."

CHAPTER FIFTY

Three nights later, Sheldon was backstage at the church, guiding the cast through the final performance of the Christmas play. When he had first started writing this play, Sheldon had no idea what a momentous few months he would have leading up to the performance. Reesey coming home. A new pottery studio. Slurs scrawled on his beloved storefront. A kidnapping and arrest. And was he the world's biggest idiot for pushing Theresa away the other night?

But no, Sheldon knew he had done the right thing, even if he kicked himself when he thought about Theresa's kisses. Sheldon needed to know whether he would have a family again, finally, or whether he would be buying a one-way ticket to Mali. He had always wanted to see Mali.

Everyone seemed on edge tonight. The first act was over, and it was just about time for the second.

"What's up with everyone?" he muttered to George. "Is it just nerves?"

George grinned unexpectedly at him. "Probably. And

maybe a bit of ebullience, since we caught the racist vandal and our town menace is gone."

"You know that's not quite true," Sheldon said. The refugees would arrive in the spring, and Sheldon knew it wasn't the last time they would experience push back about the new families.

George shook his head. "You know I know. But it's still good to celebrate the small victories."

"True. Okay, second act. Let's finish this with a bang," Sheldon said.

"Hear that, Maddie?" George called. "Sheldon wants this play to be memorable."

"I'll do my best," she said wryly.

It was Sheldon's favorite part of the play. Four homeless guys with dogs were his modern take on shepherds, and he loved the scene where the angel choir sang to the guys, who were sitting around a barbecue pit in a park, trying to stay warm.

"You should watch from out there," Francisco said, coming up from behind him. "Nothing left to do back here. Go on, get the full effect."

So Sheldon went and found a seat between Ani and Dorothy, in the front pew. The choir sang even more beautifully than they had on either of the two previous nights. Sheldon was impressed. At one point, Dorothy grabbed his hand and squeezed it. He turned and saw tears in her eyes.

The angels finished the song, and the men ran to find Jesus in the shelter.

Sheldon lost himself for a few minutes, then, in memories of shelters he had spent time in. He and his father had switched shelters so many times that Sheldon had lost count. And for the first time, maybe ever, Sheldon remembered the pile of things his father had brought to each facility. He carefully unpacked at every new space, making Sheldon's bed with the blanket his mother had made for him, putting Mr. Rumple, Sheldon's stuffed dog, on his pillow. There were Sheldon's favorite books, and a framed photo of the three of them—Sheldon, his mom, and his dad— back when they were happy together.

"You're so good at collecting things," Theresa had said. "Why do you think that is?"

And it occurred to Sheldon that he was good at making a home because his father had been good at making a home. And his father was trying to continue what Sheldon's mother had always done before she got sick. They had both tried so hard to make a home for him.

He blinked. The play was over. Sheldon started to get up to go and take a final bow with the cast. But instead of lining up, the choir was standing. Dorothy pulled on Sheldon's arm, and he sat. And then Wanda, the church soloist, started to sing, At Last, by Etta James.

"*At last*
My love has come along
My lonely days are over
And life is like a song..."

What on earth? Had they all lost their ever-loving minds? This was outrageous! It wasn't part of the play.

"*I found a dream, that I could speak to*
A dream that I can call my own"

Sheldon glowered at the stage, then looked around to see

if anyone else found it as odd as he did. But wherever he looked, people were either smiling at the choir or looking at Sheldon. He kept accidentally meeting the eyes of people who were looking at him meaningfully. He frowned.

And then Sheldon saw Reesey, standing just behind the choir, and the blood drained from his face.

"You smiled, you smiled
Oh and then the spell was cast
And here we are in heaven
For you are mine...
At Last"

No. What?

She came forward as the song ended, taking the mic from Wanda.

"I hope you don't mind me using this moment," she started, "to tell someone a very important thing." She frowned at the sheet of paper she was holding. "Actually, it's okay if you mind. I'm still going to do it."

Ripples of laughter ran through the audience.

"I could tell you all I love Sheldon in a million ways," she went on. Sheldon's heart was thudding so hard he thought it might actually stop. "But I thought I would say it in a way that is most understandable to him, and that means—because, as you know, he is very odd—that you might not understand it all that well. I'm okay with that too because this is really for him. You can ask him what it means if you don't understand." She took a breath, looking around, obviously searching for him in the crowd.

Beside Sheldon, Dorothy stood up and waved her arms back and forth. Theresa gave a tiny thumbs up.

"This is for you, Tazzy. Here's your answer:

'Don't go far off, not even for a day, because—,'

Sheldon was going to faint. He was going to faint because Theresa was standing on a stage reading the Neruda poem to him.

'Because -- I don't know how to say it: a day is long,'

She was reading the poem he had held forever in a particular place just for her. She was reading the words that meant more to Sheldon than...

'And I will be waiting for you, as in an empty station,'

He couldn't bear it, not in front of all these people. He got up and started walking toward the stage.

when the trains are parked off somewhere else, asleep."

Reesey finished and looked up, expectantly, but Sheldon was already almost to her. He bounded up the steps faster than he could have imagined this tired, heart weary man could move, and he had Reesey in his arms, off her feet.

Vaguely he heard the roaring of the people-packed sanctuary as friends and family hooted, cheered, and stomped, but he was only focused on her face laughing into his. Theresa had given her answer. Sheldon bent to kiss her.

The Lost Art of Reverie, Book One in the Aveline Series, is here.

To learn when the next Aveline book is out, sign up here!

What is the most important ingredient for a book's success? Besides, of course, the book itself?

It's what you, the Reader, says about it. Social proof. Reviews.

When people are out there, in the wilderness of the book jungle, looking for something to read, the main question they ask is, "Have other people read this? Did they like it?"

So if this book is your kind of book, and you think it might be someone else's kind of book, I will be over the moon if you leave a review on whatever site feeds you your books. Reviews can be the key to a book's success. Thank you!

ACKNOWLEDGMENTS

(AND A NOTE.)

Thank you dear reader, for following the stories of the people of Aveline!

Thanks so much again to my wonderful patrons.

Kathleen Andersen, Jessie Benkert, Molly, Donia Goodman, Rose Anderson, Erin Smith, Teresa Q., Amanda Friese, Tj and Mark, Annie Laurie Nichols, Stephanie Donnelly, Ro Keyzer, Erin Yeatman, Diane Brodeur, Alicia Wiggin, Karen Engel, and Elisha Pettit, you have encouraged me so much. Thank you!

I am always and forever thankful for the support my best friend, Chinua, gives me every day.

I'm thankful for my wonderful community, and for all the people who do such hard justice work in the world for so little reward.

A note:

If you want to read more about ASD in women, I recommend the work of Rudy Simone or Tony Attwood.

Sign up here!

ABOUT THE AUTHOR

Newsletter

If you want to join Rae Walsh's Newsletter and learn about books and new releases, sign up here. Your address will never be shared!

~

Bio

Rae Walsh is the women's fiction/inspirational romance pen name of Rachel Devenish Ford. Rae is the wife of one Superstar Husband and the mother of five incredible children. Originally from British Columbia, Canada, she spent seven years working with street youth in California before moving to India to help start a meditation center in the Christian tradition. She can be found eating street food or smelling flowers in many cities in Asia. She currently lives in Northern Thailand, inhaling books, morning air, and seasonal fruit.

~

~

Reviews

Recommendations and reviews are such an important part of the success of a book. If you enjoyed this book, please take the time to leave a review.

Don't be afraid of leaving a short review! Even a couple lines will help and will overwhelm the author with waves of gratitude.

~

Contact

Email: raewalshauthor@gmail.com
Blog: http://journeymama.com
Facebook: http://www.facebook.com/rae.walsh.author
Twitter: http://www.twitter.com/journeymama
Instagram: http://instagram.com/journeymama

Printed in Great Britain
by Amazon

38227830R00189